I Followed the Rules

JOANNA BOLOURI

Quercus

First published in Great Britain in 2015 by

Quercus Publishing Ltd
Carmelite House
50 Victoria Embankment
London EC4Y 0DZ

An Hachette UK company

A CIP catalogue record for this book is available
from the British Library

PB ISBN 978 1 78429 107 5
EBOOK ISBN 978 1 84866 902 4

10 9 8 7 6 5 4 3 2 1

Typeset by CC Book Production

Printed and bound in Great Britain by Clays Ltd, St Ives plc.

For Claudia

The fictional dating book that Cat Buchanan follows in my novel was loosely inspired by the much-loved international bestseller *The Rules* by Ellen Fein and Sherrie Schneider (Thorsons/Element, 2000). Cat's experience is very different from my own, and I very much recommend picking up a copy for anybody looking to do some research on the do's and don'ts of modern dating. Finally, I'll add that all the characters appearing in this work, as well as the dating book *The Rules of Engagement* itself, are entirely fictitious.

Joanna Bolouri x

Does a good relationship always involve living together?
Glasgow Girl doesn't think so.

When you've been single as long as I have, you start to ponder if you could ever be truly happy as part of a couple again. I'm a creature of habit now, so the thought of allowing someone into the little world I've created for me and my daughter is a daunting prospect.

Being a lone, working parent is tough, and I wonder if I'll ever have the time or the energy to direct towards someone new. Sometimes it's hard to imagine a future where I'm not doing everything alone. Still, I am a woman of a certain age and I have needs, dammit. I need to flirt and be kissed and feel wanted and cuddled by someone I didn't give birth to.

The dating part doesn't worry me; I'm sure when I meet the right man, it'll be a whirlwind of laughter, sex, sleepovers and boxset marathons before one of us spoils it all by saying something stupid like, 'Let's move in together.'

Dating? Sure, but actually living together – the committed, financially draining, I never knew you were quite this messy, TAKE THE BLOODY BIN OUT, YOUR JOKES AREN'T FUNNY, I WISH YOU HAD NEVER BEEN BORN kind of relationship – isn't high on my agenda. And I know what happens, because it's happened to me before and I'm scared it will again.

Before we even start going out, I already have restrictions set in place for a man I haven't even met yet. Restrictions like: you will never come first in my life. You won't meet my kid unless I'm sure you're not a massive weirdo (at least six months), and don't ask to come over while she's there, even if she's asleep, and then sulk when I say no. Don't bore me with tales of how mean your ex was: women with broken hearts are very aware that there are two sides to every story – however much I like you, I'm not stupid.

I think couples who are committed to each other but never actually live together have the right idea: like Mia and Woody. Actually, that's the worst example I could have given, but you get the idea. I have close friends that I wouldn't want to live with or see every single day until one of us dies – everyone needs their own space.

God, I'm a nightmare. Form an orderly queue, boys.

CHAPTER ONE

He's late. He's half an hour late.

I nervously tuck my hair behind my ears and continue scrolling on my smartphone. *That's all right*, I tell myself; *people are late all the time*. Maybe they're not HALF AN HOUR LATE on a first date, but he's obviously been held up. Could be a number of reasons – he could be stuck in a traffic jam . . . had a car crash . . . he could have fallen down a sinkhole; these things happen. I'll just continue scrolling through the BBC News website, pretending that everything's fine. The people in this bar don't know I'm waiting for someone. As far as they know, I'm just a woman, sitting in front of a table, asking it to bear the weight of her large glass of red wine. Yup, nothing to see here.

But by the time I order my second glass, he still hasn't arrived and I'm fuming. He clearly isn't coming and I've wasted a Friday evening that could have been spent cuddling up to my eight-year-old daughter, Grace, in her fluffy pyjamas, being ignored by my equally fluffy cat Heisenberg. My sister Helen is babysitting for me, no doubt feeling pleased with herself for being the person responsible for getting her unmarried sister on her first proper date in weeks –

'Just meet up with him, Catriona. Have a drink. Colin's really nice . . . arty type. Goes to the theatre quite a bit.'

'How do you know him?' I'd asked suspiciously. My sister generally only knows two types of men: those who are married and those she wants to set me up with.

'He works with Adam. He thought Colin would be perfect for you.'

'So you haven't actually met him? All you have to go on is your husband's word? The same husband who set me up with already-engaged Kevin?'

'To be fair, no one knew he was engaged.'

'Well, I'm guessing HIS FIANCÉE did! I walked past the church as they were having their wedding photographs taken. He told me he was in Chester looking after his sick mother.'

'Yes, that was shameless. His mother died years ago. Anyway, we're no longer friends with him. But Colin is definitely single.'

I look at the clock behind the bar again, shaking my head. Why did I listen to her? *Take a chance*, she'd said. *You deserve some fun!* And now here I am, drinking alone, with a terrifying red wine smile and three per cent battery life.

Fuck it. I drain the rest of my drink, pull my coat on and throw my phone in my bag. I have better things to do than wait around for a man who –

'Catriona?'

I turn around and I'm suddenly chest to face with a short, rain-soaked, gold-cravat-wearing stranger. The sinking feeling in my stomach that follows makes it clear to me that this bizarre man is Colin.

'Sorry I'm late, m'lady,' he apologizes. 'Work ran over and then I couldn't get a taxi from the West End. Can I get you a drink?'

(*M'lady?* I hate you, Helen.)

'Sure,' I reply, staring at the tiny drop of rain hanging from the end of his nose. 'I'll have a small glass of Merlot.'

He nods approvingly, strolls over to the bar and I sit back down, placing my bag under the table and clasping my hands in front of me, mentally preparing myself for the forthcoming awkwardness. He returns carrying two glasses of red and clumsily puts them down before removing his sodden tweed jacket, which looks like it weighs a good 200 pounds.

'Hell is empty and all the devils are here.'

I stare at him blankly. 'Pardon?'

'Shakespeare! I was quoting Willie Shakespeare.' He smiles weakly, running a bony hand through his small mop of thinning brown hair. 'This bar isn't the kind of place I'd normally frequent. These people . . . lots of bad grammar and tattoos, I imagine.'

I look around and see a bar full of completely normal people: two women in their twenties deep in discussion, perhaps about the fact they've both come out wearing matching tops and boots; a couple in their thirties sharing nachos; and a group of middle-aged men doing rows of brightly coloured shots, ensuring that they'll be throwing up on their own shoes by midnight. It's a normal Friday night, with normal people. That's it – one drink and I'm out of here.

'Shakespeare, eh?' I reply, adding, 'A HORSE, A HORSE, MY KINGDOM FOR A HORSE!'

I expect him to be at least moderately impressed by the only line I know from *Richard III*, but he remains expressionless, no doubt wondering just how much I've had to drink. And he's still dripping. Jesus, this man has no ability to self-dry. Silence ensues and I take an overly long gulp of wine.

Why does this sort of thing always happen to me? Am I cursed? It gives me comfort knowing that once I finish my drink I can make my excuses, but until that happy, happy moment, I'll have to continue making conversation.

'So. Colin. Helen tells me you enjoy the theatre?'

'I do indeed, but nothing too flashy. I enjoy the classics – none of this *We Will Rock You* or *Mamma Mia!* musical-theatre nonsense.'

'I love musicals,' I reply, secretly pleased that we have nothing in common. 'I know every word of *Evita*. And *Rocky Horror*.'

'I see.' He sniffs, looking horribly disinterested. 'Well, each to their own. And what is it you do for a living, Catriona? Or should I call you Cat?'

Only people I like call me Cat. 'No, Catriona is fine. I'm a journalist. Features mainly – I write for the *Lowdown*.'

'Oh, yes, I've heard of that.' He sighs, moving his arm and leaving a wet smear on the table. 'Quite lefty, isn't it? Lots of snarky feminist witterings. Not my cup of tea. Fine for a first job, but are you hoping to eventually write for a more reputable publication?'

And with that, the date is over. I've had enough. Normally I like talking about my job. I write for the *Scottish Tribune* – the biggest-selling newspaper in Scotland – on their weekend magazine and it's a great gig: one day a week in the office, hours to fit around my daughter and a shiny press award for my highly amusing column 'Lowdown and Dirty', where they give me five hundred words to rant about love, life and men, under the pen name 'Glasgow Girl'. The *New York Times* and Ellen DeGeneres follow me on Twitter, for Christ's sake! But I know this information would be wasted on Colin – he doesn't deserve to know how utterly fucking interesting I am. I push my half-empty glass into the middle of the table and stand up.

'Well, it's been lovely meeting you, but I must get home.'

'But I've only been here for ten minutes!'

I mumble something about babysitters, hoping he'll just take the fucking hint.

'Ah. I understand,' he nods, standing up and wrapping his hand around mine. 'Dear Catriona, parting is such sweet sorrow—'

'Oh, fucking hell, STOP THAT!' I announce loudly, moving my hand out from under his clammy paw and throwing my bag over my shoulder. 'Seriously, Colin, WHO DOES THAT?' I march towards the door, head down, ready to battle the rain on my short walk back to Helen's flat (where I will murder her), and accidentally barge straight into a chipper elderly man in a tartan bunnet.

'Careful, pet.'

'Oh gosh, I'm so sorry!' I cry. 'My fault completely!'

'Not to worry, hen. Lovely evening, isn't it?'

I look up at the sky. It's clear; there isn't a single cloud. It's the kind of happy sky Julie Andrews would sing about while spinning around on a mountaintop. I look down at the pavement. Dry. Colin has only been in the bar ten minutes . . . a recent downpour would have been evident.

It suddenly occurs to me that it hasn't rained at all, and I stride off towards Queens Park to thank my sister and her husband for setting me up with the creepiest mother-fucker who ever lived.

CHAPTER TWO

2007

After seven years it's finally over. We're finished.

I open the white door of my cosy three-bedroom semi, walk down the perfectly smooth path we had resurfaced six weeks ago and unlock the doors of my blue Honda. Strapping my sleepy ten-month-old baby girl into her car seat, I quietly shut the door, just as Peter angrily throws more of the black bin bags on to the front lawn. One bursts open and I see Grace's bibs and bottles spill out on the grass. I try not to react as I casually go to retrieve them; I won't let him get to me. I duck as another bag flies past my head. Defiantly ignoring this, I continue to stride towards the ripped one.

'I'll never forgive you!' he yells at me. 'Never.'

'Forgive me for what?' I mutter, stooping down to scoop up her favourite teddy-bear bottle. 'For having the guts to end this sham of a relationship? I want Grace to have a happy life, not raised by people who hate each other. I want—'

His laughter interrupts me. 'You have no idea what you want! Enjoy being a single mother, you fucking waste of space. You're an idiot, Cat. But then again, you always were. I knew that the moment I met you.' He sneers at me with such venom I physically recoil. Looking at him, I don't recognize the man I once knew: the blond stranger I met at the White Stripes gig who looked after me when I'd had too much to drink and got separated from my friends. The man who sent me flowers every day until I agreed to go out with him. The man who said I was everything to him. That man was gone.

I need to leave. I ignore the rest of the loose items strewn on the lawn, grab the last bag and get into my car. As I drive away, Grace begins to cry loudly. And so do I.

'But he was so wet. WHY WAS HE WET?!'

Helen closes the kitchen door and frowns at me for being loud when she's just put Grace to bed. Adam, her husband, snorts and puts another sweetener in my coffee.

'Maybe it was sweat?' he laughs. 'He *is* known for being a tad sweaty in the office, but it's never usually that notice-able . . . In hindsight, though, I perhaps should have paid attention to that nickname some of the female staff have for him.'

'Which is?'

'Um . . .'

'Tell me.'

'. . . "Sweaty Colin".'

I hear Helen sniggering as she sits down at their bespoke maple kitchen table, carefully placing her cup on a yellow coaster. I want to laugh but I'm too annoyed.

'For the love of fuck, this just gets worse! You've known me for eight years, Adam. Why on earth would you think I'd go for someone like Colin? Do I seem like the kind of woman who would go for someone who quotes Shakespeare and has unexplained drippage?'

Helen decides to chime in, simultaneously thrusting a piece of carrot cake into my hand. 'We have no idea what your type is, Cat!'

I take a bite of my cake and talk with my mouth full, just to annoy her. 'Peter. Peter is – was – my type.' A shower of tiny cake crumbs sprays from my mouth and lands on the table near her mug. She looks at me like I've blown my nose in her auburn hair.

'Peter? After all he's done?! I despise that man. Actually, we need to have a chat about him—'

'Oh, I don't mean him personally but, you know, physically he's my type. Blond. Tall. Toned. Looks good in tight trousers. Remember this for next time. Actually, fuck that, there won't be a next time. I trust you both with my life, but to find me a boyfriend? Never again. You're off the case.'

I see Helen glance at Adam and I know that it'll be a cold day in hell before she lets *that* happen. I quickly change the subject. 'Shall I just leave Grace to sleep here then?'

Helen nods. 'She wanted to stay here anyway. We didn't expect to see you till tomorrow. Go and have a nice evening and I'll send her over after breakfast. Your cat is here, by the way.'

'There's a surprise.' I roll my eyes. 'Good. If he's here, then he's not hiding under my bed, waiting to attack my bare feet. I swear that cat hates me – actually he hates everyone, except Grace. He adores her.'

'We all do.' Helen smiles. 'She's a pleasure.'

Grace is also very fond of both Helen and Adam, so I shouldn't grumble as much as I do. They're such a big help, but sometimes I wish that my very lovely flat wasn't directly across the hall from theirs. Helen flounces in and out of my place whenever she feels like it – moving shit around and disturbing me when I'm trying to work – but whenever I need her to look after Grace, she's there and I'm grateful. Peter would rather stick his cock in a blender than help me with additional babysitting.

I place my cup in the sink and say my goodnights. It's only quarter to ten, but I'm already planning a long, deep bath followed by a gin and tonic and a Hitchcock film. Before I leave, I quietly creep into Grace's room. The sound of her contented breathing makes my horrendous evening feel much less grim. In the gloom, I see Heisenberg curled up in a white ball beside Grace's head, guarding over her as he does every evening. I gently move him out of the way and he makes a low growling sound, to which I respond with a similarly hushed, 'Shut your furry face.' Sweeping her blonde curls from her face, I lightly kiss her cheek and breathe in her unique smell. She smells beautiful – I can't help myself; I do it again. She stirs.

'MUM. Stop it. I can feel your nose-breath on my ear . . .'

'Sorry, Grace-face. Just wanted to kiss you goodnight. I'll see you tomorrow.'

'OK, Mum. We're making pancakes for breakfast.'

'Amazing! Go back to sleep.'

'I'm going to have jam on mine.'

'Night night, Grace.'

'If you could be any kind of bear, what would it be?'

'A polar bear. Now go to sleep.'

'Night, Mum. Oh, before you go, Uncle Adam farted in the living room and it smelled like doom.'

'Go back to sleep!' I laugh, and turn to leave.

She giggles and pulls me back, throwing her arms around me before cuddling up to her teddy and falling back asleep in record time. I close the door behind me, throwing a last 'fuck you' look to the devil cat still staring at me through the dark, and then make my way back to my flat, grateful to have the rest of the evening to myself. Unlocking the heavy wooden door, I walk inside . . . followed by Helen.

'I need a word,' she whispers, pushing me into the living room.

'What has Adam done now?' I ask, draping my favourite green coat over a chair. 'Is this about his farting?'

She frowns. 'This isn't about Adam. It's about Peter.'

'Oh, for God's sake. I was winding you up when I said he was my type.'

'You don't still have feelings for him, do you?'

'No way! He's Grace's dad. That's all. I'm so over all that now.'

'I really hope so, because he's getting married.'

I stared at her for a moment in disbelief. 'What? Fuck off. How do you know this?' I can feel my face begin to drain of what little colour it has, and my lip starts to tremble. Jesus, I think I'm going to cry.

'Melanie at work is friends with Emma. She texted me a couple of hours ago.'

I sit down on the arm of the couch and shrug. I'm determined to be grown-up about this. After all, Emma, Peter's girlfriend, is a nice woman, and despite her 'mistress of the dark' exterior, she's good with Grace. 'Well, they've been together long enough. I guess it was just a matter of time. I wonder when he'll tell me. He's going to savour every bloody moment, isn't he?'

'Of course he is. Well, I'm surprised you're taking this so well. I remember how gutted you were when you asked him to marry you and he said no.'

'Yeah, thanks for bringing that up.'

'Don't be so touchy. Look, are you sure you're all right with this?'

'I'm fine,' I lie. Helen can tell it's not the truth, but tonight at least she doesn't make me admit it. She kisses me on the forehead instead and says, 'Good. I'll see you tomorrow. Chin up.'

'Oh, it's up. My chin has been up since I left him. It's *so* . . . up.'

Neither of us is entirely sure where I'm going with this, but she smiles and backs out of the room, leaving me standing there mouthing the word 'chin' to myself.

After a couple of minutes I decide that standing alone in my living room staring at the wall probably isn't the best use of my time, so I run a bath and get undressed. I walk naked through to Grace's room and grab her bunny iPod speakers, hoping that a few tracks from Regina Spektor will make everything all right again. I submerge myself in warm soapy water and close my eyes, letting the music wash over me.

By the time 'Samson' has finished, I want to fucking drown myself. Not only is he getting married, but he's going to rub my lonely, single face right in it.

By eleven, I'm wearing the panda onesie Grace gave me for Christmas, have chosen my film and am pouring myself a Baileys on ice in the kitchen. I saunter back through to the living room; drink in one hand, the other pulling at my onesie, which is riding up my arse at an alarming rate. I plonk myself down on the couch and hit Play on Netflix just as my phone starts to ring.

Withheld number. I hate that.

'Hello?'

'It's me. How did the date go?'

'Kerry? Why is your number withheld? I nearly didn't answer.'

'I'm being fucking mysterious. And on Kieran's phone. He's gone to bed so I'm using his phone and drinking all his beer. Tell me how it went.'

My friend Kerry met graphic designer Kieran Nelson in Kelvingrove Art Gallery six years ago when she spotted him wandering around with his fly open and light-heartedly threatened to call security. They've been together ever since, and if she wasn't my very best friend in the whole world I'd challenge her to a duel for his hand in marriage.

'The date? I'm already trying to forget it. Not only was he insanely unattractive and sweaty, but he was also rude, pompous and probably a Tory.'

'Oh dear God. Sorry to hear that. I was hoping you'd at least have found someone shag-worthy.' I hear her take a swig from her beer bottle and then softly burp.

'Yeah, that would have been nice. The last time I had sex, science wasn't even a real thing.' I laugh, feeling nothing but self-pity and contempt for my own, dust-gathering vagina.

'So when was the last time?'

'On the floor of my living room with engaged Kevin.' I throw a look of disgust at my laminate flooring. 'Not particularly memorable.'

'Nonsense,' she replies. 'You shagged that guy after your work Christmas party . . . What was his name?'

One of the worst sexual encounters of my life flashes before my eyes. I flinch.

'Jesus, don't you forget *anything* I do? Ugh. Chris.'

'Well, there you go.'

'Kerry, being jackhammered by someone with a small cock who works on the fish counter at Asda doesn't count as a shag.'

'OK, well what about the solicitor who finger—'

'Kerry! There's a reason I mentally delete these events and I'd advise you to do the same.'

'Never. When you eventually get married, I'll need some stories for my maid-of-honour speech. You want to come over and help me finish this beer? Or bring more?'

'No, thanks. I'm just out the bath. I have Baileys and I'm in a rotten mood. And speaking of marriage, Peter's taking the plunge.'

I hear her splutter on her beer.

'WHAT? Married?'

'Yeah, that's what I said.'

'To "Elvira"? When?'

'I have no idea when the big day is. Helen found out – he hasn't told me yet.'

'TWAT.'

'Isn't he just? He better tell me first. This is a big deal for Grace, whether she realizes it yet or not. She's going to have a fucking stepmum.'

We both remain silent for a moment and I finish my drink. I can feel my sadness rising again and I sigh loudly.

'You OK?'

I shake my head.

'Are you shaking your head?'

I nod. I want to punch the wall but I'm afraid it'll hurt, so I whack a scatter cushion before demanding, 'How is this remotely fair? He's found someone he wants to spend the rest of his life with, and I'm still alone?'

'Listen, don't let him get to you, and don't get bitter about this. I've known you since Primary Three – you're better than that. It's not a competition. You'll meet someone. I promise.'

'But what if—'

'There is no "what if". He's getting married and you're on a different path right now. Just take a moment to feel sorry for Emma. Bow your head in sympathy for the woman who will be legally bound to Peter Anderson until death or an expensive divorce.'

I laugh and start to feel better about everything – well, except this onesie, which now seems to have entered my colon. 'You're right. I'm going to watch *Rear Window* and forget about this for the evening.'

'You should watch *The Corpse Bride*. Remind you of anyone?'

'Ha, I'm going now. Speak soon.' I continue laughing after she hangs up, then refill my drink and settle down on my white corner couch, glaring at the massive chocolate stain that Grace obviously made and failed to tell me about.

Dear God, I hope it's chocolate.

CHAPTER THREE

I wake up at half past eight to the sound of Grace and Adam heading out to the shops. I hear Grace chuckle when Adam asks her if she wants to drive, then the front door closes with the kind of bang only a hyper child can produce. The sun streams directly into my eyes like laser beams through my Ikea blinds and I snuggle back down, pulling my lemon-yellow covers over my head, promising myself some new blackout curtains when I get paid. And maybe a blackout room. I need my sleep.

Knowing I have at least half an hour before Grace is back and all hell breaks loose, I let my hand wander between my legs, grateful to have some me time, but then Chris the fish man pops into my head and my hand retreats like my pubic region is on fire. Bugger, now I'm reliving every bad one-night stand, including the DJ who dribbled on my face in 1998 and the lawyer who sniffed my dirty underwear when he thought I wasn't looking. I try and shake the images off and start again, but once my phone starts to ring it's clear that my *ménage à une* is ruined for good. I don't have to check who it's from; there's only one person whose assigned ringtone is 'Loser' by Beck. I grab my phone off my bedside table. Better get this over with.

'Hello, Peter.'

'Hi, Catriona. I wanted to have a quick word.'

When we were together he called me Cat. Now he uses my full name like a disapproving parent. 'OK . . .' I reply, knowing full well that he's calling to tell me he's getting married. I prop myself up on my pillow, take a deep breath and close my eyes.

'It's about Grace. We've noticed she seems to be very tired when she's here. At bedtime she's exhausted.'

I exhale. '. . . What?'

'I said that we've noticed—'

'You're calling to tell me that Grace gets tired at bedtime?'

No mention of the engagement.

'Yes, that's correct. Wait – no, not like that. We've just noticed she seems unusually tired when you bring her round to us.'

I pause and roll my eyes so far back in my head I can practically see my own brain cells depleting with frustration. Why does he insist on doing this? He calls up for no fucking reason, asking pointless things that could easily be discussed when I drop Grace off. I sigh heavily.

'Interesting. Maybe I'm working her too hard, but that chimney won't clean itself!'

'Now you're just being facetious.'

'Peter, unless she's coming down with something, I'm guessing she's tired because she goes at a million miles an hour all day.'

'Maybe, but we've noticed this a couple of times and we're concerned.'

I start to giggle. Since Peter got together with Emma, he's seemingly become unable to think for himself. Everything is 'we', and I'm sure it's his way of reminding me that I now have two fuckwits to contend with instead of just one. To be honest though, I have no beef with Emma, despite the fact she's stupidly tall with black hair and Goth make-up, the complete opposite of my five-foot three-inch blondeness. I try to avoid black, unless it's for an evening dress or underwear. I'll never understand all that Gothic nonsense – YOU WATCHED THE CRAFT AS A TEENAGER. WE GET IT. Put some blusher on and cheer the fuck up. I guess she probably feels the same about my taste for retro clothing (but she'd be wrong).

I decide to end the call as quickly as possible. It's too early for this shit and I'm peeved that my tiny window for self-love has been slammed shut. So I pretend that I have another call coming in. 'Grace is fine, Peter. I have someone else on the line, so I have to go. I'll drop her across at two this afternoon as usual. Anything else you need to tell me?'

'No. We'll see Grace at two'.

He doesn't know I'm giving him the middle finger as he hangs up, but it makes me feel better anyway. I throw my phone on the bedside table and pull the covers over my face to muffle my screams of annoyance. Quite frankly, I'd rather start my day being water-boarded than engage in an early-morning conversation with Peter.

I lie in bed for ten more minutes until I hear the paperboy shredding the weekend *Tribune* through the main-door letter box. It's clear that the universe is conspiring against my downtime. Admitting defeat, I get up and yawn like a Munch painting.

Plonking myself down at my dressing table, I tie my hair back with one of Grace's pink scrunchies before carefully examining my face for signs of decomposition. It appears to be wrinkle free, but I'm at the age now where random lines sometimes creep up on me while I sleep, and this scares the shit out of me. My skincare regime is pretty standard: cleanse, tone and moisturize with whatever is on offer at Boots. It takes me five minutes while my coffee machine makes my morning cup of conscious, and this morning is no different. Two cups later, I'm dressed and sitting at the kitchen table with a copy of the *Scottish Tribune* in front of me and a croissant shoved sideways into my mouth. Putting the main paper to one side, I open the *Lowdown* magazine and scan my Glasgow Girl column:

Recently I've been considering online dating, but it all seems rather bleak. After I've placed my advert stating that I have unruly hair, enjoy short walks into oncoming traffic and that I'm looking for a man who owns a tank and knows all the lyrics to 'The Safety Dance', what then? If someone miraculously responds to my pathetic need for human contact and affection, we'll probably arrange to meet up and I'll have to pray that he looks like his photographs. But in reality he won't – no one ever does.

I skim down the rest of the column, then check that my editorial on stupidly expensive face creams and my interview with David Tennant are also present and correct before closing the pages, feeling entirely smug that I actually get paid for doing this. Things could have been very different.

2010

'Any news on the job front yet? Your redundancy pay must be running low by now.'

I glance over at Helen and shake my head. Sometimes she sounds more like Mum than Mum ever did. 'Nope. That magazine said they'd let me know, but that was two weeks ago.'

'What magazine?'

'The new weekend magazine that's starting . . . remember? Part of the *Scottish Tribune*?'

Helen's looking at me like this is brand-new information. In fact, she's looking at me like she isn't quite sure who I am or why I'm in her house.

'Editor wanted fresh new voices . . . had the interview last week . . . you drove me there . . . seriously? You don't remember?'

'Of course I do,' she replies, but it's clear she doesn't have a fucking clue what I'm talking about, so she changes the subject. 'By the way, Cat, they're looking for someone at the university. Canteen staff. Don't think the pay is great, but it's something and you'd get the school holidays off. Want me to get you an application form?'

My heart sinks, but I nod and tell her that would be great. As much as I'd kill for that job at the *Tribune*, I'm aware that my experience is limited; I was only at the *South Side News* for a year before it closed, so my chances of getting this are slim at best . . . but I'm a good writer! I'm sure of this. I try to imagine myself serving chips and cheese to booze-soaked students at the same university I once studied at to get my journalism degree and I want to have a little cry.

Helen frowns. I see her dark brown eyes narrow as she tries to second-guess what I'm thinking. 'There's nothing wrong with canteen work, Catriona. A job's a job.'

'Jesus, Helen, I didn't say there was! I know I can't afford to be too selective about where my income comes from, but unless I start making some decent money, I'm never going to be able to move out of my shitty rented flat. I need to aim high!'

'You can still aim high while you're putting food on the table. You're thirty-one now and competing with writers much younger than you, who will work for pennies. Maybe it's time to do something else? You can always move in here with me and Adam and save on—'

'Stop right there,' I interrupt. 'I love you both dearly, but Grace and I need our own space, however vile it is. And I'm well aware of my position on the food chain, thank you very much. I'll think of something.'

'Anyway, the offer is there. You really should consider it.'

I nod, but there's no way in hell I'm moving in with my sister. I didn't get away from one control freak to move in with another.

At quarter to two I leave Helen's flat and make my way to Grace's nursery school to collect her. It's only a fifteen-minute walk to Hillcross Family Centre, but the cold, unforgiving rain is stinging my face and making my jeans stick to my freezing thighs. It's days like this when I miss my old blue Honda, but the five hundred pounds I sold it for came in handy for food and bills. I pull up my hood and keep my head down.

Hillcross Family Centre is a charming council-run nursery, staffed entirely by women of various ages and temperaments, with the exception of John – a nursery nurse in his twenties who delights the children and confuses the parents, simply by being male. The head of the nursery, Mrs Woods, is a passionate woman with a penchant for ponchos, dancing and coral lipstick and has taken a particular shine to Grace, it seems.

'Your daughter is wonderful, Cat: one of my favourites.'

'That's nice. Are you allowed to have favourites?'

'Probably not, but I can't help it. She's a darling. Calls gravity "grabbity", which actually makes sense when you think about it.'

There's already a group of mothers huddled at the doors as I arrive. I spot Rose hanging back from the pack, standing under a massive yellow umbrella, and head towards her for shelter.

'Hi, Cat!' She moves over and lets me under, being careful not to poke me in the face with the spokes. 'I'm just standing here thinking how much I fucking hate everything.'

I love Rose. She's very funny, swears like a trooper and although she loves her son to death, she despises everything about motherhood. I met her on the first day of nursery and we instantly clicked.

'Everything?!' I grin.

'Yeah, pretty much. I especially hate this routine. Same fucking thing every day. And Jason's being so difficult at the moment; threw a fit last night at dinner because the peas on his plate were too small. THEY'RE FUCKING PEAS.

I didn't sign up for this shit. And he refused to come to nursery yesterday without his Barbie doll; went ape-shit when the teacher wouldn't let him bring it into class, in case it got lost.'

'Aww, they all have a *thing* at this age,' I attempt to console her, desperately trying to think of something weird that Grace does, but my mind's a blank. So I tell her the 'grabbity' story and hope for the best.

'Ugh, your child is normal.' Rose smirks. 'Go and stand over there with the perfect parents.'

I laugh and look over at the three flawlessly groomed women waiting impatiently at the main entrance. Janice, Patricia and Anne-Marie are the kind of mothers Rose dislikes with a passion, and I can see why. They're mean, they're pushy and, astonishingly, they're actually far more judgemental than Rose and I combined.

At last count they had at least twelve kids between them. They also have two Range Rovers, three sense-of-humour bypasses, a pug called Barnaby, at least one Weight Watchers Silver Star award and numerous ways of bragging how exceptional their completely average children are. Like on sports day. The leader of the little group, Anne-Marie's son Ben, came third behind two girls in the egg-and-spoon race. Ben screamed. Then he threw a fit and his hard-boiled egg at his teacher. Anne-Marie wasn't happy either.

'That's outrageous! Ben's an excellent athlete – that

race was entirely unfair. Ben's egg was clearly bigger than everyone else's. I'm not even sure it was a hen's egg.'

The nursery bell rings loudly, almost drowning out the sound of my phone. I scarper to the back of the queue to answer while they begin letting parents in. It's the *Scottish Tribune*. My heart leaps into my mouth as I answer.

'It's Natasha here. We'd like to formally offer you the job.'

Three minutes later, everyone else is inside but I'm still outside in the playground – punching the air like it's 1985.

I finish my coffee just as Grace rushes through the door, back from her errand with Adam and swigging from a tiny bottle of fresh orange. The house instantly becomes alive when she's here.

'Hello, my darling! Did you get your pancakes this morning?'

'Yup. Aunt Helen tried to make one that looked like Mickey Mouse, but I heard Uncle Adam say it looked like a willy, so she made me a normal round one instead.'

'Oh . . . right then.'

She pauses for a moment, tiny hands on tiny hips. 'Why don't girls have willies? Why do we have a bagina? Is it so we can sit down to pee?'

'It's a *vagina*, and it's a bit early to be discussing bottoms and peeing, Grace. Can we talk about it after I'm dressed?'

As I walk through to the bedroom and take off my

dressing gown, I hear her shout, 'Mum, Daddy sits down to pee sometimes. I saw him. He calls it a "sit-down-wee".'

'Tell him to close the door when he's in the toilet,' I reply, pulling on jeans that should have been thrown in the wash a week ago. 'That's a private thing.'

Her little face appears round my bedroom door. 'But I've seen you pee a gazillion times. And he does close the door but I go in anyway.'

This is true. I haven't been able to take a piss on my own since 2007. Or shower. These private moments seem to be when Grace invariably decides she wants to tell me something very important, or announce that she can't find a toy or, y'know, just talk nonsense and show me some dance moves. Part of me is secretly pleased that Peter isn't getting let off the hook either – that he might get a small insight into what it's like to never get a minute to yourself.

'OK, I'm getting dressed now. Why don't you go and watch telly before we go to the farmers' market? Grace, what are you laughing at?'

'Your boobs are massive. Will I have the same ones when I'm older?'

'Well, you'll have your own boobs, but not these exact ones; they're not heirlooms. Now go and play for ten minutes.'

Mercifully she doesn't ask what an heirloom is and skips back into the living room. I hear the opening credits to *Monster High* blasting out as I search for a pair of socks in the massive ironing pile that's slowly taking over the corner of my bedroom, cursing my inability to successfully cope with any kind of household chore. In my twenties, I truly believed that by the time I hit thirty I'd be wealthy enough to pay someone to clean my house while I was at work. Now I just look forward to the day I can teach Grace to vacuum.

Finally I'm dressed and Grace and I leave for the farmers' market, held on the last Saturday of every month and responsible for my newfound love of sourdough bread. Before I had Grace, Saturday mornings were used to sleep off Friday night's hangover. Now they're spent admiring home-made jam and root veg, while my childless friends have morning sex and booze-induced amnesia. I can guarantee that, right now, Kerry won't even be aware that it's morning.

We cross the street and walk along the side of the park, where tennis lessons have already begun, dogs are being walked and joggers look far too motivated for their own good.

It's quieter than usual this morning so I take my time sampling cheese and chutney from a woman in a shawl while Grace hops from one foot to the other, excitedly deciding which cake du jour looks worthy of her tiny mouth. Despite my occasional longing for a life less ordinary, I only have to look at Grace to know that I have everything that matters right here: my amazing child and an artisan bread stall.

'The fruit looks good, Grace. Why don't you get some pears? You like pears.'

'I do like pears Mum, but ONLY A CRAZY PERSON WOULD BUY PEARS WITH THEIR POCKET MONEY. I want a treat.'

'Fruit is nature's treat,' I reply quietly, knowing that this battle has already been lost. She gives me a pity look and continues hopping. She's right of course. Who the fuck would spend their pocket money on fruit? It's the weekend. When did I become such a joyless bastard?

Eventually she chooses some scones and jam to take to her dad's house before spotting her friend Caron and running off towards the swings to play. I walk quickly behind, one eye on her and the other on anyone who looks like they might be a child-snatching nutcase.

The park is quite busy so I sit on a bench and watch Grace and Caron play. She waves at me from the top of the climbing frame and I wave back, desperately trying not to be the lone overprotective mother who shrieks, 'OH MY GOD! BE CAREFUL!! PEOPLE HAVE DIED FROM DOING CLIMBING!' every time their kid climbs something higher than the kerb. I look elsewhere to distract myself.

There are three dads at the park this morning, and I swiftly rate them in order of attractiveness. The guy attempting to climb on the see-saw with his daughter is immediately ruled out for wearing turquoise skinny jeans so tight he can barely lift his leg over the seat. The second dad has the most handsome face of the three but doesn't make it to the top of my list; he's far too clean cut and so is his son – you can tell they've both been dressed by his wife, who's probably at home cleaning the house with undiluted bleach and a mouth full of Valium. So today's winner is dad number three, a tall man with enough stubble to strike a match on and a lumberjack shirt that would look better on me. His baby daughter is wearing odd shoes though, which leads me to believe he's either very tired or an idiot.

Twenty minutes later, a rather rosy-faced Grace plonks herself down beside me on the bench and wipes her nose on her sleeve.

'Can we go now?' She sniffs.

'Do you need a tissue?' I ask, rummaging around in my bag.

'No, I'm fine now.' The snot trail on her sleeve is making me gag.

'Next time, get a tissue, please,' I say, gathering up our market bags. 'That's really gross.'

She grins. 'It was an emergency. It was running down my face. Liam Kirk from school always has snotters running down his face and it's disgusting. He also told the teacher she was the b-word.'

'He sounds wonderful. Please stay away from him.'

'I don't play with him. He plays with Joseph McKenzie. Joseph's the one who brought a dead bee to school and kept it in his pocket.'

We walk back towards the house and she takes my hand as we cross the road. Apart from her cuddles, that's my favourite thing in the whole world; I know she's safe when her hand is in mine. It makes me sad that one day she'll probably rather cut her own hand off than hold mine in public. Sometimes I wish she'd stay this age forever.

At two I drive Grace over to Peter's house, or rather our old house that Peter never left and which is now also home to Emma and her vast collection of black eyeliner, crushed velvet and New Rock boots. Their beady eyes met on the 7pm Edinburgh Waverly to Glasgow Central train and three months later she moved in. It still stuns me that she's his type. Maybe she always was, and perhaps I was never his type in the first place. I ring the doorbell and kiss Grace goodbye just as the door opens, hoping for a quick escape.

'See you tomorrow, honey. Have a great time!'

'Bye, Mum. Hi, Dad, I brought scones!' she chirps, and makes her way down the hall, which has recently been painted a delightful shade of brown, instead of the lovely ivory colour it used to be. But I don't live there any more; they can do what they like. They can paint the entire house in glowing dog shit for all I care.

I quickly focus back on Peter and pretend I haven't noticed the hall or that he seems to be growing a goatee. A really patchy goatee. He's starting to look like that character from *The Lion, the Witch and the Wardrobe*. What's his name?

'Don't let her eat all of those scones.' I laugh, not because it's funny but BECAUSE OF THE BEARD. Oh, what's that character's name?!

'I won't,' he replies. 'I can't guarantee the same for me though. How are you?'

I'm always suspicious when he makes conversation that doesn't start with the phrase 'We're concerned about . . .'

'Um, I'm fine. Bye then. Have a nice evening.'

(Got it! Tumnus. Mr Tumnus.)

'We will. We're taking Grace to the cinema later.'

My mouth says, 'How lovely,' but my brain is shouting, 'GET BACK IN THE FUCKING WARDROBE, TUMNUS!!'

I'm now too far gone with thoughts of Narnia and Turkish-delight jokes so I mumble my final goodbyes and hurry back to the car. I wonder if he'll shave his beard off for their wedding. I wonder when he'll tell me he's getting married.

CHAPTER FOUR

I get back to the house and throw myself down on the couch. On the weekends I try to catch up on housework, as when Grace is here with me she can destroy a room quicker than I can tidy it. Eventually I move my arse off the sofa, feed Heisenberg, open Grace's window so he can go outside and then prepare to clean. If nothing else, it'll help me forget that bloody awful date from last night.

I shuffle the music tracks on my phone, put my headphones on and begin tidying up to the soothing sounds of the Chemical Brothers. I couldn't endure the pain of housework without tunes. Helen regularly tells me my musical tastes are ridiculous:

'You're thirty-six and listening to dance music. You're not Jo Whiley, you know.'

'I listen to all sorts of music, Helen: pop, disco, dance . . . just because it's not Michael bloody Bublé or whatever—'

'Stop right there. Michael Bublé is a god. A GOD. I won't hear a word against him.'

'I have no idea how we're related.'

I start hoovering just as Donna Summer announcing that she 'feels love' is rudely interrupted by a call coming through on my phone. It's Rose.

'Jason is making me take him to soft play. Fancy bringing Grace? I cannot tolerate that fucking place alone.'

'Ah shit, I've just dropped her at Peter's house. Sorry, love – otherwise you know I would.'

'DAMMIT, now I'm going to have to endure other people's children by myself for two hours.'

I feel for her. There's nothing worse than other people's children.

'Take some trashy magazines, have a coffee and snarl at anyone who comes near you. Y'know – what you usually do.'

She snorts. 'I know. It's just more fun when you're there. What you up to anyway?'

'Bugger all, but I'm fine with that. I'm exhausted.'

'You should get out and about! You need a man. Preferably one who works away a lot and brings you diamonds when he comes back.'

'Like Jason's dad?' I ask, knowing the answer already. 'Two weeks on the rigs and two weeks at home?'

'Ha, all Rob brings me back is washing. But he isn't around long enough to get on my tits, so it works for me. Anyway, enjoy your weekend and see you next week!'

She hangs up first and I get back to cleaning with her

words swimming around in my skull – 'You need a man.' Technically I don't *need* a man; I'm an independent single woman, successfully raising a very clever, witty child and paying my way in the world. That said, I'm pretty tired of living a passionless existence; I do crave company and laughter and impulsive sex and, well, any kind of sex really. I miss the kind of intimacy I haven't had since Peter – the kind that feels like a security blanket that's permanently wrapped around you. I miss knowing I'm loved.

So, no, I don't need a man . . . but sometimes I sure as fuck want one.

It's nearly seven in the evening on Sunday by the time Peter brings Grace home. I see that she's got pasta sauce on her chin, which means he's already fed her. It saves me cooking an hour later than planned so I'm not complaining.

'Did you have a nice time, my darling?' I barely get my question out before—

'I'M GOING TO BE A FLOWER GIRL!' she screams at me, almost bursting with excitement. He's told her.

I look at Peter. I raise my eyebrows. He looks at the ground.

I pretend I'm surprised, because Peter discovering I have inside knowledge of his life isn't worth the hassle. I even smile, despite the fact that I feel numb about the whole thing.

'That's wonderful, darling. Why don't you go inside while I have a quick word with Dad?'

She skips into her room, saying hello to the cat, and I close the front door a little.

'Congratulations, Peter.' I smile unconvincingly. 'Don't you think you should have discussed this with me first? It's a big deal for Grace too.'

'I don't *have* to discuss anything with you. I wanted to tell my daughter first.'

'Our daughter, Pete – *our* daughter. Don't pretend that you wouldn't react the same way if the tables were turned.'

'No, I wouldn't.'

He looks like a nine-year-old who's being told off, but like any nine-year-old he's determined to remain defiant as fuck. He can never just admit when he's wrong.

'Look, I have to get inside. All I'm saying is a heads-up would have been nice. It's a big deal.'

'For Grace? Or for you? Feeling a little bit jealous?'

'I'm not even dignifying that, you arrogant shit. Who do you think you are? Go away.'

'Thought so,' he says with a smirk.

And with that he walks back down the path and gets into his car while I breathe the word 'bastard' after him. It still makes me sad that someone I once loved very much now feels nothing but contempt for me. The man I thought I'd spend my whole life with is now a stranger to me, and behind my anger I can't help but feel wounded.

I go inside, put on my happy face and prepare to listen to how thrilled and excited Grace is about the wedding, despite the fact I'm still raging inside.

Sunday night is always bath night. Even though Grace would happily play in the bath for hours at a time, getting her in there in the first place is always a chore.

'Bath or shower, Grace?' I take towels from the cupboard and place them over the radiator.

'Neither.'

'Neither isn't an option. I'm running a bath now.'

'What do I get?'

'Two bedtime stories.'

'I'd get that anyway . . .'

'GET IN THE BATH!!!'

She giggles and hops through from the living room. I pour bubble bath under the running water.

'Do you think I'll get to wear a big white dress, Mum? And a tiara?' Grace hops in and starts playing with the little plastic sea creatures she got from Deep Sea World three years ago, which are now beginning to look like they deserve a decent sea burial.

'Hmm, usually it's the bride who wears the big white dress, honey,' I reply, thinking that Emma will probably wear black and float down the aisle on a broomstick. 'I'm sure Dad will let you pick a lovely dress though.'

After the bath, we make it through two chapters of *Coraline* before Grace starts to yawn. I fold down the page and kiss her goodnight, and she snuggles down under the covers. The cat is sleeping on top of her drawing table – he's so sweet when he's not being a furry dickhead.

After I've prepared Grace's packed lunch for the morning, I text Helen to remind her that she's taking Grace to school and then I head to bed too, taking *Coraline* with me. It's not that I'm tired; I just don't feel like spending yet another bloody evening sitting on the sofa in my own company. I'm starting to bore myself. I'd like to put Grace to bed and snuggle up with someone who gives a shit about my day, which, as it happens, was both tedious and swift and was filled with routine household drudgery. Everything in my life is planned. There's no excitement any more, no surprises. How I long to be surprised.

I lay out my clothes for the morning on my chair, flop into bed and begin reading where we finished up.

I hope tomorrow is a better day.

CHAPTER FIVE

I catch the 8.21 from Queens Park and manage to grab a seat beside a stubble-faced man-beast who's clutching a bottle of Irn-Bru like his life depends on it. His dark grey designer suit screams, 'I AM A MAN WHO MEANS BUSINESS!' but his crumpled face sobs, 'I AM A MAN WHO DIDN'T MEAN TO STAY UP UNTIL 3 A.M. DRINKING WHISKY.'

The journey is short, only two stops. I clamber off the train at Central station and am instantly lost in a sea of familiar, miserable faces, all of whom would rather be anywhere else than heading to work. Technically I don't need to work at the office; I can write from home and email my copy, but I know that if I don't make the effort to go in once a week, I'll become the kind of freelancer who lives in her whiffy dressing gown, only getting dressed for the school run or to answer the door to the pizza guy. Appealing as that sounds, I choose to remain a functioning member of society for as long as possible.

Just like everything else in my life, my routine rarely changes, the exception being where I choose to buy my coffee in the mornings. This depends entirely on length of queue, and today I spy only three people in line at Delice de France. This is almost unheard of, so I casually head towards it, trying not to alert other coffee drinkers to this miracle by rushing. I spot a well-dressed, haughty woman in a faux fur coat approaching the queue. Dammit, she looks as if she's about to order something they'll have to import in especially for her. I refuse to be stuck behind anyone who wants to sample every option before spending three pounds fifty, so my footsteps quicken to an 'Oh no you fucking don't' pace. I slip into the queue seconds before her, and although my face remains emotionless, inside I've just crowned myself CHAMPION OF THE FUCKING WORLD and I'm wearing her fur coat like a royal robe!

I order my skinny caramel latte and eye up the pastries, deciding on the last chocolate croissant while the barista cleans the coffee machine with a vice-like grip some men would pay handsomely for. I'm completely bewitched by this until someone taps me on the shoulder, breaking my concentration.

'Morning, Cat!'

It's my colleague Leanne.

'Ready for a brilliant day? I've been up since six – already been for a jog.'

Leanne's a morning person.

'I'm starving. I was going to . . . Look at that man over there. Is he wearing tweed? It's too hot for tweed.'

Leanne is easily distracted.

'Oh, you've bought the last chocolate croissant. Bugger. Split it with me? I really don't have time to wait in line somewhere else.'

Leanne can go and fuck herself.

'Oh, go on. I'll give you one of those hot-chocolate sachets I keep hidden in my drawer.'

I'm tempted to tell her that I'm already aware of her hot-chocolate stash and have been raiding it for the past year – and can she stop buying the hazelnut ones as they taste like shit – but instead I nod and reluctantly hand her a torn-off corner of the pastry as we walk towards the station exit.

I walk. She bounces. It was one of the first things I noticed about her when she joined the company last year. Everything about Leanne is bouncy, from her personality to her curly black hair. She's not so much a glass-half-full kind of girl; more of a girl who's simply excited to have a glass in the first place.

We stop at the traffic lights on Union Street, crushed between the other Monday-morning losers.

'Good weekend then?' she continues, stuffing the pastry in her mouth and brushing the crumbs off her navy suit jacket. 'Charlie and I went to Ikea. He bought a new computer table; hideous red thing, but it's for his office. I got—'

'Meatballs?' I interrupt.

'Ha! Of course. You can't go to Ikea without having meatballs. But I also got a new rug for the bedroom. It's so fluffy.'

'Does Charlie like a fluffy rug?' I enquire, wondering why I feel the need to turn everything into a euphemism when I'm bored.

She giggles and shakes her head. 'No, he hates them. He likes a clean area to work with. Bare floors, if you know what I mean.'

'I do, and now I'm sorry I asked.'

She giggles again before her brain takes off in another direction. 'I wonder if they've restocked the vending machine.'

The green man appears and we head down Gordon Street towards our office near George Square. I know the words 'LEANNE'S BARE FLOORS!' will now appear in my mind's eye every so often, flashing in neon seedy strip-club signage. It's going to be a long day.

The *Scottish Tribune*'s new, swanky offices are located near the squinty bridge on the picturesque banks of the River Clyde. They are expensive, clean, modern and unfortunately still being built, which means staff who write for the *Lowdown* continue to work from the third floor of the elevator-free 'Trade House' office block, while the main-paper journalists, sales and production staff are still at their comfy but crowded headquarters in Finneston. The powers that be are building the new block because they think it will be more cost-effective and productive if we are all based in the same building, but the schedule is delayed and, to be honest, I'm not there often enough to care.

The trudge up three flights of stairs never gets easier, but we've learned to cope. I plod along slowly while Leanne takes the steps two at a time because she's a fucking show-off. Her legs are in great shape though – if I put as much time and effort into fitness as I put into being a smartarse, I'd probably be leaping up the stairs too.

I swing open the office doors and I'm greeted by the usual sight of messy desks, strewn newspapers, PR freebies and the wall display of our magazine covers, which could use a good polish. Five of us work for the magazine, but it appears that only three have made it in so far today. I smile over at Gordon, our music editor. He's already on Twitter and downing a Red Bull.

'Morning, Gordon. Good weekend?'

'Nope.' He continues typing. His red hair looks as if it has been lovingly ruffled by a shark.

'Anything you'd like to share with the group?' I ask. The room smells musty. I get up and open a window.

He stops tapping for a minute. 'My fucking in-laws came to stay. How the hell my wife turned into the well-adjusted woman she is, I'll never know. Her mum and dad are insufferable. Thank Christ they live three hours away. Here, did you see that cabinet minister got caught in a brothel on Saturday? Clown.'

At my desk it looks like nothing has been touched since last week, including the coffee cup I forgot to put in the sink. Even the cleaners here are shite. I turn on my computer. Nothing happens. Oh for God's sake.

'Yeah, I heard it on the news yesterday,' I reply, thumping the side of my PC. 'Do me a favour, Gordon, and stick a journo request on Twitter for me? I need to speak to women who've had facelifts before fifty, and I can't get this bloody machine to switch on again.'

I hear him laughing. 'Is this for the magazine or for you?'

'It's for your mum.'

'Leanne's signed in – use hers. I can't have that nonsense clogging up my notifications when everyone inevitably takes the piss.'

Leanne smiles and pulls up a webpage for me. I post my request from the column's Twitter account, then log out. Last time I left myself logged in as Glasgow Girl, Gordon announced my forthcoming and completely fictional haemorrhoid surgery to my seventeen thousand followers. I'm wise to these people now.

My editor Natasha arrives ten minutes later, carrying three espressos and a green tea, which she carefully lines up on Leanne's desk.

'Morning, troops. Don't say I'm not good to you.' She opens her coffee and blows on it, looking over at the empty desk in front of Gordon. 'Patrick not in yet?'

Gordon shakes his head. 'He's out on a job. I think he's interviewing Val McDermid.'

'Nice one.' She smiles. 'Catriona, I need some new column suggestions from you this week – I think something slightly more engaging than that piece about how your cat hates men. Not sure I'm convinced that misandry exists in the feline world. Anyway, have a think and we'll talk after lunch.'

I nod and continue trying to turn on my PC, but already a slight twinge of panic has set in. I'm aware from recent online comments that my column isn't as funny or clever as it used to be, and I'm mindful that Natasha has noticed this too. I liked that cat piece! It was funny: how a white cat turned up, knocked on our front door and decided to stay so I called him Heisenberg and because . . . oh fuck it, she's right – it was shit. And he doesn't just hate men, he hates everyone but Grace.

Finally my PC decides to work and I check my emails. It's mostly PR rubbish, one from a crazy woman asking what David Tennant is like in real life and can she have his autograph and several addressed to Glasgow Girl demanding I either shut my face or keep up the good work. I delete them all and neck my espresso, hoping it'll magically trigger some good ideas. It doesn't work. I sigh, and suggest a brainstorm with my colleagues. Leanne is first in line to contribute:

'You know how you said in Saturday's column that you didn't want to do the online dating thing, but maybe you should? Plenty of material there! Lots of people meet online.'

'Yes, yes, everyone knows someone who met their other half online, but that *someone* is usually a socially awkward musician who has run out of people willing to listen to his latest song about Karl Marx on SoundCloud. No, it's all too weird and clinical. AND DANGEROUS. I don't like the thought of searching through hundreds of photos, trying to pick the one who looks the least likely to pick me up in the car that will drive me away from MY LIFE. That shit is real. I watch the news.'

Gordon laughs. 'You're so dramatic. I think you're canny enough to weed out the bad ones.'

'I'm not so sure . . . I could write about speed dating?'

He shakes his head. 'You did that last year.'

'Bugger, so I did. How about I date someone young and then someone old and—'

'Do you really want to date someone old?' Leanne interjects, squinting at me. 'He'll just bore you with tales about the war and you'll be forced to change his incontinence pads.'

'Which war?'

'All of them.'

I place my head in my hands. 'Ugh, I have nothing. My dating life is a big, dull pile of crap! It's not even noteworthy enough to write about once, let alone week after week. The last man I asked out on Twitter didn't even bother replying.'

'You ask men out? Well, there's your first mistake.' Leanne's looking at me with the face of a 1950s housewife.

'What do you mean? It's 2014. Women do that. I ask men out all the time.'

'And how's that been working out for you so far?'

'Sometimes they say yes . . .'

'But it never lasts, right? Oh, don't look at me like that. I had the same problem! You have to read *the book*.'

'There's a book? What book?'

'*The Rules of Engagement*. I swear it changed my effing life. I'm engaged to Charlie because of it.'

'Oh, is it one of those generic self-help brain-fucks, Leanne? I hate those.'

Leanne's phone starts to ring. 'It's a remarkable book. Look, just go out at lunchtime and buy it. You won't be sorry – Hello? Yes, this is Leanne.'

I swivel back round on my chair, laughing. A dating book? I don't fucking think so.

Lunchtime arrives and everyone heads off to do their own thing. I could just have the packet soup I've had in my desk since Christmas, but instead I decide to dine alfresco by buying a sandwich and sitting in George Square watching all the suits and the students go about their lunch hour. Since I'm usually stuck at home writing, this helps to remind me that I still live in a world where other human beings exist. I hope that a good hard dose of people-watching will inspire me, because I'm struggling to come up with new ideas. I'm not sure when or why I lost my spark, but I'd better get it back pronto before Natasha sees fit to fire me.

Four bites into my Mexican chicken sandwich and I start to attract the attention of several overfed pigeons, which boldly waddle over to see what I'm eating. I feel like I'm in some low-budget Hitchcock remake and I smile, until one of them does a weird flappy thing near me and I leave my bench abruptly, throwing them the rest of my sandwich as I go. I wander into Queen Street station and grab a tea before heading back to the office. Leanne's already there.

'You didn't get the book, did you?' She frowns at me and my lack of carrier bag. 'I knew you wouldn't, so—'

I interrupt her before she mistakenly thinks I care about what she's saying. 'Look, Leanne, I just don't think it's my kind of thing—' but before I can say anything else, she reaches into her own bag and hands me a small black book.

'Surprise! I bought one for you.'

This woman is unstoppable.

Resistance is futile. I take the book from her with a sigh

and drop it on my desk. I glance at the cover: 'The Rules of Engagement: Single to Spoken-for in Ten Easy Steps by Guy Wright' in gold lettering. Ugh. I want to frisbee it out of the window, but instead I smile, playing along, and open it at a random page.

> Stop throwing yourself at men. We know you're keen, but restrain yourself. If a guy likes you, he'll ask you out.

I flip through to another page:

> We want to sleep with you, but if you offer it up straight away, on some level we're going to judge you for it.

I look over at Leanne, who's grinning. 'This isn't serious, right? It's like a parody?'

She shakes her head. 'No, Cat, totally serious! I'm telling you, if you want to find someone, pay attention to every word in this book.'

'But . . . but it's ridiculous! When the hell was this written? 1892? Women being judged for wanting sex?'

'Look, men and women are wired differently. It's about getting an insight into men's minds and being able to act accordingly. It even covers women with children. Like you.'

'Oh, I feel honoured.'

'You're being very negative about this.' Leanne smiles, almost singing the words. She bites into an apple and hums. It's like working beside Snow White.

Natasha comes back from lunch, followed by Gordon, just as I'm in mid-rant about women dating on their own terms and waving the book around in the air.

'Ooh, what's this?' She grabs it out of my hand.

'It's some sexist tripe advising women on how to date,' I reply. 'Leanne thinks it's the Holy Grail of self-help.'

'I've heard about this.' She nods, reading the blurb. 'Glasgow-based author, isn't he? If I'm not mistaken, Debbie from the *Star* met her husband using this book.'

How the hell am I the only one who's never heard of this?

'Told you!' Leanne cries. 'It works!'

'Interesting. Can I see you in my office, Cat?' Natasha hands me back the book and doesn't wait for an answer. I grab my notepad and walk behind her, watching her pencil-skirted bottom wiggle towards her office. I have the feeling that I'm about to get my arse kicked for my recent substandard columns and I start to panic. She sits down and spends a minute checking her emails while I wait.

'So, your column. You know I love it and it's a valuable addition to the magazine, but lately you seem to have lost your edge and, well, your edge is what keeps your work fresh and attention-grabbing. Have you given some thought to what we could run this week? Any good ideas?'

Well, Natasha, that would be none. Zero fucking ideas.

'Hmm, let me see.' I open my notepad and flick through, hoping that something will jump out at me. There's the number Rose gave me for a painter and decorator, a reminder to buy Grace new pants and something scrawled in what looks like Farsi . . . Shit. I'm going to have to think on my feet.

'There's a new dating website for single parents. I thought that—'

'Lead time too long.'

'OK, well, I could talk about past boyfriends and compare—'

'Boring.'

Rude. 'Or I could discuss pornography and—'

'You did the whole porn debate when Cameron decided to bring in the new parental control filters. Anything else? You know that the *Standard* have that new columnist now. Her stuff isn't as funny as yours used to be, but it's doing well.'

USED TO BE? I stare blankly at my notebook and hear her give a big sigh. Oh fuck, I hate it when she sighs. Think, Cat, THINK! I could infiltrate a neo-Nazi gang? I could dabble in tantric sex . . . but I'd need a partner for that. Unlikely. Argh! I need to come up with something right now, before she sighs again. In my panic, I hold up *The Rules of Engagement*.

'OR I could do this book. I could do a weekly column where I follow these rules.'

Oh NO! Stop talking. What am I saying? Maybe she didn't hear me. Maybe she'll hate the idea. Maybe—

'I love that idea! "I Followed the Rules". It has a nice ring to it.'

Fuck. Just. Fuck.

She stands up and smiles. 'Great idea, Cat. Be funny, be enthusiastic and please be ready with a seven-hundred-word intro piece by Thursday to replace that bloody cat dirge.'

Seven hundred? That's double my usual word count. I want to argue but I have nothing to bargain with, so I bite my tongue and agree this one time. As I return to my desk, I try not to make eye contact with Leanne, who's bursting to know what happened.

'Is everything OK, Cat?'

'Not really. I'm now following these rules for my column and IT WAS MY IDEA. How did this happen?'

'I think it's a brilliant idea!'

'I blame you.'

She laughs. 'I can live with that. Who knows – you might even meet someone.'

'Anyway, I have seven hundred words to write for this week, so I'm ignoring you now, Leanne.' I take a deep breath, open the book and start reading:

> RULE 1 – *Stand Out from the Crowd*
> *There are millions of women in the world he could have; what makes you so special?*

One line in and I already hate this man. I continue down the page.

> Let's get one thing straight. Men notice women. We're not blind, but we are picky. We notice everything about you, from your hair to your glasses to your breasts, all the way down to your shoes. We don't all have the same type, and naturally what one man considers ugly another will consider beautiful. This isn't a book that will tell you that you have to look like a certain stereotype or cliché; this is a book that will empower you to stop acting like one. This book will also encourage you to forget everything you thought you knew about dating and men and relationships. You'll be the one in control; he just won't realize it.

> When it comes to getting serious about a woman, we're looking for something unique. We want to date someone who exudes a quiet confidence, who stands out from the crowd. For example, there are millions of thin, blonde women wearing fake tan and clothes from Topshop. Or you geeky girls with the thick glasses and 1940s dress sense – you're hardly original any more; what makes you special? And don't start going on about personality – first visual impressions are everything. If we're not attracted to you, we won't

ask you out and we'll never know how smart and
funny you might be.

His tips, which will apparently help me stand out from the crowd, include: avoiding being one of those tittering, vacant girls; exploiting my femininity through hair flipping and skirt wearing and, most importantly, maintaining an air of aloofness but without being a prick about it. Never at any point does he say, 'Hey, be yourself!' because apparently being yourself is the reason you're still single – a comforting thought.

I move on to Rule 2, which is subtly called 'If You Don't Ask, You Don't Get'. This must be what Leanne was going on about.

If you ask a guy out and he has nothing better to do, chances are he'll say yes. This doesn't mean that he actually wanted to go out with you; it just means he's not busy. But if you let him do the chasing, you can be confident that this man is completely interested in you and not just passing the time until someone better comes along.

As stated previously, men will notice you – it's up to you how this happens. I don't advise making it obvious that you want to be noticed – nothing screams desperation more than a woman staring at a man like it's dinnertime. Make your presence

known, but if he doesn't approach you, he's either
not available or he's not interested. Learn this truth
quickly and your life will be a lot easier.

Bemused, I close the book.

I find it hard to believe that this stuff actually works, but after a bit of research I seem to be the only one who doubts its effectiveness: of 2312 reviews on Amazon, 2300 are 'four star or above', with comments like, 'Good 4 single ladiez!', 'Arrived just in time' and 'Finally something that works!'

There are some one-star cynics, to which of course I'm naturally drawn: 'Utter nonsense', 'The author of this book should be shot' and 'FORGET FEMINISM, ABANDON COMMON SENSE AND BE PREPARED TO LOSE YOUR DIGNITY.'

But, horrifyingly, the general consensus is that the majority of readers are now happily attached thanks to *The Rules of Engagement.*

For now, I decide to keep an open mind. That said, when it comes to writing my column, I know I'm going to find it very hard to keep my snark in check.

The Lowdown magazine – *Saturday 11 October 2014*

Can dating books really change your love life?
Glasgow Girl's about to find out . . .

I FOLLOWED THE RULES

CHAPTER SIX

Kerry buries her face in the magazine and laughs loudly. We're having a rare Saturday lunch together and she's insisting on reading my column aloud, as if I don't already know what it says.

> The Scottish author using the cringeworthy pseudonym 'Guy Wright' explains that there are certain rules I should be sticking to when attempting to find a man who's also in the market for live music, romantic strolls and eventual genital contact, followed by fighting, marriage, apathy, hair loss and death.

'Oh my God, this is so wrong. How are you ever going to manage this? One rule per week, or what?'

'Well, there are ten rules and each applies to certain points in the relationship, so I guess I'll just hope the first few work, then wing it.'

She stops at a point halfway down the page. '"Be unique"? What the fuck does that even mean? You'd better not become one of those pricks who knits their own pubes into a hat and sells it on Etsy.'

'It means I have to "stand out from the crowd" so that I can be noticed by one of the seventeen single men who still fucking exist in Glasgow—'

'Sixteen,' Kerry interrupts. 'Masood from my work just started seeing someone.'

'I don't even know who that is, but I feel cheated.'

Kerry snorts and continues reading.

Making eye contact is a no-no. This isn't a job interview. I'm supposed to look anywhere and everywhere else, ensuring my gaze doesn't meet his, otherwise he'll assume I'm desperate to have his babies and drag him down the aisle, brazenly eyeballing him as I do so.

She looks genuinely confused. 'So how will you know if he's noticed you?'

'Because he'll approach me and propose right there and then. Besides, I plan to set my limbs on fire and do star jumps – it'll be impossible not to notice me.'

Finally she closes the magazine. 'I have no idea how you're going to do this with a straight face, but it's going to be HILARIOUS. I cannot wait to read the next one.'

If Kerry of all people is reacting like this, then I imagine a lot of readers are. Natasha will be thrilled.

I get up from her brand-new cream John Lewis kitchen table and switch on the kettle. The flat Kerry shares with

Kieran isn't huge, but you can tell it's owned by two people who really have their shit together. Everything matches, everything is clean and nothing is out of place. You can also tell that it's not inhabited by any children; otherwise this beautiful kitchen table would be covered in snot and crayon stickmen.

'Well, following the rules of engagement can't be worse than whatever I'm unsuccessfully doing at the moment,' I say, taking a mug from the draining board. 'You want coffee?'

'No, ta, but you can grab me a Diet Coke from the fridge. Maybe it'll actually work. Maybe this time next year you'll be happily attached and shamefully pregnant out of wedlock.'

'Well, one can dream.'

She smiles and glances at her wrist. 'Shit, it's quarter past three. I'm going to have to throw you out soon. I'm getting my hair coloured at four.'

'That's OK; Peter's bringing Grace back to mine anyway. Are you staying brown or changing it to something weirder?' Kerry's hair has been every shade imaginable, including some colours that don't technically exist.

'I'm keeping the brown for now. As much as I'm tempted to get bright white streaks, I think I'm getting a bit old for all that now.'

'I don't think many accountants have fashion colours in their hair anyway.'

She glares at me. 'I work in finance; this does not make me an accountant. And the correct answer is: "You're not old, Kerry. You can have fun hair if you like, Kerry. I LOVE YOU, KERRY."'

I pour my tea, then hand her an ice-cold Coke from the fridge. 'Of course you're not old! Thirty-five is the new twenty-five. We're both in our prime.'

'Really? So how come you're so set in your ways? When was the last time you went a bit wild?'

I think for a moment. 'I slept naked the other night. Totally in the buff. Does that count?'

'Not if you were alone, no.'

'Look, I'm raising a child on my own. If I get wild, social services gets called in. Anyway, I thrive on my strict routine; it's the only thing keeping me sane. I'll consider getting a life when Grace leaves home.' God, I hope Grace never leaves home, but I'm not admitting that to someone who has made it clear on several occasions that she doesn't understand the need for children.

We leave at quarter to four and I drop Kerry at 'Logan and Cross', the only salon in Glasgow she considers worthy to touch her hair. I carry on home, all the time wondering how on earth I'm going to successfully follow this book.

A quick stop at Tesco for snacks and I'm home. I open a packet of pistachio nuts and sit silently on the couch, shelling them one by one while staring at the black cover with the gold lettering. Finally I open the book and read

Rules 1 and 2 again. The main points seem to be: don't be too forward, eager, giggly or chatty. Basically, be *restrained*. If the author isn't secretly a presenter from a 1940s public-information film, I'll be surprised.

My darling daughter arrives home at five with tales of swimming pools and ladybirds, but Peter remains quiet, barely making eye contact. Maybe he's following the fucking rules of engagement too.

Grace eats some cold tuna pasta for dinner and we spend the evening watching a film about talking dogs before she falls asleep on my lap. Really, someone should warn you that you'll be forced to watch some of the worst films ever made when you become a parent.

I help her through to my bed and carefully put on her nightdress, hoping she won't suddenly spring back into life and demand to stay up. She doesn't. She snuggles under the covers and I lie down beside her, hoping to have five minutes of calm without the pressure of planning what I'm going to do about these bloody rules. It doesn't work. The dark room is soothing but the words '*Stop making the first move*' fizz around in my head, until a realization comes to me. In every single long-term relationship I've had, I've been the one who made the first move. And not one of them has lasted. Lewis – the boy from university, who used to kiss my neck and make me feel like I was floating, dumped me for a girl with huge tits; Michael – the man who could never commit to anything; and finally Peter

– the man who broke my heart the hardest but who helped me create the most incredible little girl. I met them, I approached them, I loved them and I lost them. Would I still be in a relationship if I'd waited to be asked out? Would I have had any relationships at all? Is the author on to something with this?

Feelings of failure begin to rise and I get up and march back through to the kitchen. I stand at the fridge, drink some orange juice directly from the carton and attempt to pull myself together, reminding myself that the ramblings of some lunatic writer aren't true just because he and several thousand others said so.

Although I'm too young to remember him, Mum always said that Dad pursued her for ages. She said that he was very handsome, but handsome men weren't to be trusted and it was weeks before she finally agreed to go out with him. They got married one cold October day at a registry office after she found out she was pregnant with Helen. Four years later, I came along. Then, on my first birthday, he went to work and never came home. We haven't seen him since, but Helen did some digging and apparently he now lives in Spain with his third wife, Jennifer. He never had any more children, probably because he didn't even want the ones he already had.

If anything, this proves that most relationships fail anyway, regardless of who makes the first move. I rarely think about my dad – it makes me think of how hard Mum's life was, and although it's been ten years since her accident, I still miss her terribly. I know she would have loved Grace.

I place the orange juice back in the fridge and wipe a tear from my cheek. Fuck night-time; I'm never this morose during the day. I'll think about this rule thing tomorrow. It's only ten thirty but I'm exhausted, so I pull on an old T-shirt and climb back in beside Grace, who is now starfishing the bed and snoring soundly. I kiss her forehead and cuddle in, ignoring the sound of the text message coming through on my phone. Right now there's nothing I need more than this cuddle.

We get up at eight and she dances bare-arsed to 'YMCA' on Wii Party while I make us some eggs and toast. I draw smiley faces on the boiled eggs and cut the toast into soldiers, feeling like a shining example of motherhood. Setting the table, I call her through to eat.

'Aren't you going to put some pants on?'

She nods. 'Someday. I want breakfast first. You don't need pants for breakfast. Or for Sundays.'

'Which egg do you want?'

She carefully examines each face before pointing to the one on the right. 'That one. The one that looks like Dad.'

'Does it?' I turn it around and, true enough, staring back at me, is a small, soft-boiled Peter. I examine the other one. It looks like Clint Eastwood. I have no idea what goes on in my head sometimes.

'Good choice,' I reply, and watch with a strange delight as she scalps it.

After breakfast I dump the dishes in the sink and take my tea over to the couch to check my phone while Grace plays. There are two texts from last night, both from Rose:

22.45: *Want to take the kids to the park tomorrow?*

23.20: *Y U NO ANSWER ME?*

I giggle and press the green Call button. There's a sleepy 'Hello?' from the other end.

'Hi, Rose. I went to bed early. I wasn't ignoring you.'

'I figured. You up for the park? I need some company.'

'Yeah, why don't we take some lunch and head to Rouken Glen? I'll drive.'

I arrange to pick them up at noon and tell Grace that we're spending the afternoon at the park.

'Do we have to go with Jason?' she asks, scrunching up her face. 'He says I'm a crybaby. *He's* the crybaby. I cried because I hurt my knee. He cried when the lunch lady gave him peas.'

'Yes, I'm aware of his pea phobia. Boys can be silly at this age, Grace; it does get better. And you like him most of the time. Just try and play nicely.'

She sighs and continues dancing while I get her clothes from her bedroom, feeling bad that I just lied to her. Boys don't get better with age; they just get taller.

After arriving at Rouken Glen and then driving around for ten minutes, we finally manage to park near the exit.

We make our way towards the swing park, and while the kids play we try to find a picnic table, but it seems every person on the south side of Glasgow has decided to spend their Sunday here too. Eventually we spy a nice spot near a tree and lay out the blanket Rose has thankfully thought to bring. She's also brought crustless sandwiches, cucumber slices, dips, olives, snacks, water and cups. Me? I've brought three Kinder Eggs, a bottle of something that resembles piss, a multipack of beef Monster Munch, some brown bananas and one napkin for the four of us.

'Should we call them over?' I ask Rose, stuffing a Monster Munch in my mouth.

'They can see where we are. They'll be over when they're hungry.'

We stretch out on the blanket, soaking up the sun like two pasty sponges. Rose sits up and nudges me, lowering her sunglasses.

'Do you see that man playing football with his kid?'

I look around. There are quite a few dads playing football with their kids. 'Narrow it down, Rose.'

'The one in the black T-shirt.'

I spot him straight away. There are also three other mothers watching him from a nearby bench. Rose lowers her voice.

'That's Billy Murphy. He's just split from his wife, Lindsay. I'm not surprised – she's a stuck-up witch of a woman. Rob plays five-a-side with him sometimes. They call him "abs".'

'Yeah, he looks fit.'

'Doesn't he just? You should talk to him. I bet he'd go out with you.'

'What, and be his rebound girl? No, thanks. Besides, he has to approach me first. And I smell like beef.'

'What? Why?'

'Because of the crisps.'

'No, why does he have to approach you first?'

'Long story – you can read all about it next Saturday. It's for work.'

She looks a bit scared. 'I don't understand. How on earth are you going to find a boyfriend if you can't chat them up?'

'EXACTLY!' I shout, throwing my arms in the air. 'See? YOU get it!'

'I don't actually, but, um, I'll look forward to reading your column.'

Jason comes back first, followed by Grace, who begs me to pour her some juice or she just might die. 'Having fun?' I ask, sniffing the bottle of piss and deciding I'm at least 85 per cent confident that it's apple juice. 'Come and eat, and then we'll feed the swans and see the waterfall.'

While the kids are eating I continue to watch 'Abs Morrison'. I'm intrigued. I'm not really into sporty types, but I'd make an exception for this one. AND he already has a child, so me having one shouldn't be too much of an issue. Maybe Rose is right, this isn't such a bad idea.

As we pack up and collect the rubbish, I notice a litter bin near where he is and decide to test out Rule 2, remembering the book's advice:

Men will notice you – it's up to you how this happens.

'I'll just get rid of this!' I announce cheerily, grabbing the bag of rubbish and heading towards the bin, knowing that I'll have to walk past Abs en route. I'll just saunter past him, where he can see me. Maybe put a little wiggle in my walk. Here goes.

I get closer, casually slowing down as I walk between him and his son. 'Don't look at him, just look straight ahead. Be cool,' I mutter to myself, as I wiggle directly into an oncoming football. It whacks me on the side of my face, I go over on my ankle and his kid starts laughing.

'HA! DAD, IT BOUNCED OFF HER HEAD!'

'You all right?' I hear him call, but it's drowned out by the sound of my own voice: 'Great, Cat! WELL, THAT'S ONE WAY TO GET HIM TO NOTICE YOU.' I'm mortified. I can't believe I actually said that out loud, so I just give Billy and his son a thumbs-up. A. Fucking. Thumbs. Up. WHO DOES THAT?

Everyone has finally stopped laughing at me by the time we reach the duck pond. If it was deeper, I'd happily throw myself in and end it all. My ear is throbbing and I want to go home.

'Where are the signals, Mum?' asks Grace.

'They're called cygnets, and they're right in the middle of that little island. Look closely and you'll see them. They're getting quite big now.'

Rose frowns as we walk slowly around the pond, passing elderly couples and families who've all brought their stale loaves and picnic scraps along. 'Trust me to cut the crusts off the sandwiches. What an idiot.'

'Listen, I just got skelped in the face by a football while trying to get a man to notice me. It's safe to say you're winning at Sunday so far.'

'Are you going to include that in your column?' she teases.

'Am I fuck . . . Jason, don't go too near the edge. The water doesn't look that clean.'

Rose swiftly yanks him back before he's head first into the pond, and we walk back towards the car, past the small but noisy waterfall hidden away at the top of a wooded area. This place reminds me of being a kid, where Helen and I would throw pennies in and wish for My Little Ponies and a VHS player, instead of the shitty Betamax we couldn't find decent films for. We'd look for bats in the trees, throw sticks in the stream and now I'm doing the very same with my own child. If this was *The Lion King*, I'd be holding Grace aloft right now, singing 'The Circle of Life' in my best Elton John voice.

By the time we get back to the car, it's almost five. I turn on the radio for the kids. They sing along to 'Happy' by Pharrell, and Rose and I both agree how, despite his stupid hat collection, we totally would. I drop them home and continue on to our flat, where Helen is out front, unloading two large spider plants from her car. Grace gets out first and runs over.

'Hi, Aunt Helen! That's nice. Why have you got two?'

'Hello, Gracey. There are two because one is for your mummy.'

'Cool. We don't have any plants.'

Helen looks at me. 'I know. That's why I bought it.'

I lock the car and join in the conversation about my plant-less existence.

'We did have a plant once. It died quickly. Anyway, I prefer flowers. They make the flat smell nice.'

'Plants provide clean air and it's not toxic for cats—'

'Stop trying to pitch it to me. You're not on *Dragon's Den*. I'll put it in the living room and be sure to take my time killing this one. Thank you.'

She frowns at me and closes her car boot. 'I read your column. I'm happy that you're proactively seeking a boyfriend, but I'm not a big believer in these American self-help books. Too touchy-feely for me.'

'The author is Scottish.' I reply. 'From Glasgow, I believe, and while I'm glad you approve, I'm only doing it for the magazine. Anyway, it's not that kind of book. It's more about turning yourself into the type of woman a man wants . . . y'know . . . reserved . . . feminine . . . devoid of all personality and—'

'Oh, don't tell me any more, Cat; it sounds awful. Just be yourself. That's good enough.' She presses her car remote and turns to leave, pausing only to squint at me and say, 'Maybe you should get a fringe? No one in this family was blessed with a small forehead.'

'Fine just as I am, eh?' I laugh. My days of being hurt by Helen's overcritical eye are long gone.

Grace has already disappeared inside with the door key, so I graciously take my new plant off Helen and make my way to my flat. I plop the plant down on the coffee table, wondering which spot looks best. In the end I let Grace decide. She opts for the top of the white bookcase so that Heisenberg won't poo in it. Wise move.

Another weekend over. I put out Grace's school clothes, then spend twenty minutes looking for her tie, which eventually turns up wrapped around the neck of a *Monster High* doll. Heisenberg goes out, Grace goes to bed and I soak in the bath for forty minutes, planning my week and removing any football dirt that might still be stuck to my face and hair. I feel so fucking conflicted about these rules. On the one hand I'm happy to have a new project to keep me busy, but on the other, my first slapdash attempt to follow the rules backfired spectacularly. From now on I must approach these rules with precision, caution and, evidently, safety gear.

CHAPTER SEVEN

Monday rolls around and I arrive in the office, twenty minutes late but ready to take on the world, one column inch at a time. The warm morning sun has produced a little sweat moustache above my lip so I pull a tissue out of my pocket and discreetly wipe it away, knowing that, at some point, this tissue was used to wipe something manky from Grace's face.

Both Patrick and Gordon are sitting at their messy desks, flicking through newspapers. I can hear Leanne on the phone in Natasha's office.

'What time do you call this?' asks Patrick, biting into a bagel. 'We've all been here for hours.'

Oh lovely – Patrick's back. He's dropped some yellowish bagel filling down his crumpled pink shirt and it's making me feel queasy. I put my bag under my desk and sit down. 'Liar. I had to do the school run this morning. Natasha not in yet?'

'She's out today. I think Leanne's talking to her. Now

that you're here, what are you working on this week?' He stares at me through small designer frames.

Patrick is a divorced first-class cunt who enjoys Russian food, James Joyce and typos in other journalists' articles. During working hours this man is the pin to my bubble. He likes to think he ranks higher than the rest of us in the imaginary chain of command he's somehow had time to invent between gin-tasting sessions and masturbation marathons. He considers himself Natasha's right-hand man – saving the world one pompous book review at a time, when he's not verbosely critiquing art shows, theatre or anything else Kerry would politely call 'wanky'.

I open my diary and try to read my own scribbled handwriting. 'Well, Patrick, if you really must know: I have two telephone interviews for that surgery piece, my column and an advertorial for some weight-loss clinic in Edinburgh. I'm also trying to get an interview with Gerard Butler. He's over here promoting next week, but no one's returning my bloody calls and—'

'They won't,' interrupts Gordon. 'I trashed that film of his last year, remember? Gave it a real kicking.'

'Oh, so you did. Bollocks. Trust you to spoil my one chance to meet him. Anyway, why do you ask, Patrick?'

Patrick looks irked at Gordon's interruption. 'Well, because I need someone to write about *The Voice* for the television section. I'm swamped and I, um, don't have the time. Leanne and Gordon are both busier than you.'

I smirk. 'Ah, you don't even watch it, do you? It offends you, Patrick, doesn't it?'

'Of course it bloody well does!' he bellows. 'But Natasha's insisting we include "relevant" television reviews along-side the "critic's choice" from BBC4, and it's not a show I'll be able to review without prejudice. It's unworthy of my time and talents.'

'But worthy of mine?'

'I assumed that as you sit at home every Saturday night, you'd be familiar with the show, that's all. Don't be childish.'

I hear Natasha's door close as Leanne makes her way back to her desk. 'Morning, Cat. Good weekend?'

Oh you know . . . drew faces on boiled eggs, went to the park, tried to appear alluring and got hit in the fucking face by a football. The usual.

I smile and nod. 'Yes, it was fine, thanks.' I turn to glare at Patrick. 'Apparently I watched *The Voice*.'

'Me too. Love that show! You going to review it for P? I would but I'm snowed under.'

'P' blushes slightly and looks down at his desk. Dear lord, I bet he has a crush on Leanne. That's why he never gives her any shit.

Finally I agree to do it because I'm the bigger person and because he'll grass on me to Natasha if I don't. Cat Buchanan: reluctant team player extraordinaire.

'OK, Leanne. I'm just about to write 450 words for "P"

while he goes to Starbucks and buys me a LARGE Americano. One sugar. Thanks, Patrick!'

He doesn't want to, I can tell, but he shuffles off towards the door anyway, clutching his scuffed leather wallet and I begin typing.

The Voice (aka *Ugly people can sing too*)
There are many things that hurtle through my brain while watching *The Voice* and sadly none of them is a .45-calibre shell from the imaginary handgun I haven't bought yet.

Despite the fact that I've only ever watched one episode, I manage to get 300 words down about the judges, song choices and contestants before finishing with a triumphant conclusion:

Who cares who actually wins the show? I watch it to see the look on someone's face when they've spent ages telling a film crew how they lost both nipples in a sledging accident, only to get no chair turns and a disappointed look from the ghost of the father to whom they've just dedicated their shaky rendition of 'Hero'.

I give it a once-over, then email my copy to Patrick, who mutters a disingenuous 'Thanks' before passing it off as his own work. Ungrateful knob. I see that the bagel filling has somehow crept from his pink shirt on to his red tie and I'm glad he'll have to spend the rest of the day looking like a badly dressed toddler.

Natasha fails to appear, but emails me at four to say that there were 179 comments on my column online, so this is definitely a goer for at least three more weeks. I steel myself and go to the website to check what people have been saying (something I try never to do as a general rule – I tend to get a little stabby if someone's mean about me). Sure enough, the comments section is filled with readers arguing over the merits of the book and wishing me luck. Well, except JohnT567, who says only, 'This woman disgusts me.' I mentally squash his tiny avatar between my finger and thumb, thus destroying him.

I could hang around the office for longer, but really there's nothing that can't be finished off at home, and I can't concentrate on *The Rules of Engagement* with Leanne chattering insistently in my ear. I need to get my arse in gear with this assignment – one failed attempt involving a football isn't going to cut it. I wish everyone a good week before directing my legs down the stairs and towards the train station. Rose has picked up Grace from school, so I don't need to hurry, but my desire to see someone who always looks genuinely happy to see me makes me put a rush on.

Rose is sitting at her green patio table with a black coffee and a closed Marian Keyes paperback, watching Jason and Grace play swing ball at the bottom of the garden. Neither has much luck actually hitting the ball, but they still embrace each fluke with a Wimbledon-like enthusiasm.

'Who's winning?' I ask, sitting beside Rose and waving to Grace, who stops to yell 'Watch this, Mum!' before going in for a killer swing that never happens.

'I have no idea.' Rose laughs. 'I think they're both equally shit at it. Good day?'

I make a groaning noise and shrug. 'So-so. You had the garden done? Looks great.' Sometimes I envy Rose. She lives a ten-minute walk away from us, but with her five-bedroom redbrick house with its huge back garden, it seems more like a million miles.

'Rob's friend Martin offered to do a bit of landscaping on the cheap for us, and I invested in some new pots and shrubs from that garden centre in Giffnock. I have now officially turned into Rob's mother; you never see the old trout without a hand trowel and a bag of foul-smelling compost.'

Grace runs over and hugs me before disappearing to the toilet, and Jason continues to practise his swing, only to hit himself in the forehead with his wooden racket. It's the final straw, and the last thing the poor racket ever sees is the side of a plum tree as it's smashed into pieces by an irate seven-year-old boy shouting, 'THIS IS THE WORST DAY OF MY LIFE.' Rose breathes the word 'fuck' and walks over to comfort her son, who's now throwing a tantrum of massive proportions. Grace returns during this spectacular outburst and whispers, 'He always does this when we play swing ball. Every. Single. Time.'

Puzzled by why Rose doesn't just take the swing ball down, I announce that we're going home and Grace and I leave quietly. I'm grateful Grace is so easy-going – I'd never be able to cope with a kid like Jason. I turn back to look at Rose, who's now sitting on the grass, cuddling her sulking child. She whispers something to him and his little arms wrap around her waist. I smile.

Grace and I walk back towards our flat in silence before Grace says, 'What did Rose whisper to calm Jason down? That she'd buy him a new racket?'

We stop at the kerb to cross the quiet road. 'Hmm, could be, but I think it was something else.' I take her little hand in mine and say, 'I reckon she told him that she loves him very, very much.'

Grace looks at me and smirks. 'Nah. I think it was a new racket.'

Later that evening, I'm sitting on the couch wondering about my next step for the rules when there's a familiar knock on my front door. It makes me smile.

When I was ten, our elderly spinster neighbour Mrs Pollock died, leaving behind a house that lay empty for two years and a rickety brown garden shed that Helen and I adopted. After mum cleaned it, painted it white and removed any potential health hazards, we officially declared it to be our clubhouse – taking several days to perfect our secret knock: essentially the 'Shave and a haircut . . . Two bits' knock from *Who Framed Roger Rabbit?* For five years Helen and I hung out there, and those will always be the happiest memories from my childhood. I think Helen feels the same; twenty-six years later, she still uses the knock.

'I know it's late, Cat, won't keep you. I just wanted to say I'm sorry I couldn't take Grace to school this morning. Staff meeting. Couldn't get out of it.' She's already sitting on the couch by the time she's finished the sentence.

I close the front door quietly. 'Yeah, you already said. It's fine – my boss wasn't in anyway. Everything OK at the uni?'

She takes a peek at the open Word document on my laptop. 'Oh sure. Just the normal budget cuts and staffing problems. How's the dating project going? Any luck yet?' She's avoiding looking me in the eye. She's up to something.

'No, but it's early days . . .' I reply suspiciously. 'Why?'

'Oh, just showing in an interest. Y'know . . . a sisterly interest . . .'

She's definitely up to something.

'Spider plant looks good there, Cat.'

She's stalling, but I'm too busy for this. 'OK, so I'm actually working just now . . .'

'Yes, of course,' she replies. 'I'll let you get on. Oh, before I go –'

Here it comes.

'– I was just wondering if you're free for dinner a week on Wednesday?'

Boom. She knows Grace goes to Peter's on a Wednesday, so therefore I'll be free.

'I'm free this Wednesday. Why not then?'

'We're busy. Going to the cinema,' she snaps. 'Has to be next Wednesday. Well?'

'Well, it depends, Helen – dinner with you or dinner with someone you're secretly trying to set me up with?'

'Just me and Adam. Thought it might be nice! No set-ups.' Her mouth is saying one thing, but her face is telling a different story: the story of a woman who is lying through her fucking teeth. But it's now nearly eleven, and if I don't get some planning done I'll be behind schedule. I unenthusiastically agree to dinner and usher her out of the door, knowing full well that next Wednesday I'll be sitting opposite the next serial killer my sister thinks would be perfect for me.

I tear a sheet of paper from my notepad, open *The Rules of Engagement* and scribble some notes on how I'm going to approach this. It's tough – most of the rules only apply if I actually have a man to use them on – so I'm still stuck at square one.

I finish around midnight and crawl into bed. Although I'm completely exhausted, my brain is working overtime. I have three days to come up with something on the rules of engagement for Saturday's column, which means I'm just going to have to suck it up and get my arse out there, however embarrassing. I could make something up . . . but Natasha can spot a bullshit story a mile off. It's hard enough meeting men when you have all the time in the world; how the fuck am I supposed to do it on a deadline?

The next evening I find myself staring blankly into my fridge, wondering what the hell to make us for dinner. I watch *Masterchef* religiously, I should be able to do this shit but I'm clueless.

Grace has already decided that pizza is the only food she will eat this evening and after surveying the limited options on offer (tomato puree, two eggs, three slices of ham, margarine and a garlic bulb that's been there for at least a year), I have to agree with her. I call Domino's for a medium pepperoni and a side of wedges, insisting they use low-fat cheese like it actually makes any difference. I then set the table and begin to write a shopping list entitled 'Healthy as Fuck', to make up for the shit I'm about to let my child shovel into her mouth.

I tip the pizza girl – her car looks as if it's being held together by rust and hope – while Grace runs through with the pizza and starts without me.

She's already peeling back the lid of the free dip when I sit down beside her. 'Do you have homework tonight?' I ask, watching her rearrange the pepperoni into a face.

'Just reading.'

I wipe my mouth on some kitchen roll. 'Do you need any help with it?'

'Can Dad do it? He helped me last time. He did a really funny reading voice. Maybe I'll just keep it for tomorrow, when I see him.'

Stuff like this kills me. When Grace was born, I never thought that one day Peter's help would be conditional, depending on which day of the week it was. Why couldn't we get our shit together long enough to give her a normal family life?

'That's fine, honey,' I say, taking my plate to the sink. 'Listen, if you don't have anything else to do, why don't we go and get some shopping?'

'No way. I'd rather die.'

'Don't say that. Well, I need to go, and I can't leave you here.'

'I'll go to Aunt Helen's. Anywhere but the shops.'

I call to make sure Helen's home, then send Grace over with the last of the pizza, promising to pick up some prawns for Adam and a magazine for Grace.

As I drive towards the supermarket a thought occurs to me: single men have to eat too. I could use my food shop as an opportunity to be seen by men, who will no doubt be overcome with desire as I wheel around my shopping trolley and seductively compare the prices of loo rolls. This could work.

I park near the entrance and take a look at myself in the mirror, immediately wishing that I hadn't bothered: skin dry and pale, mascara crumbling, pores open. All I need is a bed and a priest standing over me shouting, 'THE POWER OF CHRIST COMPELS YOU!'

Applying the emergency lipstick I keep in the glove compartment, I pinch my cheeks, hoping to look less like a corpse, and head towards the trolley park. Naturally I grab the wonkiest trolley and push it into Sainsbury's, going over the main rules of engagement in my head (*Be confident. Make sure they notice me*) and casually saunter into the fruit-and-vegetable section.

Feeling like some sort of predator, I stalk slowly up and down the aisle, trying to spot any lone men. I have a sudden vision of my future self, spying on men through bunches of bananas and tell myself to get a grip before I'm spotted by security. Even though it's seven thirty on a Tuesday evening, the only men I see are two pensioners and one tired-looking, wedding-ring-wearing dad with three unhappy children; the youngest is stupidly cute and my ovaries do a little happy dance. I remember what Grace was like at that age. I miss that.

I leave my broodiness beside the iceberg lettuce and move on to the chilled goods, where I spot an attractive man lifting a vat of milk with one strong arm. I wheel myself closer for a better look, but then remember that I'm supposed to be inconspicuous. I turn to the side, but now all I can see is cheese. My internal shouting voice becomes louder. HOW IS IT POSSIBLE TO SEE THINGS I'M NOT LOOKING DIRECTLY AT? I'm not a fucking bird.

So I decide to just walk past him. Twice. My rapid side-eye captures enough to let me know that he's mid-thirties, slightly greying and fit as hell. Of course, I have no idea if he's also seen me, and now I'm a woman walking back and forth near some cheese. He heads off to the checkout and I return to my trolley, feeling like an absolute maniac but strangely proud of myself for sticking to the plan.

I continue making my way up and down each aisle pretending to shop, occasionally stopping next to men who, unsurprisingly, don't ask me out there and then. I flip my hair. Nothing. I resist the urge to corner them all with my trolley and shout, 'I HAVE FLIPPED MY FUCKING HAIR. WHAT MORE DO YOU MEN WANT?' It has become apparent that these men either find me hideous, are already seeing someone . . . or perhaps just don't think it's appropriate to pick women up in supermarkets.

I've had enough. I throw some prawns in my trolley, grab the first magazine I see with a free toy and walk towards the checkouts, bumping trolleys with a striking man in a dark blue suit. I smile at him and say sorry. But before he can reply, I tut loudly, abandon my trolley and storm off – I've just broken a rule (no speaking first) and ruined any chance I had of marrying him.

I return home empty-handed and tell Helen and Grace

that the shop was closed. A stern glare lets Helen know not to question this obvious lie.

Back in the flat, I turn on some music, throw myself face first into a pillow and scream. I'm so frustrated. Not only do I still not have anything funny to say in my column, but I also don't have any fucking food in the fridge. I feel sorry for women who follow these stupid rules for months on end while the author, Guy Wright, lies back and makes cash angels on massive piles of money. What kind of lazy pseudonym is that anyway? That in itself is reason enough not to take the man seriously.

On Wednesday I spend the afternoon finishing off some articles for the *Lowdown* and a freelance blog post for a property website ('How to make moving day run smoothly'), as well as being ignored by everyone who works for Gerard Butler and shouting at Heisenberg when he tries to claw my sofa to death. The only thing left to write is my dating column, and I have no idea what to say. I wonder if perhaps I should have buckled down and made more of a serious go at doing these stupid rules. As it is, I'm deleting words as fast as I can write them:

~~Things haven't gone very well this week . . .~~
~~This week I set out to find my true love . . .~~
~~Glasgow Girl thinks Guy Wright is a little scrote . . .~~

This is useless. I shut my laptop, rest my head on the back of the couch and stare at my overpriced pink-and-silver butterfly lampshade from Debenhams, the one Peter wouldn't let me get because he said it was childish and weird. Of course it was the first thing I bought to furnish the flat after we split because, well, fuck him. To be honest, I haven't really looked at it properly in years and I can kind of see his point, but I'd never tell him that. Sometimes I wish I wasn't so stubborn, but not half as much as I wish that my neighbour upstairs would take her fucking shoes off before walking around.

The Wednesday-evening schedule runs smoothly – Grace goes to Peter's house, I take the car to the car wash, successfully purchase our weekly shopping (not a man in sight) and watch a little television before applying my new Clinique night cream and going to bed. I might be soft and fragrance-free, but I'm bored as fuck. If Helen hadn't been busy tonight, I know I could have at least gone over and shared a bottle of wine. But no, I've chosen to stay in and be the old fart I swore I'd never become. My boring, ordinary routine is starting to make me ordinary too. I bet Emo Emma's not ordinary . . . Maybe she's the extraordinary type Guy Wright was referring to. I bet she's a pungi-playing, cock-charming high priestess with a fucking magical vagina. Ugh, piss off, Wednesday evening and your quest to take me to the dark side. I'm not playing. I turn off the light and try not to panic at the fact I still have no column for the weekend. I really do need to start making things happen.

CHAPTER EIGHT

'I'm going to spend today being noticed. I'm going to look nice and smell nice and just walk around Glasgow, letting my enigmatic yet approachable vibes wash over all who notice me. Kerry? Are you there?'

It's 8 a.m. and I've woken Kerry up on her day off to take my very important call. I can picture her talking to me with her eyes half shut and her hair covering most of her face.

'I'm here,' she replies, before yawning loudly in my ear on purpose. 'Kieran is too – in fact he's waving at you with his middle finger as we speak.'

'Yes, I'm aware it's early. I just had to tell someone my plan so that I'd actually go through with it and not bottle it in favour of watching *Criminal Minds*.'

'Right. So where are you going to be noticed?'

'Does it matter?'

She snorts. 'Course it does. There are areas in Glasgow

where you do not want to be noticed, Cat. If I were you, I'd stick to the Southside or the West End.'

'You're such a snob!'

'Perhaps, but I don't think you're going to meet the man of your dreams outside Poundworld on Sauchiehall Street. And won't most men worth dating be at work on a Friday afternoon?'

She has a point. 'Fine, I'll jump on the underground to Byres Road and do a cafe crawl at lunchtime. Men have to leave their desks to have lunch. I'll get them when they're hungry.'

There's no reply. I'm pretty sure she's gone back to sleep, but I hold on for a second, just to make sure.

'Kerry?'

Still nothing.

I hang up the phone and shrug.

I lay out a pretty yet understated summer dress and yellow cardigan, then take a long, hot shower. The radio on the windowsill plays the censored version of 'Starships' by Nicki Minaj, but I add in the swear words with as much delight as if I was fourteen years old. After I've dried and curled the ends of my hair, I copy a Jennifer Aniston make-up tutorial on YouTube. Not my proudest moment, but the results are pretty good, and with that I'm ready to go. I feel like I've spent all morning excitedly getting ready for a date I haven't been invited on yet. I decide that after my half-arsed attempts in both the park and the supermarket, I'll give it one more chance before I declare the entire experiment a waste of time and invite women of the world to publicly burn this book.

Following *The Rules of Engagement* on the underground is extremely easy, as I never make eye contact anyway. It's just not tube etiquette. As I sit down, I catch a glimpse of the man sitting across from me and kick myself for picking a seat opposite a man with the coolest afro I've ever seen. Afros make me happy. I want to look at it. And touch it. And then congratulate him on his amazing hair. I so want to fucking smile at him using all of my face, but I don't because he's a man and Guy Wright specifically forbids the disgusting forwardness of women smiling at men. I continue staring at the advertising banners above his head, and two stops later he (and his hair) walk out of my life forever.

Emerging from Hillhead underground, I resist the urge to acknowledge a guy walking past with his baby in a papoose. Instead I lower my eyes and grin at the baby like a hormonal loon. The baby notices me. Ha, I'm fucking brilliant at this. The baby starts to cry. I speedily set off in the direction of anywhere that wailing baby can't see me.

My plan is to start at Ashton Lane, one of the trendier spots in Glasgow, then work my way down Byres Road, all the way to the next station on Dumbarton Road, with a stream of men following me like I'm the Pied Piper. That, or I'll have consumed too much coffee and it will be a stream of piss and shame trailing behind me.

I wobble up the cobbled backstreet of Ashton Lane, regretting my choice of wedged sandals, and head into Jinty McGinty's Bar. I figure I'll order a cappuccino, sit down and hopefully attract the attention of someone who isn't a nineteen-year-old student from the nearby university, which might be a long shot. It's an older crowd inside – small groups in booths and geriatric regulars – propping up the bar, so I take my coffee outside to the huge beer garden around the back of the pub. It's lunchtime and it's mobbed with people who all look younger than me. I spot a couple leaving and grab their table, thankful that I won't have to stand there in front of everyone, awkwardly holding a hot cup or, worse, trying to sit gracefully on the grass.

I take out my phone; a missed call from Kerry and a text from Peter, which I feel obligated to look at in case something's wrong:

Where is that purple dress we bought Grace last year?

I was right to check – something is wrong: Grace's dad has finally lost the plot. Last year? He seems to forget that, unlike him, children are unable to wear an item of clothing from the previous year, what with all the growing they selfishly do. Maybe he thinks I sold it to pay for Botox. Maybe Emma wants to wear it for the wedding. Maybe *he* does? Who knows?

I calmly reply: *I'm guessing it stopped fitting her and went to live in a charity shop. Before you ask, I don't have the shoes you bought her in 2008 either. Busy. See Grace at 5.*

I turn my phone off and try to relax. I'm here to meet someone new, not be reminded that I once thought I was compatible with a dress-hunting pharmacist who sits down to pee.

I drink my coffee slowly – I'm aware that getting up to order something else from the bar will result in the loss of my table – but I spend so long nursing it, it goes cold and I'm forced to push it to one side. Moments later I see a man walking towards me and nonchalantly look somewhere else so he doesn't think I give a crap (even though I do). He's coming right towards me; I can feel him looking at me. Oh fuck, is this rules of engagement shit actually working?

Be calm, Cat. Act like this sort of thing happens all the time. WAH, HE'S STANDING BESIDE ME.

'Hi. Is this seat taken?' His strong Geordie accent is rather charming.

I glance at him (nice jeans, dodgy belt, yuck – T-shirt tucked in, but when he loves me I'll tell him to stop doing that) and then at the wooden stool before casually replying, 'No. It's free.' I run my hand through my hair, waiting for him to sit down.

He utters a quick, 'Thank you,' lifts the stool and takes it over to a table where his girlfriend is already sitting. Oh fucking hell! Now I'm just the woman on her own, with a cold coffee and no extra seat. I feel like walking over, giving them my handbag and yelling – 'TAKE IT. NOW I HAVE NOTHING. ARE YOU HAPPY?'

I decide to move on from Jinty's and try somewhere else, away from Ashton Lane. It's only T-shirt-tucking wankers that go there anyway.

I head back to Byres Road and spot my next cafe across the street. I carefully cross the busy road – being pulled from under the wheels of a bus is not the type of attention I'm after.

As soon as I step foot in the first cafe, my heart sinks. It's full of women – specifically four middle-class women huddled in a booth to my left, each clutching a paperback copy of *Eat, Pray, Love*. It's an afternoon book group. Who the fuck has a book group in the middle of a weekday afternoon?

To the right of me there are four tables, one occupied by a woman who's having a pot of tea alone but is dressed to impress in navy and white. I fear we might both be on the same pointless dating quest. I peek around the side of the counter to see if there's a hidden back room, but no, just three more empty tables, a large rubber plant and the door to the gents' toilets. I consider looking in there, but before I take that drastic step, a server asks what she can get me.

'White coffee, please.'

'Sure. Large?'

'No, just a regular, thanks.'

'Can I get you any cookies, cakes or pastries?'

Oh, sure. In fact, give me all of them and I'll be the girl sitting alone stuffing her fat face while teapot lady remains elegantly cake-less and crumb-free.

'No, thanks, just the coffee.'

'I'll bring it over.'

Common sense tells me to take my coffee to go, but I hesitate. What if my next boyfriend walks in and I'm not here to dazzle him? I make a point of sitting where I'm plainly visible to everyone (men) who walks in, but it's still close enough to the book group to hear their discussion on *Eat, Pray, Love*, which means I get coffee and free entertainment. I lean in to listen:

'I'd seen the movie before I read it, and to be honest I don't remember Julia Roberts being so self-absorbed in the movie,' says the one in the scarlet top. She has cappuccino foam on her lip and no one has told her.

'I agree,' replies the woman in black next to her. The rest wait expectantly, but she doesn't say anything else; instead she clears her throat and folds her napkin into the shape of (amazingly) a much smaller napkin. The third woman chimes in.

'Well, I loved it. It was wonderfully written escapism and the closest I'll get to living in Italy or Bali. Some of it could have been written specifically for me, what with my recent divorce. It made me ask myself some pretty deep questions. What did you think, Claudia?' Divorced woman turns her head to look at the last member of the group, who's been slowly stirring her frothy coffee since the discussion began.

'Well, Louise, I thought it was awful.'

Louise sighs. 'Oh really. Honestly, the first book I pick and you're all dismissing it. It's sold over eight million copies! Would you care to expand, Claudia?'

Claudia places her teaspoon on her saucer and smiles. 'Yes, Lou, I would. Let me see . . . I got halfway through and began to question my own existence as it made me want to *fucking kill myself* because I'll never be able to unread it. *But then* I remembered I'd have to come here and relive the whole pasta-eating, God-bothering, inner-peace-finding bullshit with you three! I actually typed "I WOULD LIKE TO DIE NOW" in capital letters on Bing. Not even Google. BING!'

I actually liked that book, but now I like Claudia even more. The rest of the women are just staring at her. Louise looks annoyed. The woman in the scarlet top with the cappuccino moustache is grinning.

Claudia redirects her rage towards the woman dressed in black. 'You didn't even read this, did you, Sarah? Come on – what did you read?'

'I did read it!' Sarah protests.

Claudia narrows her eyes. '*What did you read*, Sarah?'

'. . . *Doctor Sleep*.'

'Oh, fuck this.'

I'm transfixed. Even the waitress is pretending to clean the table next to me so she can listen in. Unfortunately however, from the way Claudia is gathering up her carrier bags, it looks like she's decided to leave. She does, without saying a word to anyone. This is the best book group EVER. The rest of the women continue chatting like nothing has happened. I turn my attention back to my rapidly cooling coffee, wondering if anyone with an Adam's apple is ever going to walk in, but they already have. In fact, while I was so busy pretending not to listen to Claudia's hilarious meltdown, a man has come in, bought a coffee and *is now sitting beside teapot lady.* The right side of my brain tells me that it's likely she knows him, but the left side is insisting that HE CHOSE HER OVER ME. Regardless, I'm not staying here any longer. Time to move on.

I carry on down Byres Road, one sandalled foot in front of the other, shoulders back, determined to give this one last go before I get the tube back to where I've parked my car. I feel down but not out. Finally I'm making a real effort to meet men and I shall not be defeated. But unfortunately the weather has other plans. The gentle breeze that greeted me when I came off the train has now turned into a level-five hurricane, blowing my dress and hair in the same upwards direction, so I dart into the first pub I see and head for the ladies'.

After washing my hands with bright green soap I glance in the mirror and laugh out loud. My hair is ridiculous; my look has gone from cafe crawl to saloon brawl. My once perfectly styled curls are now snake-like tangles – if this was ancient Greece, I'd expect to be beheaded by Perseus at some point soon. Opening my bag, I take my comb and try to salvage my hair, even attempting to smooth it under the geriatric hand dryer while hanging on to the crumbling wall to my right, but it's too late. My heart and my hair are no longer up to the task of finding my soulmate. I sigh and head back into the bar.

Downhearted, I order a small orange juice and sit by the window, waiting for the wind to die down. I'm intently watching a man chase his hat across the street when I'm tapped on the shoulder.

'Penny for 'em?'

A ruddy-faced man, early forties, with a pint in his hand, is towering over me. Christ, he's tall – at least six foot five, built like a rugby player, and possibly three sheets to the wind.

'I'm Harry,' he announces, and without being asked, Half-cut Harry plonks himself in the seat beside me, exhaling loudly and blocking my view of the hat-chasing man. I stare at him in disbelief.

I'm aware that I have two options. I can tell Harry that he hasn't been invited to sit down and therefore off he must fuck, or I can take advantage of the fact that I have now been approached (albeit by an actual giant) and take this opportunity to practise some of Guy Wright's rules for being aloof, mysterious and restrained. I decide on the latter; I'm determined this day won't be an entire waste.

'Have you got a name then?' he asks, playing with a beer mat.

'Catriona.'

'Nice to meet you. I'd get you a drink, but you already have one.'

I stretch out my fingers and inspect my nails. 'It's fine. I'm leaving after this one anyway.'

Aloof badge earned.

'Not working today? I'm on a half-day. I work in insurance. What about you?' He lets out a long, beery belch.

'No, I don't work in insurance.'

'No, I mean, what do you do for a living?'

'This and that.'

And the cagey-as-fuck award goes to . . .

He takes a long drink from his pint and his hand wanders down to adjust his crotch. 'Not very chatty, are you, sweetheart?'

Call me sweetheart again and I will end you.

'It appears not.'

Oh sweet lord, this is just painful. Am I even doing it right? I'm actually grateful that the man of my dreams isn't sat opposite me, because I'm coming across as a total arsehole. Luckily for me, I suspect giant Harry is an arsehole too so I'm not overly concerned with what he thinks. He unashamedly stares at my tits for a second, then leans in and says, 'So what's a decent-looking bird like you doing in here?'

I refuse to put up with *this* shit. I need to cut this short, even if it means sabotaging my first proper rules-based encounter. He is just too vile. I finish my orange juice and politely tell Harry that I'm leaving, to which he replies, 'Stuck-up cow.' It's then that I forfeit my *medal for being restrained* and raise my voice to a level known as 'shouty'.

'Listen, you sexist prick. For future reference – you don't sit down at a table unless you're invited, you don't say *sweetheart* and *penny for 'em* unless you're in a fucking Dickens novel, and if you're going to chat someone up, make sure your nose is clean.'

And with that I exit the pub and hail a taxi to take me back to my car. Today was a waste of time. Had I *not* been following this book, I'm pretty sure I'd have been able to use my eyes to spot potential single men and maybe even have been charming enough to get them to have coffee with me, possibly dinner at the weekend. Instead I've wasted an entire afternoon not looking directly at men, before being approached by huge Harry and his amazing interpersonal skills. Is it going to be like this every time I try to meet a guy? Women meet men every single day, going about their lives and behaving normally, not perched prettily on coffee-shop chairs waiting to be spotted by the opposite sex. I'm livid. Who the fuck does this author think he is? I cannot wait to write my column this evening and tell the world that Guy Wright is full of shit.

CHAPTER NINE

Having a lie-in is my favourite thing in the world, but not when it's Monday morning and I'm supposed to be at work by nine. My cries of 'SHIT!' almost drown out the sound of the alarm I've obviously snoozed ten times as I scramble to get out of bed. Grace, who is awake and happily reading a comic, looks startled when I fly into her room at a hundred miles per hour.

'Why didn't you wake me?' I wail, looking for anyone to blame but me.

She shrugs. 'You didn't tell me to. Look at the wee puppy here, Mum. He's eating a banana.'

'No time for that, Grace-face. You'll have to get changed for school at Aunt Helen's. I'm running very late.'

I hand her a uniform, grab her schoolbag and practically hurl her across the hallway into Helen's house. 'Can you get Grace organized?' I plead. 'I have about ten minutes to get ready.'

I can see the look of disapproval on Helen's face, but

I don't have time to convince her that I'm not the worst mother in the world.

'Fine. Just make sure you're not late for dinner on Wednesday.'

'Of course not! I'll be right on time!' I reply, dashing back into my flat. It's lucky she reminded me or I'd have completely forgotten.

I throw on my suit, tie my hair back in a slick ponytail and brush my teeth while slipping on my shoes. I'll do my make-up on the train.

Unbelievably, I make the train with thirty-seven seconds to spare and even manage to get a seat. Just as I'm about to take out my make-up bag, I notice a pregnant woman standing near the doors. I count seven seated men who've spotted her and not one of them gets up for her. I'm liking men less and less these days. I close my bag again and catch her attention.

'Please. Sit here,' I say, and stand up. She smiles gratefully and squeezes past me to sit down.

'Jesus, I feel a hippo,' she says in a broad Belfast accent. 'Thanks very much for this. I'm only one stop; you can have it back then.'

'No worries. I've been there. When are you due?'

'Last week. I just want it out now. I'm getting cranky. Seriously, look at the size of me, and yet still I appear invisible to some people.'

I laugh, but she isn't finished.

'I mean, not one of these big strapping lads offered me a seat. What the fuck is wrong with the world?'

The man to the right of me looks uncomfortable. He turns the page of his paper and carries on reading, but she's spotted him.

'Carrying around another person isn't an easy job, you know!' She raises her voice in his direction. 'Your mammy would be ashamed of you. This wee girl is standing up now and you're still sitting there! Where's your manners?'

He looks at me and I swear there are tears welling up in his eyes. I can tell he's torn between telling her to piss off and being the dickhead who was mean to the pregnant lady, or caving in and offering me his seat. Lucky for him, her stop arrives and she pushes herself up off the seat.

'There you go and thanks again.' She glares one last time at the man shakily clutching his copy of the *Metro* and growls, 'Have a nice day.' And with that she's gone and I'm back in my seat, which is now lovely and warm.

Make-up complete and only slightly smudged, I disembark at Central, where the queues for coffee are miles long, so I decide to slum it and buy one at Greggs outside. The weather has turned shitty, as it often does in Glasgow, so I practically sprint towards the office.

'I've received an invite to the reopening of the Filmhouse on Friday night,' gloats Patrick before I've even taken my jacket off. He's the only one in the office so far and his creased, dishevelled appearance makes it look as though he's slept here. 'I hear they're planning to make it more art house; you know, independent films, world cinema, black-and-white oldies? The launch will be excellent: free food and drink and a chance to mingle . . . right up my street.'

His pretentiousness nauseates me, but sadly his plan to make me envious is working. I love the Filmhouse, and the reopening is all anyone has been talking about for weeks. Such a great night will be wasted on a sad sack like him.

'That's nice, Patrick. *Whatever are you going to wear?*' I mock and turn on my PC, which for once seems to be working.

'Very funny, Catriona,' he sighs. 'I'm thinking definitely nothing in that shade of green *you're* wearing at the moment.'

I open up my emails. Twelve new. The second one makes me happy to be alive.

'Ouch. Touché, Patrick!' I laugh. 'OK, I'll admit it, I *am* jealous . . . Well, I *was* until I received an invite too. Now I'm just happy. We should go together!'

'What? You didn't.'

'I did.' I smile winningly. 'I'm guessing the whole office got one too. What fun!'

He mumbles something unintelligible and stomps out, almost knocking Leanne over on the way. 'What's up with Patrick?' she asks, rubbing the spot on her arm he barged into.

'He's just found out that he isn't special. Best let him stew in the gents' for a while. How was your weekend?'

She opens a yogurt and licks the lid. 'Good, thanks. Five-kilometre run and then dinner at my parents' house. We're off to Turkey on Thursday for two weeks, so I just had a chilled one to save some cash.'

'Did you run to your parents' house or are these things unrelated? Also, you can't go to Turkey because we're all invited to the reopening of the Filmhouse and Patrick really wants everyone to be seen there with him.'

She chuckles. 'So that's why he's sulking. Ha, remember that time Gordon got an invite to that gallery opening instead of him and he called the organizers to complain?'

'God, I'd forgotten about that. Has he always been such an arsehole?'

Leanne pulls a sad face. 'Aww, he's not that bad. You guys just clash. Give him your press award. That'll cheer him up.'

'Yeah, sure. Listen, since you're away next Friday, I'm going to use your invite for my mate – is that cool?'

She nods and shovels a spoonful of Greek yogurt into her mouth, and I forward the email to Kerry to see if she fancies coming along. Free food and drink should convince her.

An hour later, I'm finishing up a telephone interview with an Edinburgh-based fashion designer who's currently in high demand after designing the dress Kelly Macdonald wore to the Golden Globes.

'Thanks, Megan, and congrats on your success! The article should be in this week, but I'll let you know if that changes.'

'Pleasure,' she replies. 'I love this magazine. Especially Glasgow Girl's column – it's hilarious!'

I grin. Sometimes I'd like to be able to announce that it's me, but Natasha advised against it early on –

'You're writing some really personal stuff here, I'd use a pseudonym . . . keep an air of mystery about you. You know what the online trolls are like – they're brutal. Once you put a name and face to your words, you make it much easier for them to judge you. Let them judge "her" instead.'

Very few people know it's my column: only the office staff – who've been sworn to secrecy – and Kerry, Rose, Helen and Adam. When I won my press award, Natasha accepted it on my behalf. I just sat there and applauded myself.

'– though my boyfriend thinks Glasgow Girl is unbearable. He calls her "The Bitch". Does she work beside you? What's she like?'

I stop grinning. 'I've never met her,' I lie. 'She just emails her column in. Unbearable? Why does he think that?'

'I dunno!' She laughs.

Well, stop laughing and go and fucking ask him.

'I'm sure she's a really lovely person,' I sigh, suddenly eager to end the call. 'I'll pass on your comments though! Thanks again, Megan. Take care.'

We say goodbye and I hang up, feeling deflated.

'I'm not unbearable, am I?' I ask Leanne, back at my desk. 'Megan Black's boyfriend hates me and calls me "The Bitch".'

'Of course not!' she answers immediately. 'Although . . . never mind. No, you're lovely.'

'Although what?! Tell me.'

'Well, you were really unkind to Guy Wright this week in your column.'

'Oh, I wasn't that bad.'

She lifts a copy of Saturday's mag from her desk, turns to my page and recites:

If you purchased this book, the author is laughing at you. Despite the fact women have been successfully dating long before he piped up with this self-helpless shambles of a book, he's clearly preying on single women who are on the edge of a dating breakdown. When you're desperate to meet someone, you'll consider anything, and your £5.99 (minus the cut from his agent and publisher) means he gets to think he's right until someone tells him he's wrong. I look forward to being that person.

'Well, maybe it's a little harsh . . .' I reluctantly agree. 'But I was pissed off. Do you know, I wasted a whole day last week, ignoring and being ignored by men, except for one horror show who called me "stuck up". I'm sorely tempted to give up.'

'Aww, Cat. Never give up! You have to keep trying! Anyway, I was just pointing out that you can be quite . . . well, blunt about things.'

I want to grab her by the cheeks and yell into her face, 'BUT YOU JUST SAID I WAS LOVELY' until I realize that perhaps these are the things that *make* me unbearable.

'What I will say is that you have to change your attitude,' she continues. 'Stop taking the piss out of it. Once you start believing it'll work, it will! I'm living proof.'

'Fine, you're right,' I reply. 'I've still got weeks of this utter sh— uh, compelling challenge left. I shall try to be a beacon of optimism from now on. In my column anyway.'

'Good for you! You'll meet someone. I just know it!' She swivels back around in her chair and carries on typing, while I give her the invisible finger.

Rose texts me just as I'm leaving to tell me Grace is happily eating fishcakes and so not to rush picking her up. As I'm texting her back, a call comes through from Kerry:

'So, this Filmhouse thing – is it going to be all arty folk who want to talk about experimental cinema and bore me into a coma?'

'I have no idea actually. It might just be media folk who're only there for the free booze. Either way, I have a spare invite and I insist you come. Otherwise I'll be stuck with work bores all night.' I smile over at Gordon who's mouthing the words 'Fuck you'.

'OK, but only if I can borrow your long green mac. I'll pop round on Wednesday to get it and we can catch up.'

'Sure, sounds great – oh wait. Sorry, I said I'd have dinner with Helen and Adam on Wednesday. Thursday?'

'Yeah, OK. Gotta get back to work. See you then!'

The day of Helen and Adam's dinner, I pick Grace up from school and bring her home to have a snack and get changed for her dad's house. I have to get her there by five thirty and then get back in time for dinner. But now that I think about it . . . I have no idea when dinner is.

'Grace, I'm popping over to Aunt Helen's for a sec. I'll just be in the hall. Don't set fire to anything.'

Helen is cleaning her flat like a woman possessed and doesn't hear me knock the first three times. I stand and wait for the sound of the vacuum cleaner to stop before attempting a fourth.

'Oh hello!' she says. 'Just a bit of tidying for tonight. You're still OK for tonight, right?'

Oh how I want to mess with her and send her spiralling into a panic, but I don't have the time or the heart. Her make-up-free face and pulled-back hair tells me she means business. The smell of chicken wafts from the kitchen.

'Helen, that smells amazing. Yes, I'm still coming. I just wondered what time . . . Hope you're not doing all this for me. You know I'm not bothered if your house is untidy.'

'Seven, and no, actually, it's for Tom.'

My heart sinks and my face takes on a look commonly known as I FUCKING KNEW IT.

'Tom who? Helen, why is there suddenly a Tom coming for dinner, when last week there wasn't?'

'I only asked him this morning. He's my new dentist. Handsome guy. English. Doesn't know anyone here. Thought it might be nice if—'

'If you sat him in front of me and tried to marry us off? Oh, Helen, I specifically asked you NOT to do this any more. You promised!'

I'm raging inside. *At dinner parties, I always end up doing all the talking and joke-cracking; it's exhausting. Now I'm going to have to spend a whole evening . . . Oh. Hang on . . .* I stop internally ranting and begin to smile.

'Not everything is about you, Catriona. This was a spur-of-the-moment thing. Besides, I think you two will get on really well . . . why are you smiling?'

'Am I?' My grin grows wider. Helen has forgotten that I'm following the rules. 'No reason.'

'Did I say something funny?'

'Not at all. I'm just really happy to be having dinner.'

She's trying to read my face but I'm giving nothing away. 'Fine,' she replies. 'I'll see you tonight at half seven.'

I go back inside and tell Grace to get ready for her dad's house while I get changed. Skimming through my wardrobe I find the patterned maxi-skirt I bought last year during my gypsy phase and match it up with a vest top and cropped cardigan. I don't want to look like I've made too much of an effort, plus I refuse to get spruced up to the nines for some middle-aged dentist and my sister.

Once we're ready, I take Grace to Peter's house, safe in the knowledge that with me following *The Rules of Engagement* to the letter at dinner, Helen's little plan to set me up with yet another unsuitable and unstable suitor will be well and truly fucked. If I'm going to meet someone, it'll be on my terms.

I plug my phone into the radio and play songs for Grace on the way there. I'm singing along to Lorde when I feel a foot poking my lower back.

'Don't kick the chair, Grace. What is it?'

'Mum, can you stop singing? I want to hear the song.'

I smirk. 'But I like singing. My singing is beautiful and perfect, Grace. I sing like an angel.'

She giggles. 'You kind of sing like a ghost.'

I pull up outside Peter's and let Grace out while I grab her schoolbag and empty packed lunchbox. She stops to say hello to the neighbour's dog before ringing the doorbell. Emma answers.

'Hi, Grace!' she chirps. She's wearing black gym trousers and a vest top that reveals her perfectly flat stomach – mine has never quite recovered from having eight pounds of baby kicking around in there. 'Hi, Cat, how are you? Peter's on his way back from work. I was just doing some yoga on the Wii board.'

Ouija board more like, I think, because I really am a childish wanker. I kiss Grace and she trots off down the hall.

'Hi, Emma. I'm good, thanks. No worries. I don't need to speak to him anyway.'

'Cool. You look nice. Off out?'

I could explain that my sister is sneakily trying to make me eat dinner with someone I've never met because she finds it odd that I haven't been in a relationship since Peter, but instead I blurt out: 'Yes, I have a date! He's a dentist. He's very keen but I'm keeping him on his toes.'

'Oh good for you!' she replies, trying not to sound patronizing but failing miserably. I wonder if she can hear the little voice in my head shouting, 'CAT, YOU LYING SHIT. YOU HAVEN'T EVEN MET HIM YET.'

'Yep, so I'd better get off.'

I make a gauche *cheerio!* hand gesture as she closes the door, then head home to meet my new imaginary fucking boyfriend. Please don't let him be weird.

I can hear Helen laughing as I linger in the hallway out-side her door; she's using her 'Isn't everything fabulous!' laugh, which she saves for social engagements, instead of the usual snorting chuckle I love so much. OK, here goes: this is my opportunity to really start doing the rules of engagement properly, no more messing about. No talking first, no flirting, no reasonless chattering, no giggling. Just smile, be cool, get this inevitably uncomfortable evening over with, and with any luck I'll have plenty of material for this week's column. It would be nice to try this stupid experiment on someone I fancied for once, but after my run of horrible luck with Helen's previous set-ups, I completely expect to be sat across from a pearly-toothed hobgoblin.

I smooth my hands down over my skirt and adjust my bra strap just as Helen pulls the door open and drags me inside.

'Tom's in the living room,' she whispers. 'He's been here for ten minutes. Get in there and introduce yourself!'

Here we go. I pause for a second, then say to Helen, 'I do believe that would be considered too forward. Overly keen. If he wants to know who I am, he'll ask.'

It takes her a second to understand me. Then she remembers. She frowns, and her whisper turns into a low growl. 'Cat, you are NOT following these rules tonight. I know you'll just take the piss to annoy me, and you could end up ruining something very special!' We're still standing in the hallway, whispering furiously at each other.

'I told you not to set me up again, Helen. Besides, this is my job. I have no choice.'

She wants to throttle me, I can tell. If this had happened twenty-five years ago, I'd have a dead arm by now.

'Don't you ruin my dinner! I've spent ages preparing everything,' she warns me as we march down her recently mopped hallway. 'Tom is—'

'A cat's name?'

'STOP IT. Tom is *charming*. When you see him, you'll forget all about this column nonsense. Trust me.'

She pushes open the living room door and trills, 'She's here everyone! Catriona, this is my dentist Tom Ward. Adam, can you help me with something in the kitchen?'

'Smooth, Helen,' I mutter under my breath, then follow it up with a generic 'Hello!' which applies to everyone and definitely not specifically to the man who's sitting beside Adam. The man who has just made my face flush spontaneously. Holy fucking fuck, he's handsome. Shit. No one looks like that in real life. I wasn't prepared for this.

The dentist stands up, smiles and shakes my hand, which gives me approximately four seconds to take in as much as possible before he finds me creepy (and I break the rules); dark blond hair with a hint of red, brown eyes, wide smile and, of course, perfect teeth. Oh my. *Hello, Tom.*

'So, Catriona, you live across the hall?' he asks, as I sit down on the couch opposite him.

'I do!' I reply, delighted that he initiated conversation and that therefore we don't have to participate in a staring competition until one of us caves. He has a lovely voice, but I find his accent hard to place. South London, perhaps?

'Helen says it's just you and your daughter?'

I wonder what other information Helen has been

divulging from the dentist's chair. Income? Bra size? Did she tell him that the meaning of my name is 'pure' or 'chaste', which at the moment is pretty fucking accurate?

'Yes, just the two of us . . . oh, and our cat, Heisenberg.'

Behind my smile, I'm singing *Just the Two of Us* by Bill Withers. Maybe someday this will be Tom and me. The man clearly has no idea who he's dealing with.

'Heisenberg? Really. After the physicist?' He crosses his legs and I find myself briefly mesmerized by his left knee.

'Ha, uh yeah, that's what I tell my kid anyway. Better than saying her cat is named after a fictional meth dealer.'

He smiles, but he isn't laughing.

Whoops. *Don't try to be funny. That's his job.* Oh Christ, not only am I not supposed to make jokes, he has no idea what I'm talking about. I have been set up with the only person on Earth who hasn't seen *Breaking Bad*. What fresh hell is this? I momentarily forget myself and stare at him hard, then decide I'll forgive him this one time. Fortunately at this moment Helen saves us both by telling us dinner is ready.

The layout of my flat is identical to Helen's, but unlike me, she has used her floor space wisely. In front of her living-room window she has a dining table, whereas I have a long white horizontal bookcase, which blocks out the light and is crammed full of books I'll either never get round to reading or just can't bear to throw away.

I sit opposite Tom, a large roast chicken stuffed with

haggis between us. Helen pours me a small chardonnay, which I elegantly sip, allowing everyone else to make small talk around me. We haven't even started dinner before Adam is on my case:

'Jesus, Cat, are you feeling all right? I don't think you've ever stayed quiet this long. Saying that, you're staring at the stuffed neck of a chicken. Quite unnerving.'

'Oh, I'm fine, Adam, and the chicken looks great. Good job, Helen.'

Tom agrees. 'It looks wonderful. I've never had haggis. Are you a fan, Catriona?'

If he wants to know something, he'll ask. OK, Guy Wright – one point to you.

'Aye,' I reply casually. 'It's gorgeous with some whisky sauce.'

Fucking hell, could I sound any more Scottish? Maybe later I'll cross swords and pas-de-basque myself towards the nearest unicorn.

Helen serves Tom first as Adam quizzes him about his job. Personally I want to quiz Adam about his own choice of horrible striped T-shirt, but I'm sure Helen will have beaten me to it.

'So why did you decide to work up here, Tom? Surely the money's better down south?'

Tom nods. 'It can be, but there's more to life. After the divorce, I didn't see the point in hanging around. Besides, commuting four hours every day was taking its toll on my sanity.' He shrugs, a playful smile on his perfect face. 'A former colleague of mine, Ameera, runs a practice and needed a partner –'

We're all staring at him. His ability to hold court is quite impressive – I can tell that even Adam is considering shagging him.

'– and here I am.' Tom laughs and continues eating, seemingly oblivious to the fact we're all completely infatuated with him. He examines the haggis on his fork carefully before taking the plunge.

'What do you do for work, Catriona?' he asks.

More questions. This is a good sign.

'I'm a journalist. You like the haggis?' Am I allowed to ask questions? Oh well, too late.

'I do. Who do you write for? Newspapers? Magazines?'

Oh God, stop asking me about my job. I might have to write about you.

'Magazines,' answers Helen. 'She's very talented. She writes—'

'– whatever they want me to!' I quickly interrupt. 'Just a newspaper supplement, nothing exciting.'

'Oh, I'm sure it is,' Tom reassures me. 'Though to be honest, I only read the *Independent*, if I read newspapers at all. I watch Fox News on cable, and occasionally BBC News.'

Oh fuck, he thinks I'm a serious news journalist. I'm not even sure who the Prime Minister is. On the bright side, this means he won't see what I've written about him in this week's column. I'll call him Mr X, just in case.

'Oh, well, I mainly cover features, reviews . . . that kind of thing. No major world events, I'm afraid.' I'm trying to play down my role at the *Tribune*. This is very unlike me. Sort of disconcerting, but bloody hell, I'm actually starting to like this guy AND I promised myself I wouldn't cheat on the rules this evening.

The rest of the meal goes well; profiteroles for dessert and a massive cheeseboard. I'm conscious of keeping my side of the conversation to a minimum. I'm reserved – 'No more wine for me, Helen.' Charming – 'Did anyone see that documentary on the creator of Elmo from *Sesame Street*? It was delightful!' And a liar – 'Why, yes, I do enjoy the opera.' (Must listen to some opera.) Maybe I'm not my usual, funny, giggly self but, amazingly, it seems to be working. At least I hope it is . . . I suppose it's very possible that Tom just finds me endearing. As in, I'm sure the sheep that ended up as our haggis was endearing too – doesn't mean he wants to date it.

I help Adam clear away the dishes while Tom and Helen head over to the couch for coffee. The kitchen is a disgrace.

'Bloody hell, Adam. Did Helen accidently cook a grenade? If Gordon Ramsay was here, he'd be shutting this place down.'

Adam carefully sets down three expensive dinner plates and throws some napkins in the bin, which is already overflowing.

'Now you decide to pipe up? Honestly, Cat, what the hell was with you tonight? That poor guy was doing everything to get your attention and you didn't even seem to care.'

'What?' I ask, wondering if we were at the same dinner party. 'He was not! He was just making conversation. Besides, you know I'm following these stupid rules. It's like playing hard to get for the insane.'

Adam fills the glass cafetière and places it on a gold tray beside some square-cut shortbread. He's using the expensive coffee and it smells divine. 'Cat. He's into you, you know. I'm a guy, I can tell these things.' And with that he winks at me and carries the tray through to the living room.

Jesus, do all men consider themselves dating experts? I remain in the kitchen and take a moment to collect my thoughts, which are along the lines of, *Oh, I hope he's interested* . . . But wait, if he *is* interested then he's interested in a haggis-loving mute who lives across the hall from her sister, whose hobbies include nodding and smiling and apparently opera . . . but, but . . . he's so attractive! I bet he won't even think we're compatible. Maybe we aren't. I mean, I know that when I return home, I'll be dancing around to the White Stripes in my underwear, while he's definitely the type to be watching *Newsnight* fully clothed . . .

Before people begin to wonder where I am, I return to the living room and see that Helen and Adam are sitting together on one couch, leaving me to sit next to Tom on the other. I catch the conversation halfway through – Tom is talking about his 'good friend Kathryn' –

'It was an amicable split. Kathryn and I had been together fifteen years, just time to move on. We're still very close.'

'Not like you and Peter, eh, Cat?' Adam smirks and sticks some shortbread in his big fat mouth.

When you first start dating, don't mention your past relationships. It might make you seem bitter or, worse, infatuated.

'Perhaps not at first,' I reply, trying hard to be diplomatic. If anyone else had been sitting beside me, I'd have been shouting, 'THAT PRICK? NO CHANCE!' but tonight I must act like a grown-up. 'It's a work in progress. We'll get there.' Translated this means, *Eventually one of us will die.*

Helen has had the same grin plastered to her face since dinner, and I can tell that behind those bright blue eyes she's still scheming and secretly wondering what style of hat she'll buy for our wedding. The conversation lags a little and, though it's painful to drag myself away from the handsome dentist, this is a sign that it's time for me to go.

'Well, it's been a wonderful evening, but I have a pile of work to be getting on with.' I place my cup on the table and smile at Tom. 'Really lovely to meet you, Tom.' I say this because it *was* lovely to meet him. It would have been even lovelier if he'd taken his shirt off . . . then his trousers . . . but fuck it, this will have to do.

He shakes my outstretched hand. 'And you, Cat. I should be leaving too actually. I have a patient coming in at eight a.m. for oral surgery.'

Helen glowers at me – she knows I'm about two seconds away from making an 'oral' joke and ruining her life. I bite my tongue.

Helen sees us both out, with Adam shouting his good-byes from the living room. As she closes the door behind us, I breathe a sigh of relief and fumble through my bag for my keys. The evening went off without a hitch, I now have some material I can use for the –

'Cat, would you like to have dinner on Friday?' Tom's voice echoes down the hallway, causing a thousand butterflies to take flight from the pit of my stomach. With my hand still inside my handbag, I turn my some-what confused face towards him.

'Dinner? With me?'

'Yes. On Friday. Are you free?' He's standing very close to me.

I hear a muffled squeal from the other side of Helen's door.

'Actually, no, I have a work thing that evening. I might be able to do Saturday though, if that suits?' My voice is cool but inside I'm far from it. Inside I'm running down the street shouting, 'A MAN ASKED ME OUT! I MIGHT GET TO HAVE SEX THIS YEAR!' I feel my cheeks colour.

Good lord, he looks so delightfully sexy. I want to drag him by the tie into my flat and insist that he . . . I don't, of course. I just smile back; hand still in my bag.

'Saturday's fine with me. Can I have your number?'

'Sure, it's 0783—'

'Oh, shit. Sorry, Cat, my mobile is in the car. I can give you mine?'

Guy Wright's words scroll in front of my eyes like the opening scene from *Star Wars*.

Let him take your number but don't take his. Women have no boundaries when it comes to texting. Before he knows it, you'll be sending him 170 smiley-faced texts a day and crying when he doesn't respond quickly enough.

'That's OK, I'll write mine down.' My hand stops looking for my keys and reroutes into the zipped pocket of my bag where I keep my notebook. I flip through to a blank page, scribble my mobile number down, then tear it off and hand to him, like a fucking BOSS. I'm getting the hang of this.

He examines the number before slipping it into his right pocket. 'Great. Well, I'll text you and we can sort the details?'

'Sure,' I reply. I want to kiss him. Goddammit, I want to invite him in. I want to point to the left and explain that my bedroom is literally just through that wall and it hasn't seen any action in *months*. Then I remember that my bedroom is a mess, there are dirty dishes piling up in the sink and Grace has probably forgotten to flush the toilet again, leaving me to exclaim, 'That's not mine!'

'OK, well. Goodnight then, Cat.' He leans in and we do cheek-kissing before he walks away with my phone number, promising again to call. I count to four before Helen flings open her front door and peers at me with a face like a Disney villain.

'Things going according to your evil plan?' I ask. 'Will you be taking my voice in payment?'

She quietly closes the door behind her. 'Actually, I thought you'd blown it with your one-word answers and complete lack of interest, but your silly rules seem to have worked. With my help, of course.'

'Don't get ahead of yourself here. He might not even call, and I'm certainly not going to be sitting by the phone. I doubt I'm his type.'

Helen throws her head back and laughs. 'Just this once, can you think outside the box, Cat? You know what they say – opposites attract!'

'But you're missing the point, dear sister. Tom thinks I'm quiet – reserved even! Don't get me wrong, I'm totally into him – for once you were right . . . but what happens to his opinion of me when the real me tumbles out, wild-eyed and swearing? I can't keep her hidden forever.'

'I know.' She laughs. 'He'll run a mile. You'd better make sure you at least shag him before that happens.'

'My thoughts exactly. Did you see his—'

Adam's stubbly face appears around the door. 'Is anyone going to help me clear away these dishes?'

Helen sighs and about-turns. 'OK, grumpy. Night, Cat. Let me know when he calls you!'

'Night, guys . . . I'M NOT HOLDING MY BREATH, YOU KNOW!'

Moments later, I'm inside my flat, pouring myself a Baileys and doing my best not to check my phone. He probably hasn't even made it home yet.

At quarter past twelve, I turn off the television and get ready for bed. Face washed and teeth brushed, I slip under the sheets and turn off the light. I enjoy the silence, letting my mind drift off for an impressive twenty-two minutes before I bring my phone through to the bedroom and check for a message. I could easily continue checking for the next three hours, but instead I turn it off and close my eyes, refusing to be the kind of woman Guy Wright blames for her own singledom.

CHAPTER TEN

Thursday arrives with a whimper. The anticipation of this date with Tom is weighing heavily on my mind and it's a distraction I don't need as I still have this week's column to write.

I throw on some jeans and direct my car towards the nearest drive-through Costa but not even a toasted teacake and latte is enough to make me the slightest bit perky.

I greedily scoff my buttery teacake on the drive home while my latte cools, and by nine thirty-five I'm on the couch with my laptop and my reference copy of *The Rules of Engagement*. I begin to type:

This week I met someone. Imagine a cross between Ewan McGregor and Jude Law – I'll wait while you finish hating my good fortune.

I pause for a moment and recall Tom's face. It's a happy moment. I keep typing.

Fifty words in and I'm already referring to the book to read up on what will be required of me on what will technically be our second date. The book advises that I shouldn't read too much into the fact that this man wants to see me again, and I certainly shouldn't become overly excited by this:

> *Most women turn up on dates hoping to be swept off their feet, but the majority of men are just planning to eat dinner and maybe get laid.*

Temporarily forgetting about my column, I read on. Who cares if the rules worked on Tom that one time; this man is a MONSTER. The book's basic message is essentially 'fuck romance'. He's telling women that there is no Prince Charming – there is only a man who will one day decide that out of all the women he's met, he finds you the least annoying.

> *Keep the second date light-hearted. Don't discuss heavy or personal topics.*

Like what? Ebola? Politics? Rodgers and Hammerstein? My feelings? My brain begins to create countless scenarios where I have the potential to fuck everything up:

How are you, Cat?

Cold. Emotional. I FEEL EMPTY. How are you?

Returning to my column, I warn my readers that 'emotion = danger' and, according to the rules, they are not to discuss anything thought-provoking, lest they upset the poor man's equilibrium. Thirty minutes later, I close the book and finish off my column.

> In any case, Mr X and I are scheduled to go out for dinner on Saturday (the day this column comes out, so you'll have to wait until next week to find out if he actually called me or if I spent the evening at home alone singing 'Soulmate' by Natasha Bedingfield into my cat's face).

Reasonably happy with my effort, I email it to Natasha, not expecting a response unless she wants something changed. With that out of the way, I turn on Radio 1 and begin washing up the breakfast dishes. Fearne Cotton's show has just started but I'm not paying attention to who's on in the Live Lounge because I'm SURE I just heard a message come through on my phone. I scramble to turn off the taps.

Three and a half seconds later, I'm leaping across the room to snatch my phone off the living-room table. No new messages . . . no new messages but also *no signal*! I wave it around in front of the window for a few seconds until the bars appear.

Nope, definitely no new messages.

I throw my phone on the couch in disgust and slink

back to the kitchen, sickened that I've so quickly become a phone-checking desperado. This book is turning me into the type of person I used to make fun of.

As arranged, Kerry comes over after Grace is in bed. Kieran has gone up to Aberdeen for work and she's bored stiff. I think she hates her own company – I couldn't say the same for me, but when you're a single parent it's not like you have much choice anyway.

When Kerry and I were at school, we were very different. We first became best friends in primary school. We stayed close throughout high school, where I excelled at English and history but failed miserably at maths and science, two areas Kerry shone brightly in. There was no reason for us to be friends; we liked different music, different films and even different boys, but when we get together everything just clicks. She keeps me sane. She was, and still is, the yin to my yang.

Remembering my promise, I reluctantly hand over my green mac, warning her not to spill anything on it because it's the only thing I've ever been able to afford from Selfridges. I make myself comfy on the couch and look around for my nail polish.

'So, exactly how good-looking *is* good-looking?' she asks, looking through my bookshelves. 'Jesus, Cat, you don't have one non-fiction book in here. How many horror novels does one person need?'

'All of them,' I reply. 'And Tom is absurdly good-looking. Like, Hollywood hot.'

She picks up a book and scans the back cover. 'Brad Pitt hot or Jared Leto hot?'

'What? Um, Brad Pitt.'

'But you don't fancy Brad Pitt.'

'Yeah, but Brad is more wholesome-looking. Like Tom. Jared Leto looks like he'd fuck you then murder you.'

She puts *Gerald's Game* back on the shelf. 'You need to stop reading this shit. So you're seeing him on Saturday? That'll be good. Who's looking after Grace?'

'It's Peter's weekend. Well, we're supposed to be going for dinner, but Tom hasn't called yet.' I finish painting my toenails blue and start on my fingers.

'He will. Then before you know it, you'll be all, "Yeah, this is my boyfriend the doctor."'

'Dentist.'

'Whatever. He saves teeth. It's still important. And it's a free meal.'

'No, the book says I *have* to go Dutch. So essentially I'm buying myself dinner and eating it in front of a dentist.'

'Why do you have to split it? He invited you!'

'To prove I'm not a gold-digger, skint or cheap. Otherwise I'd be likely to keep my purse in my bag and be all, "GARÇON, ANOTHER LOBSTER! HE'S PAYING!" Actually I wouldn't get lobster anyway; it's hard to look alluring when you're cracking the shell and ripping meat out of a dead crustacean.'

'Can I destroy that book when you're finished, please? It's turning you into a moron.'

'I know, but—'

'Wait, Cat, was that your phone?' We both stare at each other for a second before I lunge for it. It's a text from an unknown number. I throw the phone at Kerry, then bury my face in a cushion. 'You read it. I can't look!'

'Fucking hell, Cat. It's not a pregnancy test, it's a text. Right, it says: *Hi Catriona, it's Tom. I've booked the Grill on the Corner for 8pm on Sat. Can meet you there? If not suitable, let me know.*'

Smiling, she hands me back my phone and does a little dance. 'Woohoo! That place rocks. Just promise me you won't have a fucking salad or something. Women who eat salad on dates are *the worst*. It shows you're shallow and empty inside.'

I enjoy salad, especially warm chicken salad with chilli dressing and croutons, but there's no point explaining this to carnivorous Kerry, the woman who would happily devour rare steak for breakfast.

I read Tom's message for myself, then wait ten minutes and type:

Sounds fine. See you at eight x

I stare at the message. 'Kiss or no kiss?'

'No kiss. He didn't send a kiss.'

I delete the *x* and press Send. It's done.

'So this is happening then?' I laugh. 'What the hell am I going to wear?' I suggest my white summer dress with the tiny flowers, but Kerry has other ideas.

'That dress makes you look like a mum.'

'I *am* a mum, Kerry.'

'Yes, I know, but you don't need to dress like one. Heaven forbid you remind him of his mum; you'll *never* get a shag. What about your red one? Your boobs look marvellous in that.'

'Is red really a first-date colour? I read that—'

'Man, you're really over-thinking this rules stuff,' she interjects. 'Look, just wear what you feel good in.'

'OK.'

'Except that white dress.'

'FINE.'

'Glad to be of service. I'm going to shoot off now, but I'll meet you outside the Filmhouse tomorrow for the launch thingy.'

She leaves quietly, so as not to wake Grace, even though Grace would sleep through a stampede of singing bison. Regardless, it's fun to watch Kerry try to tiptoe in wedges. I settle down on the couch to watch the episode of *American Horror Story* I recorded last night. I'm looking forward to tomorrow evening. It should be fun.

*

Grace helps me zip up my red dress and messes around with my make-up as I get ready for the Filmhouse opening.

'Lipstick is only supposed to go on your lips, Grace. You've drawn an entirely new mouth on.'

'Am I sleeping at Aunt Helen's all night?' she asks, putting brown eyeshadow on her cheeks.

'Yes, honey. I don't know what time this will end.'

'But I'm going to Dad's tomorrow. I'll miss you.'

My heart sinks. 'Look, how about we go to the cafe for breakfast before I take you to your dad? Then you'll be back on Sunday night and we can watch a movie together before bed. Sound good?'

'Can we watch *Tangled*?' she asks with a massive grin.

'Will you let me sing along?'

She thinks for a moment. 'How about I let you mime?'

'Deal.'

With the taxi en route to pick me up, I give Grace a massive kiss and send her across the hall with a bottle of wine for Helen as thanks for helping me out. When she sees me, Helen practically pounces on me.

'Did he call?!'

'What? Did who call? I have to run; the taxi will be here in a sec.'

'TOM, OF COURSE!'

'Jesus, calm down. Yes. We're having dinner tomorrow. I'll pick Grace up in the morning. Stop dancing, Helen. It's only a date.'

She gathers Grace into a hug and I run down the front steps to catch my cab.

Kerry's already waiting for me when I pull up outside the Filmhouse. She stoops down to peer in the window as I pay the driver, waving wildly as if she hasn't seen me in weeks. Keeping my knees together, I gracefully exit the taxi, ensuring the fortified gusset on my body-shaper tights remains unseen.

'I thought you'd never show up!' she moans, hugging me hello. 'I've been standing alone here for at least five minutes. Loads of people have gone in.'

'You look amazing!' I gush, looking her up and down. Kerry isn't just wearing my mac, she is *wearing* it. It looks far better on her than it ever has on me – I know that by the end of the evening I'll be telling her to keep it. She grins at me because she knows this too.

'You're wearing your red dress! I thought you'd be keeping it for your date tomorrow.'

'I haven't decided what I'm wearing for tomorrow. And if you give me shit about the white one again, I'm going to take back that coat.'

She smiles and zips her mouth as I pluck the printed invitations from my handbag and hand her one. 'Right, hopefully this won't be too painful,' I say, looking around for familiar faces. I don't recognize anyone. The journalists are easy to spot – most are still in their work clothes and all are carrying mobiles and leather bags. They have that look that says: 'Please let the bar be open or this won't end well.' There's a smattering of photographers and what looks like the entire cast of *Hipster – the Movie*. No sign of anyone from work yet, but Patrick is undoubtedly already in there, swigging Scotch and challenging the arts editor of the *Evening Herald* to a pissing contest.

Kerry pulls open the heavy main doors and we walk into the lobby, which looks exactly like it always did, except they've ripped up the old blue carpet and replaced it with marble-effect flooring, which makes my black heels clunk rather than clop. I take a press pack from one of the two women standing beside the ticket desk just as a small, smartly dressed man politely requests that we all make our way to Screen 1.

'You're not doing the rules tonight, are you?' Kerry whispers.

'Nope,' I reply. 'I'm here as me, not as Glasgow Girl.'

I haven't been here since I was a teenager, and I'm feeling nostalgic as hell. The old two-screen Filmhouse closed in 1995 after the massive multiplex round the corner nicked all its business, but I used to come here often as a kid because they'd let anyone in to see anything, regardless of age. I saw my first on-screen sex as a twelve-year-old Doors fan and didn't shut up about it for at least six weeks.

Through the glass to the left I can see they've built a small trendy bar area, replacing the old confectionary stand, formerly run by a sixty-nine-year-old woman called Maggie who was blind as a bat. It used to smell like popcorn, hot dogs, rank cheese and, occasionally, spilled booze from someone who'd snuck in some of their dad's beer, but now everything smells brand new. Gone are the paintings by local artists that used to line the narrow walled corridor between screens – they've been replaced with oversized B-movie, world cinema and grindhouse posters, suggesting that this place is clearly for grown-ups and won't be showing a Disney film anytime soon.

Kerry and I line up and slowly move through the hefty double doors of Screen 1, the larger of the two screens, and sit in the third row. The old grey seats I remember so fondly have been ripped out and replaced with huge comfy dark-blue velvet ones, with black cup holders and headrests. Whoever refurbished this place has done an amazing job, but I still pine for the old place.

The small but smartly dressed man introduces himself as Adrian and welcomes everyone before launching into a somewhat dull speech on why he and his business partner Dylan decided to reopen the Filmhouse. I want to shout, 'BECAUSE OF MONEY!' but I don't; I just flick through the press information until it's time for wine.

'Dylan will be along directly,' Adrian says, looking somewhat peeved that his partner isn't here on time for their grand opening. 'The information is in your packs, but also please feel free to direct any questions you have to him or me. In the meantime, if you'd like to move along to the bar, we have some refreshments waiting.'

Kerry is the first one standing and I giggle, but she's quickly followed by everybody else. As we turn to walk along the row of seats, I spy both Gordon and Patrick near the back of the cinema, chatting. Gordon makes a 'mine's a pint' gesture at me, and I nod, turning away before Patrick spots me and decides to place an order as well.

Kerry asks for a glass of rosé, then grabs a table while I make my way to the bar. Everything is free and everyone is happy. There's a table set out with snacks and sandwiches on the right, and the two women who handed us press packs are now hovering, ready to collect glasses. Gordon catches me at the bar and helps me with the drinks as we walk over to join Kerry.

'I got you Staropramen. That all right?'

'Yeah, cheers, Cat. I'm only staying for one. I need to get back.'

We sit down beside Kerry, who's busy reading through my press information. She and Gordon have only met a handful of times but they always get along famously.

'How are you, Kerry? Having fun?' He leans over and hugs her. 'Nice to see you. The place looks great, though live-music venues are more my thing. More sweaty, less pretentious . . . Interesting mix of people here, but a little too "art school" for me.'

She sips her wine and nods. 'I bet they're all talking about how *creative* they are. Creative types are generally up their own arse; sometimes I have to pull Kieran out before he gets lost up his own arty rectum forever.'

'Hey!' I snarl at her. 'We're writers. That counts as creative, right? Are we included in your hate campaign?'

'Nah, you're not *that* kind of writer. You're not reaching into the depths of your soul to write some Twitter sonnet about a lamp post or a fig or something. Basically, until you utter the words "I'm self-publishing a fantasy novella" we can remain friends.'

I giggle and look around the bar, wondering which of the guests will make it on to Kerry's hit list by the end of the evening. Gordon finishes his pint with impressive speed.

'Right, I must be off, ladies.' He smirks and pulls his man bag over his jacket. 'Date night with the wife.'

Kerry laughs. 'I might have known! The only thing to pull a man away from free beer is the promise of sex.'

'Too fucking right. Have a good night, you two!' I watch him push his way through the crowded bar and feel disheartened that the only thing I have waiting for me at home tonight is my lunatic cat.

One hour later, we're sitting at the same table and we're on to our third glass of wine. The bar is still lively and I count at least twenty people all battling their own personal fashion demons.

'What do you think he does?' I ask, surreptitiously pointing to a thin man wearing a cowl-neck top and leather trousers. 'Artist? Dancer?'

She casually glances over. 'He's wearing sandals. I'd say professional hipster. Or wanker. Same thing really. Probably runs a coffee shop and shags his roommate, then wears her clothes to social gatherings.'

We do this a lot. Judgy little fuckers that we are.

I knock back the last of my wine. 'At least he's shagging *someone*. Right now, I'd gladly trade my fashion sense for a regular sex life.'

Kerry gasps. 'You would not! That's the booze talking.'

I look down at my fabulous dress. 'Good point. Anyway, what about him?' I continue, making side eyes towards a stylish man in the corner, clearly trying to hit on a girl who's already looking bored. 'I'd say he's the manager of something really unimportant. Like shoes. He's the regional manager of shoes.'

Kerry narrows her eyes. 'Hmm, I've seen him before at a BBC event I went to with Kieran. Sean something—'

'Sean Semple,' interrupts a male voice. 'He's head of the graphics department at the BBC. Terribly nice man, but sadly no hope of getting off with that woman.'

I look over my right shoulder and spot a dark-haired man in his late thirties standing behind me. I quickly scan his face, Terminator-style, trying to size up this rude eavesdropper: jeans, blue shirt, wide brown eyes, a few freckles on his cheeks, heart-shaped mouth. He's not classically good-looking like Tom, but still every single part of my body approves. Tom has some competition here.

He shouts Sean's name and waves before bending down to whisper in my ear, 'And I think you'll find that shoes are *very* important. I'd rate them highly, alongside penicillin and water slides. And, for the record, your shoes are hot.'

He's both flirting with me AND he talked to me first! I can't think of anything to say in response, so I smile and sip my cava. I glance over at Kerry, who's grinning like a fool, under the assumption that I'm three seconds away from announcing that I want to ruin him. I *do* want to ruin him. She steps in to help.

'And who might you be?' she asks. She loves forward men, especially the good-looking ones. Me, I usually just find them arrogant, but Jesus, he's attractive. Kerry is still smiling widely and I know what she's thinking because I'm thinking it too. Our filthy minds are in sync. Of course, she's completely devoted to Kieran and she'd never play away, making her the perfect wingwoman.

He takes a sip of his Budweiser and smirks. 'You tell me. Don't I get the benefit of your psychic abilities?'

Oh great, now he's flirting with Kerry too. My wingwoman is too alluring for her own good. I feel a bit miffed. It's like the universe never wants me to get laid, ever again.

She looks him up and down and then thinks for a moment while I keep quiet. He's still standing close to me and I'm almost eye level with his crotch. Oh God, I wish I could see straight through his clothes. I'm starting to forget what a real-life penis looks like.

'Actor,' she finally declares. 'You have that air of self-importance.'

He laughs. 'Wow, you're really bad at this. Not even close. Self-importance? Ouch.'

He sits down in Gordon's old seat, his leg casually brushing against mine. It's very possible that I might implode. He looks at me for a second. 'You were much chattier before you knew I was here. Cat got your tongue?'

'My name is Cat. So . . . y'know. Kind of . . .'

What the hell am I saying? This man is making me nervous.

Kerry face-palms and I'm on the verge of grabbing my coat. He just laughs. 'Hmm. Well, I can see why you keep quiet, Cat.'

'So if you're not an actor, what is it you do then?' I ask confidently, trying to redeem myself. 'I'm guessing marketing or PR? You look comfortable in this environment. Ha, maybe you organized it. If so, terrible wine and boring speeches.'

'Wrong again,' he replies. 'I actually hate this shit – half of these people are morons. Adrian invited most of the guests, so it's his fault really. Anyway, you're both terrible at this game, so let me put you out of your misery.'

Suddenly he jumps upon his chair and commands the attention of the room. 'Ladies and gentlemen! Apologies for my tardiness. I am Dylan Morrison, co-owner of the new Filmhouse, and I'd like to thank you all for coming to what Adrian and I hope will be an exciting and lucrative venture. I won't bore you with another speech, so please get back to your drinks and enjoy the rest of your evening.'

He sits down to applause and takes a long swig from his beer. 'Unfortunately, I'm going to have to go and mingle now, but it's been a pleasure.'

Kerry and I sit open-mouthed as he swaggers off towards the middle of the room, instantly surrounded by people who've been waiting all night to meet him. I can't take my eyes off him. Kerry laughs. 'I did *not* see that coming. I really like him. You should marry him. We could come here for free.'

I'm laughing too. 'You called him *self-important* and I insulted his business partner AND the booze. Maybe we should leave.'

She thinks for a moment. 'You're probably right, but let's have one more drink first? Be a shame to see this awful wine go to waste.' Before I can answer, she's heading back to the bar and I nip to the toilet.

On my way back to the bar I bump into Patrick. He's nursing a whisky and chatting to three women, who strangely enough don't seem in any hurry to get the fuck away from him. His intoxicated face is the same colour as his dark-pink tie.

'Did Gordon leave already?' he asks. 'I was hoping to share a cab with him.'

'Ages ago. He had plans with his wife.'

Patrick looks displeased but continues sipping his whisky. 'Not to worry.'

'Where do you live?' asks the woman to Patrick's right. 'I can drop you.'

Patrick looks as amazed as I do. 'Near the Saltmarket,' he stammers. 'And that would be great.'

For fuck's sake, it look as if even Patrick will be getting some action this evening. I leave him to it and head back to my table, where Kerry is once more chatting to Dylan. I'm stunned he came back. Perhaps we didn't offend him after all. I reclaim my seat and take a sip of the wine Kerry's placed in front of me.

Dylan smiles at me. 'So, we've established what I do for a living, and Kerry was just telling me she works in finance. What do you do?'

'I write for the *Tribune* supplement,' I reply. 'Features, interviews, that kind of thing.'

'Interesting.'

'I work beside him.' I point over to Patrick, who's just heading out the door with his female friend. How the *hell* did he pull?

'Him? That's odd. I asked him who you were and he said he'd never seen you before in his life.'

'Yes, that Patrick is such a joker!' I reply drily.

'You asked who Cat was?' Kerry interjects with a grin. 'And why might that be?'

I feel my face go red. He pauses for a moment, then chuckles. 'Because I wanted to know! I didn't send the invites, remember.'

I'm secretly elated that he asked who I was. He totally fancies me—

'But sadly, ladies, I must be leaving.'

Or maybe not.

He takes a final slug from his beer bottle before placing it down on the table in front of me.

'Oh. Right. Anywhere nice?' I ask, feeling sad that the handsome man is going away.

'Home,' he replies. 'My bed is calling. I've done my bit here – they won't miss me.'

I try to find some words – any words to keep him there just a few moments longer – but in my somewhat inebriated state, all I manage is, 'That's a shame.'

He pulls on his jacket and shakes Kerry's hand. 'Pleasure to meet you.' With those final words he turns around and starts to talk to Adrian. I stare across at Kerry, and she gives me a 'What the fuck is that all about?!' look.

'Did that just happen?' I ask, bewildered. 'He totally blanked me.'

'Um, he's staring right at you now, Cat.'

I swing around and, sure enough, he's facing me, hands in pockets. Smiling.

'You coming?'

'What?'

'You heard.'

I laugh. But he's still standing there. Waiting.

'You're not serious?'

'Oh, I am. Come with me. Bring those shoes.'

I shake my head. 'You're crazy. That's not going to happen. I don't even know you! I'm not going anywhere with you.'

My head knows this is the correct course of action, but still my vagina is practically dragging him out the door, shouting, 'I'LL DRIVE.'

'What do you think, Kerry?' Dylan loudly continues. By now a few people are starting to stare.

Kerry glances at me. 'Well, Dylan, I think that you should take good care of my lovely friend tonight, or me and everyone else in this room will hunt you down and chop your cock off.'

'Sounds fair.' He laughs.

Kerry puts on my green jacket and knocks back her wine. Then she leans over and whispers, 'If you don't see him naked, I'll never forgive you.'

I hold on to her sleeve. 'But I have a date tomorrow! I can't do this!'

'Of course you can! You have a DATE, not a boyfriend. You can go back to your rules and be on your best behaviour tomorrow. Now go and have some bloody fun for once.'

I'm speechless as she marches away, leaving me to decide on my own. Dylan is still smiling. God, he's handsome. I stand up and clear my throat.

'I hope you have decent coffee.'

As we walk towards the lobby, I'm pretty sure I can hear applause coming from the bar.

We don't speak on the taxi ride to Dylan's house. 'Pompeii' by Bastille is playing on the radio and I sing the lyrics in my head to drown out the sound of my nervous heart beating in my chest. This is surreal. This is happening! In the not-so-distant future I will be naked and he will be naked and –

'£9.80, mate.'

We're here. Cathedral Road. A quick glance out of the window while Dylan is paying reveals a row of tenement flats in a street dotted with expensive cars, and a brightly lit Italian restaurant called Gustoso. I open the door and step out before I lose my nerve completely. Oh shit, this is happening.

Dylan follows me out of the taxi and we pause on the pavement outside his flat. He's looking at me but I'm not ready to meet his gaze. 'Shall we?' he says, motioning towards his front door. I smile and nod.

The hallway is nothing special. Clean but basic. Stone walls, a couple of bikes outside flat 0/1 and a tiny dehydrated plant outside 0/2, which reminds me I need to water my spider plant. We climb the stairs to the first floor, Dylan's perfect arse leading the way before stopping outside 1/1. I'm already trying to imagine what his home is like inside. I bet it's a gadget-filled bachelor pad bedecked with randomly placed Ganesha statues and tapestry hangings to show he's well-travelled both physically and spiritually. Actually, I bet it's nothing but a massive shag pad, scattered with cushions stuffed with his previous conquests' used knickers.

He reaches into his pocket for his keys and I take a deep breath. He turns and grins. He knows I've been checking him out. 'Coffee, wasn't it?'

I follow him into a square hallway with dark wooden flooring, spotlights on the ceiling and five doors leading off to different rooms. There's a smell of vanilla coming from a plug-in near the front door.

'Just through to the right, Cat. I'll put the kettle on.'

I wander through, park myself on his couch and sink in. Holy shit, I'm comfortable. The room is nothing like I thought it would be. Bright and airy, lots of plants, and an old-fashioned record player in one corner. He does have a massive wall-mounted flat screen, but the most impressive aspect of the room is the large mahogany bookcase that sits against the left wall. This man is a serious reader, which of course makes him a million times more attractive, if that's possible. I creep over to have a look. You can tell a lot from the books a man keeps, and I want to find out exactly who I'm dealing with. I tilt my head and run my finger along the spines; Irvine Welsh, Chuck Palahniuk, Dickens, King, Koontz, David Nicholls, Tolkien –

'There's another bookcase in the bedroom, if you want to peruse that next.'

I spin around as if I've been caught reading through his emails. 'What? Oh no, sorry, didn't mean to pry. I just like books.'

'Coffee's ready.'

I spot a small tray with two black cups and some milk and sugar sitting on the coffee table. So far there's nothing about this place I don't like, but the night is still young . . . he could have a waterbed and a sex swing waiting in the next room.

He puts on some music from an iPod dock.

'Doesn't your record player work?' I ask, plopping a brown sugar cube into my coffee.

'It does, but I don't use it very often.' He takes off his jacket and hangs it over the back of a chair. 'I only have really old LPs – you probably wouldn't enjoy them.'

'Why not? What kind of music are you into?' I sip my coffee, thinking that this whole scenario is much more civilized than I expected. 'Please don't tell me you have a stack of really shady eighties bands on vinyl.'

'Hey! I can get just as excited by an eighties pop tune as I can by Frank Sinatra or Daft Punk. Although I draw the line at country. Even Johnny Cash can't make that shite cool. The vinyl is mostly from the seventies.'

I notice that while he's been talking, he's also been unbuttoning his shirt. Before I can say anything more, he's taken it off and is laying it over his jacket. Fucking hell, he's confident, and one look at his torso makes me understand why. His abs are toned and his skin looks peachy . . . but I guess biting isn't an option on a one-night stand.

'Um, you seem to be undressing.'

'I do, don't I?' He sits down to take off his socks. I place my coffee cup back on the tray and decide to join in.

'I like Johnny Cash.' I kick off one of my shoes, praying that my big toe hasn't tried to liberate itself from my tights. '"Rusty Cage" is a genius song. And John Denver wrote some amazing stuff.'

His socks are off and he's standing up. 'Don't tell me you're a Taylor Swift fan too? Dixie Chicks? If you mention Shania Twain, I'm throwing you out.' He watches me peel off my tights and I straighten to meet his gaze.

'As it happens, I *do* like Taylor Swift, but I'm also very involved with Johnny Cash. Are you really going to criticize my musical tastes when you've got Jessie J on your iPod?' I reach behind to unzip my dress.

His hand moves down to his belt buckle and he smiles.

'Yeah, I'll let you have that one. Though "Price Tag" is a tune . . . Do you need help with that?'

I have one hand behind my neck and the other trying to grasp for the zip, which is caught on the fucking fabric. I must look like a really shit contortionist, so I laugh and nod. Dylan walks towards me and I can see the little line of hair running from his belly button and disappearing under his undone jeans. My heart begins to race.

'Turn around,' he says forcefully.

Don't sing the next line from 'Total Eclipse of the Heart'.

I turn and face the other wall and suddenly he presses his body up against my back, moving my hair out of the way. I can feel his breath on my neck. He tugs slowly at the zipper and it slides down, followed by my dress, which pools around my ankles. As I step out of it, I hear him kicking off his jeans. He puts his hands round my waist and firmly pulls me into him.

Christ, he feels huge. The teenage girl in me wants to swing round for a look at his bulge, but he's kissing my neck and running his hands over my breasts and stomach and I'm torn between never wanting this part to end and throwing myself down on the ground in a happy tantrum, yelling, 'PUT YOUR PENIS IN ME THIS VERY SECOND OR I MIGHT JUST DIE!'

Suddenly he spins me around and grabs my hand. I subtly try to stuff my tits back into my bra as he leads me along the hall to his bedroom, but eventually give up when I become transfixed on his very naked arse. He has a better arse than I do.

His bedroom is dimly lit but the light from the hall lets me see that it's very spacious – several prints hang on the dark walls, and the carpet feels soft and inviting between my toes. I stand beside the bed while he closes the door behind him. It's pitch black.

'Should we turn a light on? I can't see a thing,' I ask quietly.

He takes my hand again and pushes me gently on to the bed. 'I don't want you to see this. I want you to feel it.'

He gives me the softest, slowest kiss. Soft lips, soft tongue – one hand holds the back of my head and the other undoes my bra like a lingerie ninja. His kisses continue down my body, and by the time his mouth is between my legs I'm pretty sure I'm going to pass out, because this is outrageously good. Then it happens. Dylan makes me come so hard, I want to have a little cry, but before I can offer him a standing ovation and a knighthood he wraps my legs around his waist. Two hours later we're three condoms down and I've had the best sex of my life. I'm lying next to a man who's vaping on an e-cig and has turned me into a shuddering wreck. I'm a dishevelled mess. He nudges me.

'You've gone all quiet again. Are you thinking about Taylor Swift?'

I laugh and move my hair out of my face. 'Yes. I'm hoping

she'll write a song about this. Actually I was thinking how glad I am that I'm not working tomorrow. I think your penis might have broken me.'

'Was that a compliment? Aww . . . it's been a while then, hasn't it? You just need to get back into the swing of things.'

'How the hell did you know that? Oh God, was I really rusty? Was it like shagging the Tin Man?'

He laughs loudly. 'Hardly. It was memorable to say the least. Call it intuition. I'm wise in the way of the woman.'

'Your modesty must be a real burden.' I roll on to my side and glance at his bedside clock. 'Shit, is that the time? I have to get home. I promised my daughter I'd take her for breakfast in six hours.'

'I didn't know you had a daughter. What's she like?'

I sit up and feel around on the floor for my underwear. 'I don't discuss my kid with men I've just met . . . but she's tremendous. Where the hell is my bra?'

Dylan turns on the bedside lamp, gets up and walks towards the door. 'But you're not with her dad any more?' he probes, taking his robe from the back of the door. I feel sad when his perfect arse disappears under it.

'No,' I reply, checking under the bed for my MIA underwear, 'but I'm looking for daddy number two, if you're up for the job?'

'Very funny. Just making sure I'm not going to get a visit from an irate husband in the dead of night . . .'

'Oh here they are!' I retrieve my bra and knickers from inside his duvet cover. 'No, we've been apart for years. In fact, he's getting married soon, while I'm single and following some stupid dating book for my column, which is never going—'

'What column?'

Oh shite. I start putting on my knickers, frantically trying to think of something to change the subject. I'm certain he can see the look of panic on my face.

'You're Glasgow Girl.'

I snap the waistband of my knickers. 'Never heard of her.'

'You've never heard of the columnist who writes for your magazine?'

Oh fuck off, Sherlock Holmes. I hook my bra behind my back and quickly pull the straps up. 'What I meant to say was—'

'Stop digging, Cat. Your secret is safe with me. I'll make some tea.'

He's not smirking any more.

A few minutes later Dylan's making tea in the kitchen while I un-smudge my make-up in the bathroom mirror, periodically chastising myself for letting my secret out. When I get back to the living room, he's laid my dress on the back of the couch and is texting on his phone.

'Updating your Facebook relationship status?' I ask, hoping my feeble attempt at a joke will somehow reverse time.

'Nope, just ordering you a taxi. I said you were going Southside – you can direct the driver.'

What the hell? I'm not even dressed yet.

'How efficient of you. Do you have them on speed dial?' I ask, pulling on my dress and managing to zip it up first time.

He walks to the window and peeks out of the blinds. 'Well, you said you had to get home.' I approach him at the window and wrap my arms around his waist, but he wriggles free. 'Taxi shouldn't be long. Got everything?' His tone has suddenly grown cold.

I take the hint and collect my belongings. 'Not a problem. I'll wait downstairs.' He doesn't object, only nods and walks me to the front door, kissing me on the cheek like I'm his fucking auntie.

I feel wounded. He could at least have kept up the charade of being a normal human being until I left his bloody lovely flat. It's obvious he has no intention of asking for my number.

'Oh, and Cat? Good luck with your column. I'm sure that somewhere out there is a cowboy who'll appreciate your country-music tastes.' He's laughing at his own joke now and it wasn't even that funny.

'I have one tomorrow night actually. A date, I mean. So, you know, I have options . . . and I refuse to be defined by my interest in ONE musical genre, you big snob. This was just . . . I have no idea what this was. I'm going. Tell Jessie J I said hi. Oh, stop laughing.'

As I creep out into the hallway I'm greeted by un-welcoming cold air and distressingly bright fluorescent lighting. I keep my head down and my heel-clopping to a minimum as I begin my walk of shame down to the waiting taxicab. 'Nice to meet you, Cat!' he yells after me. 'I'll see you around.'

'Doubtful!' I call back, and I make a mental note to avoid the Filmhouse for the rest of my life. Thirty minutes later I'm home, in bed, asking myself just one question:

What in the name of fuck just happened there?

It's nearly 3 a.m. but I text Kerry anyway because I'm full of bewilderment, annoyance and a variety of words which I must share with her immediately:

MEN ARE WEIRD. Great flat, incredible sex but then he turned into a cold, arrogant prick because I write stuff. HE HATES COUNTRY MUSIC. What was I thinking?

I plug my iPod into Grace's bunny speaker and turn on Johnny Cash, silently berating myself for going home with the wanker of the week.

CHAPTER ELEVEN

Despite feeling worse for wear after my night with Dylan, I take Grace for breakfast as planned. As I step outside into the morning the light dazzles my eyes and I slip on a pair of sunglasses, not caring how pretentious I look. We pop across the road to Fee's Cafe where I grab a table in the corner and Grace happily plonks herself down on the comfy brown sofa.

'I want sausages, Mum. And some toast. But not the toast with the seeds. *Real* toast. The white kind.'

I don't protest. Instead I call the waiter over and let a delighted Grace order for herself, before I ask for all the caffeine with an extra shot.

Grace swings her legs, eats her sausages and tells me important things about Lego ninjas while I nod and nurse my coffee. I know it's not only the effect of the wine last night that's making me tired – it's the fact that I haven't gone three rounds with anyone and crawled into bed at 3 a.m. for a very long time. This is a young woman's game;

what am I playing at? I'm not twenty-two any more; I'm hurtling towards forty at breakneck speed. And what the hell was Dylan all about?

'Mum? MUM.'

'Sorry, Gracey. I was, um . . . thinking about your Lego men. What did you say?'

'I was asking if I can have a muffin to take to Dad's.'

'Sure – one of the small ones though. You've just demolished a grown man's breakfast.'

'Can we go to the big toy shop after this? Marie from school said they have about a million loom bands.'

'Yes, OK, for a wee while, but we have to get to your dad's by three. I'm going out later.'

'Aunt Helen told me you have a date.'

'Your Aunt Helen has a big mouth. It's just dinner.'

'You should wear your white dress. You look pretty in that.'

'Kerry told me not to.'

'Kerry is kind of weird.'

'You're a very smart girl.'

She agrees and skips off to choose a muffin while I text Peter to let him know what time we'll be there.

Peter is pottering around in the garden when we get there, wearing cargo trousers and an overly tight T-shirt. Grace immediately gravitates towards the garden shears as if she's being pulled there by a tractor beam.

'Do not touch them, Grace,' Peter says, without even turning around. 'They're sharp.'

She changes course and instead runs inside with her blueberry muffin. We all live to see another day.

'Jeez, you look rough,' he says, now looking directly at my dark-circled eye sockets. Cheeky bastard.

'Oh, I'm fine, but never mind *me* – have you been working out?!' I ask him in my best 'astounded' voice.

'Me?' he asks, surprised. He looks down at his stomach. 'No . . .?'

'Didn't think so . . . Anyhow, must dash!'

'Yes, you must be struggling out here in the daylight, Anne Rice!' he retorts, looking pleased with himself.

'You do know she just *writes* about vampires. She isn't actually one herself.'

He doesn't answer, just carries on pulling weeds, but I can tell he'll be kicking himself when I leave.

'Always a pleasure, Peter. Anyway, I have a date to get ready for. Text me when you're bringing Grace back tomorrow.'

I get to the restaurant at eight on the dot, wearing my white dress because Kerry isn't the boss of me; Grace is.

The overly animated hostess greets me and takes my coat, telling me that 'the other party' hasn't arrived yet and 'Would I like to have a drink at the bar while I wait?'

'Hell, yes,' I tell her, quite seriously, and grab the

cocktail menu with both hands while she points me in the direction of the booze. I'm still a tad thrown after last night's escapades. I know it's unlikely that I'll ever see Dylan again, but it doesn't stop me thinking about him naked . . . Jesus, I'm about to have a date with wholesome, handsome Tom and I've brought along the sarcastic naked man with an enormous penis who now lives in my head. I need that drink.

I scan the cocktail menu, impressed with just how many ways there are for a person to get completely fucking legless. I'm pretty sure getting pissed before your date arrives is frowned upon by Guy Wright, but given the circumstances, I really couldn't give two hoots what the book says about that. The 'Porn-Star Martini' looks good, but no way am I asking for that – I'm not on a fucking hen night.

'Pear and Apple Martini, please.'

The barman nods and begins the laborious task of carefully mixing something that will be thrown in one go down my throat, hardly touching the sides.

I lift my fancy glass and sink into a soft leather couch, watching the door for Tom's arrival like a nervous Labrador. Thankfully I'm not the only person waiting alone so I don't feel the need to whip out my phone and pretend to text someone just yet. I take a long drink of my martini and begin to calm down and remember why I'm here. The rules of engagement are back on. I got side-tracked but this is my opportunity to redeem myself. All I have to do is pretend last night never happened, remember my rules and play it cool.

Ten minutes later the door opens and Tom walks in. He gives his name to the hostess and then waves over, smiling. A group of women standing at the bar are unashamedly staring at him as I saunter over to greet him with a walk that says 'WINNER'.

'Sorry, am I late?' he asks, kissing my cheek. He smells of Armani.

'Not at all,' I reply, even though he is. 'Great to see you.'

Perfect start. Not too eager and just friendly enough. Bonus points for not straddling him.

The hostess leads us into the main restaurant, where a nervous young waitress named Lorna seats us beside the window. Outside there's a drunken man in a black suit, trying to light his cigarette at the wrong end.

'Our special tonight is pan-fried sea bass,' recites Lorna, handing us two large white menus. 'Can I bring you some drinks?'

I'm about to ask for a gin and tonic when Tom cuts in –

'We'll decide what we're eating before we choose wine. Just some water for the table at the moment.'

Lorna nods and goes to fetch some while I debate whether grabbing Tom by his shirt collar and yelling, 'LET'S NOT DO THAT EVER AGAIN, SHALL WE?' into his face is appropriate first-date etiquette. I'm sure such a thing would be frowned upon by Guy Wright – but seriously? Is this the 1950s? I decide to bite my tongue.

Tom smiles at me, like a man who likes to decide things on behalf of women.

'You look very nice, Cat.'

'Thank you,' I reply courteously. 'You too.' It's true.

'Your dress is pretty. Very simple.'

Simple? This cost £99 in Monsoon. It's a fucking work of art. I just smile, but he realizes what he's implied.

'Sorry, I meant classy – not simple. I'm just nervous; I think I've forgotten how to do this. Forgive me?'

Unbutton your shirt and I'll think about it.

'Of course, don't worry!' I reassure him. 'Let's order, shall we?'

We both take a few minutes to look at the menu before Lorna returns.

'I'm going to have the sirloin. Medium rare,' Tom announces. 'Have you decided, Cat?'

What I really want is a big fuck-off burger with hand-cut chips and onion rings, but *The Rules of Engagement* states I must '*maintain my air of refinement*', which is hard to do with relish running down my chin. I order a rump steak, well done, and a side salad, and plan to get chips on my way home.

'Can we have a bottle of Merlot too? Oh, wait, how rude of me. Do you like Merlot, Cat?'

'Yes, that's fine with me.' I thank Lorna as she takes

the menus away and feel a little silly for judging Tom so quickly. For all I know, his ex-wife liked him to take charge over dinner. I wonder if she liked him to take charge in the bedroom too . . . Dylan was pretty confident . . .

'Cat?'

Tom's voice jolts me back to reality.

'Oh, I'm sorry. What did you say?'

He laughs. 'You were miles away there. I asked if you had a good day?'

If it wasn't for my strict guidelines, I'd tell him how Grace and I went to Hamleys and had a light-sabre battle which Grace won, but caused the untimely deaths of Peppa Pig and a giant panda who were caught in the cross-fire. Then I would share how Grace and I sat on green beanbags in Waterstones and read about Vikings, before she went to see her dad, who was dressed like a nineties boy-band member. But I'm wary of talking overly much and breaking the rules, so instead I reply:

'I did. Spent it with my daughter – you know, usual stuff. And you?'

Tom tells me all about his day in detail: the gym, catching up on paperwork, looking online for a new sofa . . . because he's *allowed* to talk about himself and he does it very well, coming across as an actual person and not a vacant stuffed dummy with no personality or interests.

Dinner is actually rather pleasant, as is the con-

versation. Tom grew up in Sussex, he met his ex-wife
Kathryn at university and they married at twenty-two.
No kids, no pets and one older brother, Stephen, who
lives in Germany. I tell him about my life in minimal
detail – he already knows I have a daughter, a cat and a
meddlesome sister who lives across the hall. He thinks
this is intriguing.

'How did *that* happen?' he asks. 'I mean, I get on with
my brother, but I don't think I'd like him living so close.'

'The previous tenant went into a nursing home,' I
respond dutifully. 'Helen found out before it went on
the rental market and it seemed like a good idea at the
time . . . I mean, she can be intrusive at times, but she's a
huge help with Grace.'

Despite my tedious demeanour, he doesn't appear to be
bored in the slightest, even declaring over the wine that,
'It's so nice to meet someone who doesn't feel the need
to talk just for the sake of it.' Bah, it's starting to feel like
Guy Wright might be on to something here.

As our empty coffee cups are taken away, Tom asks
Lorna for the bill, which she promptly brings over. I
reach into my bag and pull out my purse, plus an old
tissue, which I quickly stuff back inside. Tom sees this and
motions me to stop.

'Put that away.'

'The tissue?'

'No, silly, your purse. I'll get this.'

Ugh, here we go. I'm not supposed to let him pay on the first date.

'No, let's go halves. Please? I'd feel better if we did.'

No, I fucking wouldn't. I'd rather spend my fifty pounds on something new and sparkly, but that's not allowed.

'Well, on one condition,' he replies. 'You let me pay next time.'

THIRD-DATE ALERT. I hadn't even considered this. I was too busy trying to both follow the rules AND not think about Dylan. But Tom is a lovely man – he's kind and gentle and handsome as hell. PLUS dating Tom can help me rectify last night's unfortunate 'situation'. Dylan was just a mistake. A well-endowed, charming, infuriating mistake.

'That would be great!' I reply warmly. 'It's a deal.' I know that I'm grinning stupidly, but I can't help it. I'm now one step closer to being felt up by a dentist.

Tom and I both hand over our cards to Lorna who splits the total between the two and hands us our receipts. Tom leaves her a ten-pound tip and she's so grateful she thanks him twice. I retrieve my coat on the way out, which Tom helps me slip into, and seconds later we're outside on Bothwell Street, awkwardly wondering what to do next. I decide to call it a night before I recommend we both get pissed and blow my cover.

'Give me a call during the week,' I say casually. 'We can arrange something then.'

'You don't want to grab a nightcap somewhere?' He looks surprised that I'm leaving so soon. I'm more surprised that he's used the word nightcap after 1970, but still, it seems my 'whatever' attitude is working.

'No, sorry. I have to get Grace early,' I lie. 'But maybe next time?' I spy a taxi approaching with its light on and raise my hand. 'Do you want to share a cab?'

Before long we're sitting in the back of a cab, heading towards the Southside.

'I don't even know where you live,' I say as we pass the O2 Academy. 'Oh, look, Paloma Faith was playing tonight!'

'Hmm, she's a little bit crazy for me,' he remarks. 'I'm more of a Mumford and Sons man myself; and I'm renting a house in Newlands. For the moment anyway.'

I love Paloma Faith. Mumford and Sons? Oh sweet Jesus.

'Newlands is lovely!' I reply overenthusiastically. And by 'lovely', I mean 'expensive'. I wonder what his house is like. I bet it has a conservatory.

The taxi makes its way through the unusually quiet Southside streets, past the local boozers and supermarkets before stopping outside my front door as directed. I offer Tom money for my fare, but he refuses to take it. I make an informed decision not to spend ten minutes stubbornly insisting 'YOU SHALL NOT FUND MY EXTRAVAGANT LIFE-STYLE, SIR!' and put my purse back in my bag.

'Well, thanks for a lovely evening.' I tuck my hair behind my ear and feel rather coy. Which is weird. Last night I was having my dress unzipped by a man I just met, and tonight I'm nervously wondering whether a goodnight kiss is appropriate or even allowed. However, before I have time to deliberate, Tom leans in and kisses my cheek.

'I'll call you this week. I had a great night, Cat.'

'Me too. Speak soon.'

I exit the taxi and wave as he's driven off towards Newlands. I can still feel his kiss on my cheek and I sigh. Once inside, I let Heisenberg in through the window. He completely blanks me and heads for the kitchen. I follow him through and open a tin of cat food, talking to myself as I spoon it out. *Actually, it was a really great night. He's intelligent, kind and handsome.* I leave the obnoxious furry one to feast on his beefy jellied mush and retreat to bed thinking, *Maybe calm and composed is exactly what I need.*

For once, it's Kerry who wakes me up at the ungodly hour of 10 a.m. on a Sunday.

'Get up and meet me for lunch. I need to hear everything that's been going on.'

I sit upright, rubbing my eyes. 'I would, but I don't plan on getting dressed today.'

'Unacceptable. They're doing Sumo Sundays at Yo Sushi. All you can eat for twenty pounds. You don't really expect to have liaisons with two different men and think you can just NOT GIVE ME DETAILS.'

'I would have called you when—'

'Cat, this is the most exciting thing that's happened to you in two years. Now put some fucking clothes on and I'll pick you up at one.'

The shopping centre is packed full of people who somehow think it's normal to be vertical on a Sunday. Kerry has insisted that I don't utter a word about my shenanigans until we're sitting at a booth and she's ordered a spicy tuna and cucumber hand roll. As we wait for a table, she tells me that her boss Jessica was caught shagging the new temp Emma in her Fiat Punto.

'Everyone is talking about how she's abused her position of power ... I'm just shocked that on *her* salary Jessica only drives a fucking Punto.'

'I miss working in a really busy place,' I moan. 'There's never any work gossip in my life. I'm either working from home or in that tiny office with those four maniacs. I cannot wait till we all move into the new premises.'

'Yeah, it's a good laugh, although I've been there nine years and I still don't know everyone's name. There's one guy I speak to every day and I *think* his name's Jim, but secretly I call him Prince cos he's really tiny but you still would.'

'Good to know.'

Our server is a twenty-something man with a dubious moustache and a blue plastic watch. 'Can I get you green tea or miso soup?'

I order soup and watch the tiny dishes move past on the conveyor belt. Kerry points out that green tea tastes like shit, and the waiter doesn't disagree. I grab some ebi nigiri from the belt and reach for the chopsticks.

'That's all you ever eat in here.'

'Not true!' I protest, snapping the chopsticks in half. 'I also eat cucumber maki and those dumpling things. I'm just not that crazy about sushi. I'm always starving afterwards.'

'I'm starving now. Grab me those inari pockets, will you? Fucking hell – look! There's Karen Stevens. She hasn't changed much.'

I turn in the direction of Kerry's glare and see our old high-school classmate briskly walking towards the exit. She's wearing very high over-the-knee boots that keep slipping on the smooth floor.

'I wonder if she's still a gigantic bitch,' I muse, secretly hoping she'll fall on her arse. 'Remember when she brought in those pro-life leaflets to school because Allison Brown had an abortion? Wicked cow.'

'She works in recruitment now,' Kerry says through a mouthful of sushi. 'So I'm guessing the answer is yes.'

The waiter brings my soup in a small brown bowl. I thank him but he isn't listening. Kerry pours herself some fizzy water from the table tap. 'Anyway, I didn't bring you here to talk about Karen Stevens; I want to know what happened with your two boys.'

'Ugh, where do I start?'

'Start with the Filmhouse man . . . *Please* don't tell me he was shit in bed. I'll be crushed.'

I grab my second plate off the belt. 'He wasn't; in fact he was sublime. You know the way one-night stands are usually all awkward and . . .'

'Rushed?'

'Exactly. This wasn't. This was slow and exciting. It was like he was determined to make sure he blew my mind. We had a connection. Well, until . . .'

Kerry is staring at me intently. 'Well?! What happened?'

'Afterwards he went all weird. Distant, y'know? Like he'd just spent hours making sure every part of my body came into contact with his tongue, and then he was all "See ya!" and pushing me out the door at two a.m. If we'd had an average time, I could understand it, but up until then I really thought we'd clicked. I did let it slip about the column though; that might be the reason.'

Kerry drops her chopsticks and frowns. 'Why would he care about you writing a column? I think it's more likely that he's just a prize wanker. He could have at least pretended to give a shit until you left.'

'EXACTLY!' The waiter with the blue watch glances my way and I lower my voice. 'So let's just say, I don't expect I'll be hearing from Dylan any time soon.'

'Shame, I had high hopes for him. I told Kieran I thought you had met *the one.*'

'Oh, behave. If I end up with a shithead like him, I'll kill myself. Tom is a much better prospect.'

She picks up her chopsticks and hits them off mine. 'Yes! Fuck Dylan right in his sexy, sexy face. This Tom one sounds much saner.'

'He is, and he's very polite . . . and sweet! There's a lot to be said for sweet.'

'Sweet?'

'Yes. A gentleman.'

Kerry purses her lips together and sits quietly.

'Oh, come on, what the hell is wrong with sweet? Kieran is sweet!'

Kerry laughs. 'Sweet? On our second date Kieran whispered in my ear that he was going to shag me until I couldn't walk. His words, not mine. See? You're blushing now and so was I. Those are not the words of a "sweet" man.'

'Perhaps if I wasn't pretending to be so bloody repressed, he would be more forthcoming . . .'

Kerry grins. 'That boy is going to get a fucking shock when you finally unleash. You sure you want to keep doing it this way?'

I pause and pour some more soy sauce into my little bowl. 'Not really, but I am nothing if not dedicated to my job. Besides, Tom's handsome as hell. I have a strong, sexual need to see where this goes.'

Kerry picks up a pink-rimmed plate and makes a face

at the contents. 'I can tell you how this will go, Cat. He'll fall madly in love with the prim and proper you, until one morning he'll catch you dancing in your pants to Azealia Banks with your hair in bunches and he'll have you sectioned.'

'That's unfair. I defy anyone to listen to "212" and not dance like they've been tasered.'

'I agree, but Tom might be hoping he wakes up to a girl who tiptoes around to "Tubular Bells" in the mornings.'

'I'm not Linda Blair, Kerry.'

'Oh, you know what I mean. Something inoffensive and twinkly.'

I have no idea what she means.

Kerry drops me back home at three, promising to call later. I plan to creep back into bed for an hour before Grace comes home, but Helen corners me in the hallway.

'I can't believe you haven't let me know how your date with Tom went.'

'Jeez, Helen, it was only last night. Give me a break.'

She places her hands on her hips and frowns. 'That doesn't answer my question. You didn't blow it, did you?'

'No! It was great. He's really nice. We'll be meeting up again.'

Her frown vanishes and her face explodes with happiness. 'THAT'S WONDERFUL! I KNEW HE WAS THE MAN FOR YOU!'

'Christ, calm down. He hasn't proposed.'

'Oh, I know. I'm just pleased you're getting another date. It's hopeful!'

'Yeah, I suppose it is.' I take the keys from my pocket and begin unlocking my front door. 'We'll see how it goes. What are you up to today?'

I turn around but she has already vanished back inside, presumably to excitedly report to Adam that her sister isn't such a lost cause after all.

I've hit the mid-week blues and find myself ignoring three copywriting jobs I'm supposed to be finishing up in favour of drinking a frozen margarita I found at the back of my freezer while half watching an episode of *Criminal Minds* I've already seen. Secretly I know I'm distracted because it's Thursday and Tom still hasn't been in touch to arrange our next date. I'm becoming one of those women who might as well be pacing the streets of Glasgow, dressed in a sandwich board that reads: 'WHY THE FUCK HASN'T HE CALLED?' Should I text him? I have his number stored from the last text; I could easily drop him a 'Hey, are we still on for this week?' light-hearted, no pressure, dripping with desperation text . . . No, I'm not fucking allowed to, so what can I do?

I call Kerry.

'He's probably just busy. It happens. Call him.'

'I'm not supposed to call him.'

She sighs loudly. 'Get the book and tell me what it says.'

I grab my copy of *The Rules of Engagement* and turn to Rule 4 – *'Don't Harass Him.'*

'It says, *"By texting or calling him every seven minutes, you're telling him that you have nothing else going on in your sad life."'*

'Ha ha, does it really say that? What else?'

I'm a little annoyed that she finds this all so funny. '"*Stop making it easy for him. Let him do the work*,"' I continue. 'This is so bloody clichéd. So, what? I should make it hard for him? Like go into hiding?'

'You should challenge him.'

'Challenge him to what? A duel? Turn my life into one long episode of *Takeshi's Castle*? Is that challenging enough?'

Kerry snorts down the phone.

'And what if I *do* call him? Would it really be so bad? What's the worst that can happen? I interrupt him watching fucking Babestation?'

'Calm down, Cat.'

I toss the book back on to the coffee table. 'This bloody book is turning me into a prize idiot, and I still have very little to write about this week, other than Saturday's uneventful dinner date. I need more!'

'Listen, if he doesn't call, then fuck him. I'm sure your editor will understand that you can't force these things.'

'No, forcing it is exactly what she'll expect me to do.'

'Right, well. Oh! Before I forget, Kieran and I are going to some actor's birthday party in the West End on Saturday night. Do you have Grace?'

'No, she's at Peter's. Which actor?'

'Beth someone. Kieran knows her. I think she was in *EastEnders* once? I'm just about to google her so I can pretend I'm familiar with her work. Want to come?'

'I don't want to be a third wheel. I won't know anyone. I can see it now: you and Kieran getting all kissy and me standing in the corner wondering why I came.'

'Oh, say you'll come,' she pleads. 'It'll be you and me in the corner while Kieran talks about design with the rest of the arty twats. I need you to come. He always forgets about me at these things and I end up getting far too pissed to compensate.'

'Hmm. I dunno. I have an article due and—'

'Fuck work. We'll pick you up in a taxi at seven. And let me know if he calls!'

Then she hangs up the bloody phone before I can argue. She always does that and it always works. I switch off *Criminal Minds* and begin writing my column for Saturday.

The Lowdown magazine – *Saturday 1 November 2014*

I Followed the Rules

Glasgow Girl has some news.

I had my second date with Mr X this week. Yes, I know. I'm awesome. Quieten down . . .

As I describe my date with Tom, it occurs to me that although I wasn't funny, entertaining or even particularly charming, I didn't spending the evening vying for his attention either, so I'm begrudgingly giving Mr Wright a point for that. I end the column in my usual cynical manner:

> Date three is on the cards, and hopefully at the end of all this I'll either have a brand-new boyfriend or just be much, much older than I once was.

Forty-seven delightfully distracting minutes later, I email the copy to Natasha, feeling pleased that writing about Tom has taken my mind off him and all of the reasons he might not have called.

WHY HASN'T HE CALLED?

The next morning, I'm sitting at the table writing an advertorial for a handbag company when Natasha phones.

'Hey, Cat; I've got your copy for Saturday's mag.'

'Everything OK?'

'Yes! Online comments are increasing every week. I just wanted to check you've got something exciting lined up for next week?'

'Oh, of course. I have another date with Mr X in a couple of days,' I lie. 'I'm sure things will start to get, erm, exciting!'

'Great. I'll look forward to it. Speak soon.'

Bollocks. If that fucking dentist doesn't call, I'm up shit creek. As if writing about handbags wasn't bad enough, this conversation has officially ruined my morning. I glance at the clock on my laptop – 11.30, which means it's coffee time. I save my Word document and switch on iTunes. Sometimes music is the only thing guaranteed to lift my mood. While I'm putting the kettle on, the shuffle function decides to play *Ring of Fire* by Johnny Cash, and my desire to sway is suddenly overridden by thoughts of Dylan and his contempt for country music. Then I start thinking about how he began undressing, how he unzipped me, and by the time I get to him holding me down on his bed, the kettle has boiled and I'm so aroused I want to dry-hump the kitchen table. Damn him. I wonder if he ever thinks of me.

Instead of me driving Grace to Peter's house, he picks her up – they're going to the new American diner that's opened in town. Grace decides to wear her best frilly dress, along with a leather jacket and some plastic shoes, and I don't object. There will be plenty of time for wearing clothes that actually match each other when she's a grown-up. I wave her off and start getting ready for the birthday party Kerry is dragging me along to.

An hour later I'm wearing a pretty polka-dot dress, killer heels and frantically painting my nails before the taxi comes. This party had better be worth it; I could have been in bed watching *Orange Is the New Black*.

The taxi arrives at five past seven. I grab my black poncho and hurry towards the front door, almost tripping over Heisenberg in my rush to get out. He miaows while doing a little sprint towards my bedroom and I'm sure I'll come back to find he's spitefully pissed in my slippers for having the cheek to be walking where he was.

It's a surprisingly chilly evening, but I run the risk of messing up my perfectly set curls if I attempt to pull this poncho on, so instead I gallop over to the taxi, mumbling, 'cold, cold, COLD!' until I'm safe and warm inside the car. I climb into the back seat beside Kerry and say hello. Kieran, who's busily tapping on his phone in the front seat, doesn't look round but manages a short 'All right, Cat?'

'Fine,' I reply, giving Kerry a hug. She smells like a mixture of Gucci Rush and hairspray. 'So, Kieran, tell me about this party.'

'Friend of mine. Beth. Birthday party.'

'What's she like?'

'She's very nice, very loud and very sensitive about her age. Apparently this is her forty-second birthday but I reckon it's more like her fiftieth. I'm forty and she's waaaaaay ahead of me in the ageing department.'

Kerry makes a miaowing sound and playfully slaps him

on the back of the head. He turns round and purrs. God, those two are sickening.

'And she's an actress? How do you know her?' I ask, glancing at Kerry's jeans and trainers and wondering if I should have dressed down. 'Have you been secretly treading the boards?'

'No. I used to go out with her daughter Hannah,' he replies. 'A few years ago now.' He roots around for some money in his Diesel jeans. Kerry glares at the back of his head, clearly annoyed by this revelation.

'Did you now, Kieran? So essentially we're going to your ex-mother-in-law's party? Will there be a big fuck-off reunion between you and Hannah?'

Kieran sighs. 'We were never *that* serious, Kerry, and I've seen her since we split. She's just a mate. Behave yourself.'

The taxi pulls into Woodlands Drive and stops outside number three. Kerry gets out first, quickly followed by me, while Kieran pays the driver. She fixes the bow on the pink champagne they've brought for Beth.

'You OK?' I ask her quietly.

She smiles and whispers, 'I love it when he tells me to behave – it's so masterful. Anyway, I've seen Hannah before – she looks like Gary Busey AND she still lives with her mum. Nothing to worry about.'

I laugh as Kieran exits the taxi and we all make our way into the flat.

I can hear the party from the stairwell as we climb the

stone stairs to the third floor. The door is ajar so we let ourselves in and are immediately greeted by an unenthusiastic dog, pounding music and the sound of a woman shrieking with laughter.

Kieran grins. 'That's Beth. Come on, I'll introduce you.'

Beth Hope, real name Elizabeth Dick (changed ten years ago for obvious reasons), is a petite brunette actress who shares a spacious three-bedroom tenement flat with her blonde daughter Hannah and their astoundingly lazy greyhound, Harry. Although I didn't recognize the name, her face is instantly identifiable; she's one of those actresses that pops up everywhere, from bit parts on soap operas to adverts for car insurance, and although I want to yell, 'I KNOW YOU! YOU PLAYED THAT ABUSIVE MARKET TRADER ON *EASTENDERS*! I WATCHED THAT! YOU WERE MUCH LARGER THEN' I bite my tongue and shake her hand politely, thanking her for inviting me.

'Thank you all for coming! Girls, take that bottle into the kitchen and grab yourselves a drink. Kieran – how the hell are you? Have you seen that dreadful light installation at the CCA? Hannah's just taking coats to the spare room; she'll be back in a second. CAN SOMEONE GET HARRY OFF THE COUCH, PLEASE?'

Kerry and I walk out of the living room and across the brightly lit hall. There are a small number of guests in the kitchen, most of them propped up against the black fitted worktops, with a few sitting at the kitchen table, swigging from plastic wine glasses and beer bottles. Kerry places the pink champagne beside the other twenty-two bottles of birthday fizz and lifts an open one, pouring us both a glass.

'I told you!' she announces quietly. 'It's always the same at these things. We'll see Kieran in a couple of hours when he remembers he actually came here with us.'

'Doesn't that bother you?' I ask, looking around for some orange juice to add to my horribly dry cava. Two women leave their seats at the table and we grab them, knowing we'll be here for a while.

'Not really. His close friends are lovely and fun, but his wider circle of artistic bores leaves me cold a lot of the time.'

'You two really are so different,' I remark. 'And for someone who hates creative types, you're dating a graphic designer and your best mate is a writer. You can't hate them *that* much.'

'It's the pretentiousness I hate!' She laughs. 'That wankerish air of superiority that seems to cling to some people who've read some tricky books or think having a three-hour conversation about the position of a light bulb is acceptable. They're just not silly enough for me and I'm probably too uninspiring for them. I'll never be anyone's muse.'

After three glasses of wine we finally decide to mingle a little, making our way towards the music blasting from the living room. My sensible head is telling me that any minute the police will show up because of the noise, but my feet appear to be dancing already.

I spot Kieran talking to Hannah, and Beth is getting twirled around the dance floor by a younger man in a trilby. Harry the dog is still claiming his rightful place on the couch, but I have the feeling it won't be long before someone gets pissed and sits on him. Surprisingly, Kerry doesn't make a beeline for Kieran, choosing instead to start a conversation with a guy hanging out beside Beth's antique display cabinet. I stand alone for a moment, taking it all in. Kieran waves me over.

'Hannah, this is Cat.'

I shake Hannah's hand but all I can think of is Gary. Fucking. Busey. Of course Hannah looks nothing like Gary Busey. Well, maybe the teeth, but oh shit, I want to laugh.

'Hannah is a very talented artist,' Kieran informs me. 'Most of the paintings in here are her work.'

I look around the living-room walls at the splodgy modern art while Hannah beams and waits for praise. The last time I was forced to lie about art was when Grace brought home her Primary Two art book, filled with hand-prints and stick men . . . only Grace's were better.

'Amazing,' I reply. 'I've never seen anything quite like them.'

'Thank you, Cat. I try to capture the brutality and honesty of my life in my work. It's cathartic, but I do sometimes wonder why I put myself through it. Oh, look, there's Lynne. Forgive me – I must say hello.'

Hannah flounces off and I glance at Kieran, who's trying very, very hard not to lose it. I'm not so controlled.

'HA HA, you shit! You totally set me up. Whoever the hell Lynne is, she just saved me from being horribly rude to a terrible artist. I thought you liked all this arty stuff?'

'Normally I do, but these are awful. Her paintings sell very well though,' replies Kieran, still laughing. 'Admittedly her mum buys a lot of them, but still, she has quite the following.'

'Like Charles Manson?'

'Pah. Hannah is lovely, but sadly she's rapidly disappearing up her own arse. She used to be much more down to earth. Shame. Anyway, where's Kerry?'

I point towards the antique cabinet, where Kerry is now dancing with the random man. Kieran doesn't look the least bit bothered; he's actually smiling.

'She's doing this on purpose. First the argument about Hannah and now the flirting. She wants me to get annoyed.'

'But why?' I ask, watching Kerry pointedly make eyes at the man, who clearly can't believe his luck. 'To make you jealous?'

'Well, yes. And because she knows I'll use the paddle on her when we get home.'

'Paddle? Like an oar?'

He raises an eyebrow. 'Not quite, Cat.'

It takes me a moment, but I get there.

'JESUS, KIERAN! I don't need to know that!'

'I assumed you would already . . . You guys share everything, right?'

'NOT THIS!'

'My bad.' He shrugs. But as I watch him watching her, I get a little pang of jealousy. He's looking at her the way Dylan looked at me that night. Sheer fucking lust. They still both want each other just as much as when they first met, and I can't even make it past the first shag.

Before I manage to completely depress myself, a tiny woman in yellow squeezes past me to turn off the stereo before belting out the first line of 'Happy Birthday' so loudly I get a fright. Everyone joins in, and Hannah enters with a love-heart-shaped cake, mercifully not inspired by her art, topped with five candles and a sparkler. Just as Beth starts her speech, I see Kieran sneak over to Kerry and whisper something in her ear, while the random man looks on unimpressed. I have no idea what he's saying, but the smirk on her face gives me a clue. I turn back to Beth, who's now drunkenly waving the sparkler around like it's the fifth of November.

'Please make sure you take some cake, and thanks again for coming!' she slurs. 'You all spoil me, you really do.'

Everyone cheers, the dog barks and someone puts on Paul Simon's 'Graceland'. Time for another drink. I meet

Kerry in the kitchen – she has obviously had the same idea.

'Nothing makes me want to drink more than Paul Simon's solo stuff. More wine, Cat?'

'Yeah. I need to pee though. Where's the loo?'

'Door at the end of the hall. You got any powder with you? I'm feeling shiny.'

I chuck my bag at her. 'It's in my make-up bag. Back in a sec.'

The bad thing about house parties is the queue for the bathroom. I'm second in line behind a man wearing red jeans, but already I'm hopping from foot to foot, hoping I don't sneeze or laugh before it's my turn. Luckily for me, he's quick, and I breathe a huge sigh of relief that I won't be known as Pissy Pants by a room full of strangers. Suddenly there's a loud knock on the door.

'I'll be out in a minute,' I yell, looking around for the toilet roll, which has unrolled itself halfway across the floor.

'It's only me!' Kerry shouts back. 'You got a message from Tom! Hurry up, this is killing me.'

Fuck! I expertly reach across for the loo roll while ensuring my arse hovers above the toilet seat – I don't trust my pelvic floor not to unleash hell on Beth's lovely bathroom tiles. Hands washed, I rush back to the kitchen, where Kerry hands me my phone sheepishly. 'You'll have to wait for sixty seconds. I couldn't guess your stupid passcode and I've locked you out.'

'You were going to read it?!' I guess I'm not really sur-prised; I'd have done the same. We both sit and stare intensely at my phone until it lets me in again and I click on the envelope symbol.

Down south on family matter but will be back next week. Tom x

'Well, at least he texted,' I say. 'And there's a kiss this time. Maybe his granny died or something.'

'Maybe he's with his wife.' I can always rely on Kerry to say the words I don't want to hear.

'*Ex*-wife!' I interject. 'They're divorced.'

Kerry moves in closer. 'She could be having second thoughts and he's rushed to London, armed with cham-pagne, hoping for reconciliation.'

'I hope not. I hope it's something serious. Ugh, now you've got me rooting for a death in the family, Kerry.'

'Here's to dead grannies!' she toasts. 'May his reasons for blowing you off this week be unspeakably tragic.'

I clink glasses with her and down the rest of my cava. Panic is setting in. Without Tom, there is no column and – more importantly – I haven't seen him naked yet. That would be the real tragedy. Kerry has a dreamy little smirk on her face.

'Stop thinking about Kieran's paddle; this is about me.'

'What? That's . . . How did . . .?'

'He told me. You are a pair of monsters and now I have to live with that image in my head forever.'

Kerry snorts and blushes a little. 'He's quite the oversharer, isn't he? Don't be mean, and don't knock it until you've tried it. Being blindfolded and—'

'There's a blindfold too? Jesus, you have this whole sexy, submissive thing going on. I feel impressed and mildly uncomfortable at the same time.'

'Yes, well . . . Did you meet Hannah? More wine?'

I hold out my glass and Kerry fills it halfway. 'Nice deflection, Kerry, and yes, I met Hannah – and admired her artwork.'

We stare silently at each other.

Kerry speaks first. 'Do you think she painted them with her feet or her mouth?'

'Hard to tell,' I reply, casually looking around to make sure Hannah isn't standing behind me. 'I'm more inclined to think Harry the dog did them.'

There's a crash from the living room, and moments later Kieran appears at the kitchen door. 'Beth's fallen over. She's fine, but I think the party's over, ladies. Grab your coats.'

We hover in the doorway as Kieran says his goodbyes, and then make our way back down the stairs and try to call a taxi. The cold night air adds at least seventeen units to my blood-alcohol level and I'm forced to sit on the kerb until either the taxi arrives or the street stops spinning. The journey home is a bit of a blur, but with a little help from Kerry, I make it to my front door without incident.

'You sure you don't want to crash with us tonight?' she

asks, taking away my keys as I try to open the letter box. 'Will you be OK alone?'

Without waiting for an answer, she opens the door and turns on the hall light. I throw my handbag in the direction of the living room. 'I'll be fine,' I mumble. 'I'm going to make toast.'

'Oh Christ, don't cook anything. Just go to bed.'

We clumsily hug goodnight before I locate my bedroom and throw myself into bed. I hear Kerry locking the front door and then the jingle as she posts my keys through the letter box.

As I drift off, I feel the soft thud of Heisenberg jumping on to the bed beside me, quickly followed by a whack on the head from a sturdy paw. I fucking hate that cat.

CHAPTER TWELVE

'You know I'm loving your column, Cat,' Natasha announces as I take a seat in her office on Monday. 'I understand that it hasn't changed your life, but I do feel that you're being a tad overcritical with regards to the author.'

'Am I?'

She lifts a copy of the magazine, already open at my page. '*If Guy Wright isn't a friendless, loveless Neanderthal, I'll be very surprised.*'

I laugh. 'He deserves it! He's filling women's minds full of shite that only exists in his own twisted world. He's trying to turn us into robotic—'

'He's been in touch,' she interrupts, handing me a printed email. 'Seems he reads your column.'

'You're kidding?' I laugh.

'Nope, have a look.'

From: Wright, Guy
To: Carling, Natasha
Subject: Glasgow Girl

Dear Natasha,

Would it be possible for you to give me a call regarding Glasgow Girl's current columns involving my book? I feel there are matters we need to discuss.

I look forward to speaking with you at your earliest convenience.

Guy Wright

I hand her back the email. 'Well, when you speak to him, just tell him that—'

'We've already spoken. He's quite charming. And keep the email, you might need his number – you're meeting him for lunch today.'

My stomach flips. 'Seriously? WHY?'

'Because even though I offered to meet with him, he was insistent on meeting you personally. Be good for the newspaper – he very rarely speaks to the press apparently, despite all the hype.'

I think back to all the ridiculous hoops I've had to jump through lately and cannot believe I have to have lunch with that horse's ass. 'But, Natasha, he can't meet me . . . I'm anonymous!'

'So is he. Table is booked for twelve thirty at Yen. We're paying. Go and see what he wants. Push for an interview.'

I stand up, email in hand, feeling confused but intrigued. I've done so many interviews, but never one where I've been on the receiving end of the heat.

'And Cat? Be nice, please.'

I nod and shuffle out of her office. Why does he want to see me? Is he going to bribe me to be nicer about him? Is he going to sue me? Shit, maybe he's going to punch me in the face over crispy beef and noodles. Still, at least I'll get to tell him what I think of his book – not that he doesn't know already.

I give Kerry a call at her office, hoping she'll be able to calm me down.

'Listen, you know that dating book I'm doing?' I say, lowering my voice so Patrick doesn't hear me. 'The author has summoned me to lunch. Stop laughing!'

'I'm sorry, but why the hell did you say yes? You've been a complete bitch about his book!'

'I don't have a choice. He arranged it with Natasha and she's making me. I'm dreading it, to be honest. I bet he's some middle-aged man with a spray tan and hair plugs who thinks he's God's gift.'

'Probably. Just keep your cool. Don't yell at him.'

'Of course not. Anyway, I need to shoot off. Will let you know how I get on.'

As lunchtime draws near, I slip into the ladies' room to freshen up my make-up. I don't want to look like I've made an effort for him, but I don't want him to be staring at the spot on my chin or my shiny forehead all through lunch. I apply some concealer, freshen up my blusher and run a brush through my hair, annoyed with myself for giving a shit about what he might think of me. One final look in the mirror and I'm ready to meet Guy fucking Wright. I hope he's ready to meet me.

'Table for one?'

Dining alone, madam? Would you like to see our single-as-fuck specials menu?

I glance around the brightly lit, half-empty restaurant, searching for a man sitting alone with an ego the size of Australia for company.

'No, I'm meeting someone. Table is booked under "Wright".' I feel a little nervous and wipe my clammy hands on my grey suit. Thank God I wore it today. I love this suit. It makes me feel like I'm in charge. I feel like Melanie Griffith in *Working Girl*.

'Ah yes, follow me.' The young waitress leads me to a table at the back of the room. I spy a table of three women and a couple sharing dumplings in a booth, but no sign of a dating Nazi. I breathe a small sigh of relief and order a glass of wine. I don't care if it's lunchtime; if I'm going to be forced to endure this slimy idiot for the next hour, I'll need a drink.

I take out my notepad and phone and hunt around in my bag for a pen, instead finding three lipsticks I'd forgotten about and a tiny Moshi Monsters figure that looks like a pirate. I start to panic and dig deeper. There must be a bloody pen in here. What kind of fucking journo goes to a meeting without a pen?

'Hello, Cat.'

Startled, my head whips around at lightning speed.

'Dylan!'

Be still my beating loins. He has a lager in one hand and a giant grin on his smug, kissable face. I haven't seen him in daylight before. I haven't seen him since . . . Oh shite, now I'm back in his bedroom and he's pulling my legs over his shoulders and I'm blushing. He's grinning and I'm a flushed, pen-less fool holding a Moshi Monster.

'You all right?' he asks, knowing full well I'm more than flabbergasted to see him.

'Yes. Fuck! You surprised me! Sorry, how are you?' I'm strangely overjoyed to see him, but how can I get rid of him before Guy Wright turns up?

'I'm very well. Is this a bad time?' He smirks, looking at the little plastic figure I'm holding. 'Are you on one of your famous dates? He's a little on the short side.'

I throw the Moshi bastard back in my bag and compose myself. 'No, actually I'm working. I'm waiting to interview an author, if he ever shows up.' I take a gulp of my wine. 'I can't find a damn pen. It's going so well already.'

'I have one you can borrow.' He reaches into his coat pocket and hands me a brushed silver pen. 'Here you go.'

'I can't take this; it looks expensive. Can I pawn it afterwards . . .?'

He laughs. 'Just give it back to me when you've finished your interview.'

'Sure, OK. Thank you, you're a lifesaver. I'd hate to look unprepared in front of this knob; I'm in his bad books as it is.'

'Oh? Sounds intriguing. Who are you meeting?'

'I'm meeting an author . . . oh, hang on . . .'

I spy a man in his late forties wearing a bottle-green suit entering the restaurant. He's dressed like a wanker; it *must* be him.

I tuck my hair behind my ear and mutter, 'Right, OK, I think he's just arrived. I'll be about an hour. Where are you sitting? I'll come over after.'

'I'm sitting right here.'

Dylan places his drink on the table, takes off his jacket and sits down across from me.

What the fuck?! He can't sit there. I try and shoo him away.

'Sorry, but, um . . . what the hell are you doing?'

He signals to the waitress that he's ready to order. 'Well, I'm having a meeting with the woman who has been happily shitting all over my book for the past few weeks. Oh, and some Thai beef.'

'Very funny. Look, you have to go, this guy is—'

'Me,' he interrupts. 'Oh! How rude of me.' He holds out

his hand. 'Guy Wright, bestselling author of *The Rules of Engagement*. Published five years ago and translated into fifteen languages. Millions sold.'

The man in the green suit sits down at the table with the three women. I look back at Dylan, who's still holding out his hand. I have no idea what's happening. I. Just. Stare.

His hand retreats and he laughs. 'Natasha said you might be a bit defensive, given my book hasn't helped you in the old love department and you're still convinced it's nothing to do with you . . . Oh yes, please, can I have the Thai beef and another lager? The mute in front of me will have another glass of whatever that is and the Kung Po chicken. Just nod if that's OK, Cat. Cat?'

I didn't even see the waitress standing impatiently beside me – food is the last thing on my mind, but I nod to make her go away.

Neither of us speaks for about thirty seconds, but then he smiles at me and I cave first. 'Why didn't you tell me who you were? Why all this?'

'I'll admit, I was tempted to tell you that night, but, well, this is much more fun. Besides, we'd just had sex – it wouldn't have been gentlemanly.'

God, he's smug. I want to stab him with his own pen.

'You're in no danger of being thought of as gentlemanly. You practically threw me out of your flat!'

'That was just a bonus.'

He leans back in his chair and I desperately try to push it over using my mind. The waitress arrives and gently places our meals and a pitcher of water on the table. Dylan thanks her while I glare at him.

'I don't buy it.'

'Buy what?' he enquires, breaking his chopsticks down the middle.

'That this was just some weird coincidence. That you just happen to take home the woman who's been slagging off your book. I call bullshit. You planned this, didn't you?'

'You make a good point.' He pincers some rice. 'And the answer is – not entirely.'

'What do you mean? Stop bloody eating and explain yourself.'

'God, you're demanding. Look, I knew Adrian had invited everyone from the *Tribune* so I thought there was a good chance the writer who'd been dissing my book might come. I was intrigued to find out who she was.'

'And you didn't know it was me?' I grab a glass and pour myself some water. My mouth feels like it's made of cotton wool.

'Well, Glasgow Girl is anonymous, and you were very open about being a journalist . . . to be honest, I thought it might be your friend Kerry – I didn't buy the whole *works in finance* story. She doesn't look the type.'

Sounds plausible.

'As for taking you home – believe it or not, I invited

you because I was attracted to you. If YOU hadn't given yourself up, I'd have been none the wiser.'

I'm not even hungry, but I find myself on autopilot, eating the chicken he's ordered for me.

'So why am I here, Dylan? I understand that you're angry that the bad lady called you on your bullshit, but I stand by every word I've written. You should grow a thicker skin. I do hope you don't stalk every critic.'

He takes a sip of lager, seemingly unfazed by my remarks.

'I'm not angry. A little irked perhaps – any author is by a bad review – but not *angry*. I'm just curious. Your columns don't pose any sort of threat to me. This book paid for my lifestyle. I bought that nice pen, invested in a business I happen to really enjoy and I own a lovely flat. You remember my flat, right, Cat?'

I do. I remember the smell of vanilla and the feeling of the bedroom carpet on my knees and ... DON'T GO THERE, BRAIN. STAND DOWN, STAND DOWN. ABORT! I drink some more water, struggling to retain my fighting stance.

'Jesus, you're egotistical, but at least I have something interesting to write about this week. How does "*self-obsessed author tricks journalist into bed*" grab you?'

He's laughing, but I get the sneaky suspicion it's not *with* me.

'That would be fun, Cat, but I was thinking something

more along the lines of *"Journalist is full of shit and writes full and public apology to the handsome author with outstanding hair."* You see, you broke Rule 6 and yet continue to blame my book for the fact you can't find a proper relationship.'

My mind stops trying to maim Dylan and searches for Rule 6 in my memory banks. Nothing. Hang on – I only read up to Rule 4. Why the fuck didn't I read the whole book before I started this?

'But I didn't get to Rule Six!' I blurt out. 'I have no idea what that is.'

'Rule 6 – don't sleep with him straight away,' he replies, spearing some beef with his fork, and eats, motioning me to do the same. 'You should try some of this beef – it's really good.'

'But that only applies to dating. We weren't dating!'

'Doesn't matter. The whole point of your column is that you don't break the rules. And you did. Game over.'

'Look, what the fuck do you want from me?'

Without hesitation he replies, 'I want to make a deal. You had a date the other night, correct?'

'Yes, but that's—'

'You followed my rules?'

'Well, yes, but—'

'Good, then the deal is you continue to follow the book until the end of your column series, but you follow it properly. Do it like you mean it. And just to show that I'm not a bad sport, I will personally help you out . . . as your own "dating guru", so to speak. You'll get your man and I'll get to see you publicly apologize for trashing my book.'

'But there might not even *be* another date . . . What if he doesn't want to see me again?' I ask, thinking that this might actually be a possibility. The date was two days ago and now he's disappeared 'south'.

'If you did what I – sorry – *the book* told you to, he will. And you're sexy. He's definitely asking you out again.'

'Don't try and flatter me; it won't work.'

'Sure it will.'

'And, wait, what the hell do you get out of this?' I reply defiantly.

He takes another mouthful of lunch. 'Well, I get the pleasure of proving you wrong. So, what do you think? It's either that or I tell your editor, your readers and everyone with a Twitter account that we had a very, very dirty one-night stand and you therefore cannot be trusted.'

'You'll slut-shame me? Seriously?'

'Easy, girl. No, don't be ridiculous. What I *will* do is journo-shame you. That's worse. It seems you've attracted quite a following, but no one wants a journalist that makes shit up—'

'That's why we have authors,' I goad.

'Please don't interrupt. Anyway, once I tell them what you've been up to, your loyal readership will know you're a fraud. Remember Julianne Bowers?'

The manipulative little wanker has a point. I *do*

remember Julianne Bowers. She was a popular health writer for *Hey!* magazine who followed the Atkins diet for her column at the height of its popularity. Every week she swore to thousands of readers that it was complete tripe, but then a photo of her dining at Prezzo with yards of tagliatelle hanging out of her mouth appeared online, and she was dropped. No one knows where's she's working now. I cannot believe that shagging Guy Wright could be my downfall. He could be *my tagliatelle*.

'Fine, I'll do it,' I reluctantly agree. What choice do I have? 'But I think you're a devious arsehole, let's be clear on that.'

'Yes, I thought you might. I've already run it past Natasha. She loves the idea. I didn't tell her the full story obviously. I just told her I thought you might need some help sticking to the rules, and being the good guy I am—'

'Are we finished here?' I reach over and take my notepad, tossing it back into my bag.

He looks taken aback. 'What's wrong, Cat? You hardly touched your food. Aw, are you mad at me?'

'Thanks for your time, Dylan – sorry, *Mr Wright*. It's been delightful.'

'Pleasure,' he replies. 'I look forward to working with you. Can I have my pen back now?'

'Can you fuck!'

I toss my bag over my shoulder and march swiftly through the restaurant, past the lunchtime diners and straight downstairs to the ladies' toilets, where I lock myself in a cubicle and take several long, deep breaths. I can't believe this is happening. Not only do I have to follow his bloody rules, but now he's going to be my fucking personal advisor?

I trudge back to work and Natasha immediately waves me in to see her. She's finishing up on a phone call so I sit across from her and gaze around her office, which always smells of a combination of Very Irrésistible Givenchy and the popcorn she relentlessly munches on during the day. She covers the mouthpiece on her phone to speak to me.

'Sorry about this. Alexander from payroll's being a twat again . . . hang on . . . what? . . . I don't care if you heard that! I meant it. Sort my fucking expenses out, you useless prick.'

She hangs up and gives herself a little shake. 'Honestly, that man makes me livid. Anyway, tell all! What was he like? Did he explain his idea for how to progress your column?'

I want to say, 'Well, he's like a big attractive, untrustworthy bastard who just happens to be the man I shagged on Friday,' but instead I say, 'Not as bad as I expected really. And yes, I'm sure his input will be invaluable.'

'Wonderful. Glad you're on board, Cat. We both know your column hasn't been as popular as it once was, but with the reaction so far to *The Rules of Engagement*, it looks like it's back on track. Even Caitlin Moran shared a link on Twitter. It seems Guy's book has been a blessing in disguise.'

I smile and make sounds of agreement through gritted teeth.

'Oh, and don't mention this to the rest of the staff – I promised Guy we'd be discreet. Now, I've emailed you three features to do, so if you could crack on with those, and I look forward to reading your next dating column. I know you can't force these things, but in the interests of entertainment . . .'

Christ, how the hell am I going to get Tom to meet me again if I'm not allowed to contact him? I can't submit another piece about waiting around for something to happen. 'Yes, of course,' I reply confidently. 'It'll be great.'

I get back to my desk and grab my phone from my bag, desperately hoping that a message from Tom wanting to meet up again before my copy is due has miraculously appeared. No such luck. And now Patrick is staring at me.

'Can I help you with something, Patrick,' I ask, 'or are you hoping I'll tell you what Natasha and I were discussing?'

He clears his throat. 'Was it a personal matter?'

'Nope.'

'OK then. Ah, was it about the Scottish awards for—'

'Nope.' Jesus, this man cannot take a hint.

'Tell me later?' pipes up Gordon from the photocopier.

'Oh sure,' I lie, just to piss Patrick off. And it works.

'You're so bloody childish!' he moans. 'Piss off, the pair of you.'

I suspect Patrick's missing Leanne and her perky breasts, but I have more important things to think about . . . like how to meet up with Tom without hounding him. I reach into my bag for *The Rules of Engagement* and scan through the pages, looking for a clue . . .

> *When you start dating, be keen but don't overdo it.*
> *Appearing overly keen is the equivalent of turning*
> *up to a date in a wedding dress embroidered with*
> *the names of your future children.*

This man has a fucking screw loose. I grab my notepad, and the email Dylan sent to Natasha earlier falls out.

'Right,' I think. 'Smart-arse has offered to help, so I'll let him.'

My fingers begin texting:

OK Maharishi, here's a dilemma: how do I get this guy to meet me without my instigating it? I can't wait around forever, I'm on a copy deadline. Cat

I don't hear anything for two bloody hours, until I'm on the crowded train home and he calls me.

'Maharishis were spiritual leaders, you know, not dating experts.'

'Wait, how can you call yourself a dating expert when you've told me twice that you don't date?'

I move down the train and out the way of a man who smells like he's shat himself, ending up beside a women standing up, reading *Cosmopolitan* with both hands. I admire her balance.

'Let's just say I've had plenty of experience. Anyway, to answer your question, I suppose you'll have to sneakily find out where he'll be and then bump into him. I wouldn't normally advise this, however; you should be waiting for him to—'

'Deadline, Dylan.'

'Fine. What does he do for a living?'

'He's a dentist. Not mine, my sister's.'

'Interesting. Think you can convince your sister to make herself an emergency appointment?'

The train bumps to a halt and the woman beside me almost falls over. Ha!

'I guess so, but I don't really see—'

'She'll go there with her bullshit toothache, and when she's done she'll announce she's forgotten her purse and call you to drive down with it. If he wants to see you, he will appear when you arrive. Then you act like you're not that bothered to see him, but in a sexy way. I'd give it an hour tops before you hear from him.'

'That's awfully devious,' I reply, impressed and disgusted at the same time. 'You really are horrendous. But fine, I'll try it.'

I hang up before he has the chance to do it first and

get straight on the phone to Helen, sure she would fake her own death if it might help me get together with Tom.

Helen's fake appointment is at half past twelve the following day. She calls me at ten to one, shrieking dramatically, 'YOU MUST COME IMMEDIATELY. I APPEAR TO HAVE FORGOTTEN MY PURSE!' forgetting that I put her up to this in the first place.

'Aye, all right, Meryl Streep – I'll be there in ten minutes. Does Tom know I'm coming?'

She lowers her voice. 'Yes! He asked how you were. Hurry up – there's people in the waiting area.'

I pick up Helen's purse from the table, charge out the door and dive into my car like Dave Starsky (bet he wishes he was cool enough to pull off the tight plunging V-neck top *I'm* wearing). The surgery is only a few streets away, but it's raining so I decide to endure the one-way system for the sake of my hair. Andie MacDowell might have got her man by braving the pissing wet weather, but I'm not risking it. I park up right behind Helen's car and dash through the front door of the dental surgery, unnecessarily ringing the bell to announce myself. I look around the pristine waiting room for Helen but there's no sign.

'Can I help you?' asks a stern-faced woman behind reception. Her name badge says 'Margaret'. She must hate that bell, I think. She's rocking a hair bun so tight, I'm getting a sympathy headache.

'Yes, hello, I'm looking for my sister. I have her purse.'

'And does your sister have a name?'

'Sorry, yes. Helen Walsh.'

I smile sweetly but her face remains unchanged. I admire her dedication to being a po-faced bastard.

'She went to the bathroom. I can give her the purse if—'

'No, I'll wait for her. But thank you.'

Nurse Ratched goes back to typing and I take a seat beside a man who's clutching at his swollen jaw. After five minutes of listening to the clock ticking on the wall, Helen finally appears and flings her arms around me like I've just announced I'm going to pay off her mortgage. I whisper in her ear, 'Take your time – Tom must be in with a patient. I'm not leaving until he's seen me, so I can ignore him and then expect his call!'

Helen slowly fumbles around with her bank cards, stalling for time. The receptionist is staring at us, and eventually her burning death glare forces Helen to pay £10.20 for a deep clean she didn't even need but endured for me.

I've just about given up hope when a door opens and Tom appears behind a puffy-mouthed woman who attempts to settle up with Margaret. He looks happy to see me.

'Cat, I heard you were coming down! I told Helen she could pay next time, but she insisted on calling you.'

'It's no problem,' I reply, flicking my hair over my

shoulder. I smooth down my top and his eyes scan down to my cleavage. Boom! Gotcha.

'You looked nice. *Look* nice.' He's stumbling over his words. This is exciting. I turn and face my sister, who is beaming at the pair of us. It's time to move before I say or do something stupid.

'We'd better be going, Helen. I have that thing to get to.'

'What thing?'

'I told you earlier? That meeting?' Jesus, she's the worst fucking mind-reader ever. 'Anyway, nice to see you, Tom, and thank you. I like your white coat.'

I turn and walk away with a wiggle that would make Monroe blush and a creeping suspicion that this shit might have just worked.

I have time to nip home before I pick Grace up from school and my phone beeps as I walk through the front door. Excitedly I press the tiny envelope symbol.

Well?

Ugh, it's from Dylan. There then follows a quick succession of texts.

I'm just home. Think it went well. Will have to see.

The book works. He'll call. Stop being so negative.

I want to reach into the phone and pull him through, scrotum first.

Your book makes no sense. I hate it. DO YOU READ ME? I HATE YOUR STUPID BOOK.

There's no reply at first and I start to think he's offended until:

If you really don't understand, come by tomorrow and I'll go over everything with you. I'll train you up, grasshopper.

Fuck off, Mr Miyagi. I'm not going back to your gigolo pad. Besides, maybe Tom will ask me for a date on Wed.

My phone rings. It's Dylan. THIS IS NOT THE MAN WHO IS SUPPOSED TO BE CALLING ME.

'Even if he does ask you, don't rush to meet him the very next evening. He needs to believe you're busy and have a life. When's your deadline?'

'Friday at the latest. And again, that is a stupid rule.' I open the fridge and grab a yogurt.

'Why is it stupid?

'Because being keen is not a character flaw!'

'Hmm, fine, you can see him Thursday then.'

'I have a kid, for Christ's sake!' I reply, spooning Müller into my mouth. 'I can't just go swanning off every bloody evening.'

'. . . What's that noise? . . . Are you eating?'

'Yes.'

'God, you're worse than I thought. What the fuck is it? Soup? I can hear metal clanging off your teeth. Don't do that with him.'

I bash my spoon on the handset. 'You are so obnoxious. And it's yogurt! Yogurt is silent! Only you could hear someone eating the quietest food ever.'

'Look, Cat, we made a deal, and you promised you'd do this properly. Wednesday night. Seven. Bring the book. If you can't remember the address, text me.'

He hangs up and I continue with my yogurt. As much as going over to his flat pains me, I'm going to settle this *Rules of Engagement* nonsense once and for all. He's so infuriating and so bloody certain that he's right about everything.

Then, miraculously, Tom texts.

So great to see you. Sorry we couldn't chat longer. Can I take you to dinner on Wednesday?

I'm about to reply YES, YES, A THOUSAND TIMES YES! when I stop and evaluate the situation. Dylan got this one right. I did what he said and Tom texted. Just like Dylan said he would. Ah! This is nuts. I wait for a couple of minutes and reply as if I don't care one way or the other. That's what I'm supposed to do, right?

Can't do Wed. Very busy. Could manage lunch on Thursday?

He speedily responds:

Great. 1pm suit? I'll find us somewhere nice.

I'm so delighted I do a little jump and spill yogurt down my top. How classy. I do need help.

I pick Grace up from school at four on Wednesday, later than usual as she's decided to give football a try and participate in an after-school game held in the gym. When she climbs into the car, her face tells me that it didn't go very well.

'Ryan Rogers missed the ball and kicked my shin. The lady in the office put a plaster on it for me.'

'Aww, honey. You all right? Does it hurt badly?' I inspect her little leg and laugh at the smiley face she's drawn on the brown plaster.

'It only stings a little. I didn't cry. Ryan drew that to say sorry. I think he's my boyfriend now but I haven't decided.'

I wonder if *'Let him kick you in the shin and then draw on your plaster'* is listed anywhere in *The Rules of Engagement*, because it seems to be working well for my daughter.

I glance at the time and realize I'm running late for Dylan's 'love clinic'.

'That's nice. Listen, Grace? I'm going to drive you to Dad's now. We won't have time to go home first. I've brought your stuff.'

We arrive at Peter's house, but he doesn't even bother coming to the door. Instead I'm greeted by Emma, dressed all in brown, looming over me like a perfectly toned Wicker Man.

'Hi, Emma. No new homework, but Grace needs to go over her maths again. She's stuck on her division.'

'Oh, no worries. Lucky for you, Grace, I'm the Maths Master.'

What a fucking stupid title to give yourself. What next, the Spelling Sultan? The Algebra Assassin? Surprisingly, Grace finds this funny. I sometimes doubt she's actually my child.

I thank Emma politely before kissing Grace goodbye and continuing my journey to Dylan's house, miffed that it's my one free weeknight and I'm spending it studying his bloody book. I remember exactly where he lives, but I text him anyway in some sort of cunning ruse to convince him that night isn't still etched in my brain.

In the early evening light, the street he lives on looks nicer than I remember. There are well-kept communal gardens across the road, and the restaurant I noticed last time now looks chic and inviting. I ring the intercom and he buzzes me in.

At the top of the stairs I spot him standing at the open door in jeans and a checked shirt, smiling. The same seductive smile he used on me that evening. 'Hey, Cat. Glad you could make it.'

'I don't want to be here, you know,' I announce loudly as I enter. 'We did it here. It could trigger all sorts of shit. This flat could be my 'Nam.'

Dylan laughs loudly as we head into the living room. 'Did you bring the book, you maniac?'

Dammit. 'Shit, no. I've left it at home.'

He gives me a disapproving look, then pulls open a drawer in the bottom of his bookcase and motions for me to sit on the couch.

'I'm very aware that we "did it", Cat, but I'm pretty sure we can control ourselves this time.' He stops rummaging through his drawer and raises an eyebrow. 'Unless you don't want to, that is? I mean, it was pretty hot.'

'Certainly not! I slept with you when I didn't know what a terrible shit you were. I have a Tom now. A very nice, HONEST Tom.'

'I'm just messing with you. Relax. I don't remember you being this uptight.'

And now I feel stupid. I cross my legs and sit quietly. There's a beer on the table next to an empty takeaway pizza box. Pig.

'Found it.' He hands over a copy of *The Rules of Engagement* and sits beside me. 'I knew I had one somewhere.'

I take the book from him. 'How can you only have one copy of your own book? If I wrote a book, I'd be sitting on chairs made from copies of it and wallpapering my room with the pages.'

'Meh,' he replies. 'I wrote it five years ago. The novelty wears off pretty quickly. After I lost interest in writing, I lost interest in this.'

'Are you sharing with me, Dylan? Is there some deep, dark secret you're going to disclose to me next? Did a bad lady kill your creativity?'

'No, I'm just making conversation. I'm getting another beer before we get started. You want one?'

'OK, but just one. I'm driving.'

I start thumbing through the book as he leaves for the kitchen.

'I'll need snacks to soak up the alcohol!' I shout after him. The least he can do is feed me.

It might be an awful book but, begrudgingly, I can't help but admire him for writing one at all. I can barely reach my weekly word count. He returns and hands me a packet of crisps and a bottle of Bud, raising his in the air to clink mine.

'Here's to helping you and your Tim,' he toasts.

'Tom.'

'Same thing,' he continues. 'And, also, to showing you the error of your ways and . . .'

I open the crisps and my crunching drowns out the remainder of his sentence.

We decide to discuss the book chapter by chapter, beginning with the main rules, before going on to finer points after. This works for about twenty seconds before the discussion gets heated. He just won't admit he's full of shit.

'This makes no sense to me whatsoever, Dylan. Look at this for example: *Rule 4 – Don't harass him. Men don't chat or text like women do.* I mean that's nonsense for a start! I know plenty of men who text more than I do.'

He shakes his head. 'Women are notorious for hassling men over the phone. It's all, "What you up to?" and "Thinking about you!" and "Look at this dog I saw in the park". Men don't like that. Stop the calls and texts or he'll look for someone else, I guarantee it.'

I laugh. 'Like who? Someone who doesn't own a phone? OR A VOICE? If we like you, we want to chat – what's so wrong with that?'

'It's too needy. You need to make him wonder where you are, what you're up to. If you're sending him smiley faces and pestering him, he'll know you have nothing else going on in your life but him.'

'See? That's your problem! You tar all women with the same brush in this book. "*Rule 8 – Accept us for who we are.*" I mean, really?'

He opens another beer. 'This stuff happens all the time though, Cat. You'd be surprised. You're not happy with our job or our haircut, or our choice of footwear or the fact that we actually like wanking as much as we like shagging. Women aren't perfect either, but men accept this much more easily. In fact, we expect it. A sure-fire way to put a man off is to tell him he isn't good enough the way he is.'

He says this with such conviction that I become suspicious. Has this man been fucked over by someone who hated his haircut? He's obviously been told off for wanking too much at some point. He can see me considering all of these things.

'Let's get to work,' he deflects. 'We're getting nowhere and you're on a time limit. So, when are you seeing Tom again?'

'How did you know he got in touch?' I ask. He raises an eyebrow. 'Oh, don't look at me like that. Fine – we're having lunch on Thursday. And I know how to act – don't speak too much, don't skip the food and only order dessert, don't suddenly announce I'd prefer a summer wedding – all that stuff.'

He turns around on the couch to face me properly. 'Uh, it doesn't say anything in the book about only ordering dessert.' He starts to laugh. 'I'd find that quite endearing actually. Even on a second date.'

I down some beer. 'Well, if you count the initial blind-date set-up at my sister's house, this'll be number three . . . ooh, third-date rule!'

He takes the beer out of my hand. 'Number one – calm down. And number two – that's my beer.'

God, he's a dick.

'And, number three, there *is* no third-date rule,' he continues. 'It's more like a fifth-date rule. A kiss on the third date is fine, but no groping, finger banging, oral or naked-ness whatsoever, and *especially* not during lunch. Make him wait. If he already cares about you, when you eventually have sex he'll be far more likely to see you again.'

'You sound like my mum,' I joke.

'Well, your mum's obviously very wise.'

'She was,' I reply.

Cue the awkward silence. I wish I hadn't said that. He didn't need to know that.

'Oh, I'm sorry.' He looks sombre. 'Can I ask what hap-pened?'

'Car accident, ten years ago. I don't really want to talk about it.'

'No, of course.' I can tell he doesn't want to argue with me any more. Surely he isn't developing a conscience? That's no fun. I get up to use the loo. 'I'll be back in a second, and then we can return to this.'

His blue and grey bathroom is tastefully minimalist but somehow cosy. However, his toilet seat is freezing and I finish peeing in record time, then take a quick peek in the mirrored medicine cabinet while I'm washing my hands. Nothing out of the ordinary; some condoms (unsurprising), painkillers, a shower cap with bananas on it (twat) and a roll of plasters. He doesn't have a bath, but instead has a wet room which looks like it cost a fortune and I imagine has seen a lot of soapy sex action over the years.

When I return to the living room, he's stretched flat out on the couch, playing with his phone. When he sees me, he sits up and chucks it on the table.

'Get a good snoop then?' he asks.

'I have no interest in snooping,' I lie. 'Shall we get back to this? I don't want to be here any longer than necessary.'

'Take a seat and stop pretending this is so awful.' He swivels his legs round. 'Now, where were we? Ah yes, the next date. As I said, this time things can be more relaxed, but there are still subjects you should avoid completely.'

'Such as?'

'Marriage . . . kids . . . Well, you can talk a bit about your own, but don't bore him.'

I tut. My kid is fucking fascinating.

'Then there's the future. Don't talk about the future. It'll make him think you're already choosing a wedding dress and planning ahead.'

'No future talk – got it. What about *Back to the Future*? Is that OK?'

He smiles. 'Only the first one – the sequels weren't great. Oh, and don't mention diets or a dream you had or bodily functions—'

I laugh. 'Bodily functions? You mean, like farting or poo or *wee-wee*? But what if I'm French?'

'You're not French, and you're not taking this seriously, are you?'

'*Non.*'

'Fuck this. Fine, I'll tell you exactly what to do.'

He draws up a cunning third-date plan for me. Third-date lunch should be more casual than second-date dinner, but under no circumstances should I act like I would with my friends. I must not morph from being polite and reserved to the annoying woman who takes selfies with her starter and swears profusely, like I apparently do. I can offer to pay on this one to show I'm not a gold-digger, but he should decline to let me – if he doesn't it means he thinks he doesn't have to impress me any longer, in which case he should be dumped immediately. Under no circumstances should I be my sarcastic, sceptical self.

'Got all that, Cat?'

'I don't take selfies with my starter,' I mutter. 'Main course, *maybe*. And yes, I've got all that.' I stand up and sigh. 'This just seems like a lot of hard work on my part.'

He looks puzzled. 'Who the hell said you wouldn't have to put in any work? I mean, I'm assuming this guy is worth it?'

'Of course he's worth it,' I snap. 'He's extremely handsome and successful and he likes me, so he's obviously very, very smart. Now, unless there's anything else, I must be going.' I pick up my handbag and rise from the couch.

'Now? You don't have to rush off.'

'I've been here for an hour and it's past my bedtime. Can I take this book as a spare?'

'Sure. Did I mention that top looks great on you?'

'I know, but I didn't wear it for you. I wore it for Tom earlier.'

'Then it's no wonder he asked you out again. Damn.'

'Stop trying to flirt, and STOP staring at my tits.'

Dylan's eyes move north and he escorts me to the door. 'You're right, I'm sorry. Pleasure as always, Cat. Let me know how it goes and we can discuss the next course of action. Oh, and one more thing . . .'

I turn back and he moves in closer to me, making me

step back against the door. The faint smell of his after-shave makes my tummy flip. Leaning in, he whispers, 'Play nice in your column this week.'

He doesn't move his mouth away from my ear straight away, instead choosing to linger there, his body touching mine, and in that moment I feel, pressed into my hip, exactly what he's thinking about. This entire power-game scenario he's created is turning him on, but I intend to leave Dylan and his erection alone in the hall. He doesn't get to fuck me twice, regardless of how good he smells. I sidestep left and grab the door handle.

He looks a little surprised that I'm not tearing his clothes off and mounting him in the hallway, but doesn't try to stand in my way.

'Control yourself. I'm into Tom. That's what all this about. Remember?'

He laughs. 'Sure you are . . . That's why you've hardly mentioned him all night, right? Have a nice evening, Cat.'

ARGH! He's so fucking arrogant! As he's closing the door, I yell from the stairwell 'NICE SHOWER CAP!' The text from him two minutes later reads: *Fucking snoop.*

Tom texts to tell me he's taking me for lunch at the Waverly Tearooms, which suits me as it's close to home, and if I do end up paying, it won't cost me a bloody fortune. I'm excited as I stroll down Shawlands Cross towards the restaurant. The sun is shining, the natives are friendly and I have on my new purple wedge shoes, shoes that I'm so in love with I would one day like to knock them up and marry them. As I prance round the corner I see Tom waiting outside and I'm tempted to run at him in the hope he'll be equally excited, lift me in his hands and spin me around, but I reconsider. Wedges really aren't made for grand running gestures anyway. However, his face lights up when he sees me and that's good enough.

'Wow, you look great. Very pretty.'

I graciously thank him. He also looks very nice in his grey shirt – which he does – but he's nowhere *near* as fancy as me. I win.

'Cat, I'm really sorry about last week. I had to visit my dad. He had emergency heart surgery.'

I can gauge from his expression that shouting, 'YES! I FUCKING KNEW IT WAS SOMETHING SERIOUS!' wouldn't be the smartest move I've ever made, so instead I frown and say 'I hope he's doing OK', which of course I do; I'm just also happy to know it had nothing to do with me being a rules-following borebag.

'Thanks,' he replies. 'He'll be fine. My ex, Kathryn, was a big help – she still has a lot of time for my family.'

Kathryn? Oh, that's just perfect.

He pulls out my chair and we sit outside for lunch. I peer at the menu while he continues to describe what a fucking superstar his ex-wife is and how she's a selfless angel – an angel who appears to be ruining my third date from several hundred miles away. I need to distract him.

'I'm starving!' I blurt out. 'Shall we order?'

'Of course,' he replies. 'Sorry if I'm going on and on. It's just been a hellish week.'

Oh God, I've turned into one of those high-maintenance women who doesn't give a fuck about anything except her lunch. I need to redeem myself and quickly. I place my hand on his. 'Don't be silly,' I say. 'I'm happy to listen, I'm just aware you have to get back to work soon.'

He's looking at my hand on his and he's smiling. I might have saved this one, but I still have the rest of the date to get through.

I refrain from asking inappropriate questions while I tuck into my club sandwich, despite the fact I really want to know if he's ever screwed on his dentist chair, if he still harbours feeling for his ex-wife and how much perfect veneers like his would cost? Instead we chat about the weather, life in London, life here, and generally avoid anything salacious that might go against Dylan's bloody rules of engagement. This means I also avoid mentioning marriage, the future, unborn children, bumholes, bridesmaids, Pot Noodles or areolas. For my own sake I take care to skirt around questions regarding my job, making sure he's unlikely to ever read the magazine, and pretend that Peter and I are jolly old friends who share a deep understanding and respect for each other.

Throughout lunch I'm like a perfectly trained conversation maestro and it's working; he even touches my hand again when he excuses himself to go to the toilet.

I watch him walk away and I reckon I have three minutes tops to text Kerry and let her know that he made actual physical contact with my hand skin of his own free will.

On date with Tom. We touched hands. I feel about 15. Like Molly R in Pretty in Pink but without the shitty home-made prom dress that everyone hated.

By the time I've typed this, I can see him coming back and I panic, quickly pressing Send, then throwing my phone into my bag like it's covered in spiders. If he notices, he doesn't mention it.

'Sorry, Cat, I need to get back to the surgery,' he apologizes, 'but it's been really great. Again.'

I take out my purse and offer to pay, but as Dylan predicted, he refuses. 'I said last time that this was on me, and it's only some sandwiches and coffee. Please, let me.'

This time I don't protest. Part of me wants to tell Dylan right away that it all went to plan, but I think I'll let him dwell on it for a few more hours.

I walk Tom to his car, refusing a lift on the grounds that I live within walking distance, and also that I really need to fart. I omit this second bit for Tom, but it doesn't make it any less true.

'I'd love to keep seeing you, Cat. Shall we do this again?'

My stomach high-fives my heart and I immediately agree. He then takes my hands and continues, 'I think you're very special, Cat. Dignified. But I want to know more. Who is Cat? Who is this woman I see before me?'

My stomach reconsiders and this time boots my gag reflex in the balls. He didn't just say that, did he? Please tell me he didn't just cheese the fuck out of me. Where did this crap come from? My ears are offended.

With my hands still in his, I look down at my feet, afraid I'll laugh in his face. Maybe he's just nervous, and if this type of misguided sentiment is his only fault, I'm sure I can nip it in the bud later when –

'*Rule 8 – Accept us for who we are.*'

Oh, shut the fuck up, Dylan.

'I'm looking forward to getting to know you too, Tom,' I reply in the most diplomatic way I know how. 'Let me see when I can get a sitter next.'

He leans in and kisses me. It's pretty good. It's the type of kiss that you know won't cause explosions or even erections, but his lips are soft and he doesn't try and tongue my face into oblivion.

'Until next time then, cutie.'

He gets into his BMW and starts the engine. I fart and curse him at the same time. All while smiling and waving him off like a navy wife on shore. As soon as he's out of sight, I call Kerry at her office.

'Hey, Ringwald, how did it go?'

'Cutie. He called me fucking *cutie*.'

I hear Kerry laughing and it starts me off too. 'He called me cutie and asked me, "*Who is Cat*?" Honestly, I wanted to scream.'

'Wait, what? That's hilarious. Is he still alive?'

'Yes, I pardoned him. But he'll need to knock that shit off. How can I allow myself to commit to someone who talks like that?'

'Fuck, I could advise you better if I knew what he looked like. He might not be handsome at all; you might be wrong.'

'Google Southbank Dental. Tom Ward. His photo is on their website.'

I hear her tapping on her keyboard. I begin walking back towards the flat. My purple wedges are rubbing against my heels. I should have agreed to a lift home.

'Holy shit. You're not wrong. Is that his real face?'

'YES!' I cry. 'You see my problem?'

'You lucky bitch. First Dylan and now him. You're on a roll here.'

'Well, technically Dylan didn't actually fancy me like—'

'Oh shush, of course he did, and you fancied him. Him being a sneaky fucker doesn't mean he wasn't attracted to you.'

'What should I do about Tom?'

'I don't know. Do you think you can shag some sense into him? A few nights of dirty sex might make him reconsider this poetic bullshit.'

'I'm willing to find out.'

'Good. Listen, got to dash, but I'll call you later.'

She hangs up on me and I continue home, hobbled by my soon to be ex-favourite shoes.

School's out at three and I meet Rose at the gates. We decide to take the kids to a local soft-play so they can exhaust themselves, and we can catch up. As we enter Captain Clown's Play Emporium we're greeted by a host of screaming pre-schoolers and an overpowering waft of fish fingers and beans. We sit down beside an elderly woman who looks utterly horrified. It's clear that Granny has mistakenly volunteered to bring little Johnny here, unaware of what horrors await her, and now she's quietly hoping a mild stroke will end this madness.

'Ever notice how stupid the name of this place is?' Rose muses. 'How the fuck can he be a captain AND a clown? Coffee?' She wanders over to the food area, leaving me to ponder this. I look over and spy Grace disappearing into the ball pit. Jason is manoeuvring across a rope bridge with only one sock on, little beads of sweat forming on his brow. Rose returns with the coffee and I point her in the direction of Jason.

'Aww, he thinks he's Indiana Jones,' I say, laughing.

'Aye, if Indiana Jones was an seven-year-old shitebag.' She grins at me and shakes a packet of brown sugar. 'Oh, by the way, Rob is home tomorrow.'

'How long for? It feels like a million years since I last saw him.' I like Rob. He's a gentle giant of a man with a massive beard and a passion for real ale and Bernard Matthews's Mini Kievs. They met when Rose was dating George's friend Alan in college and he introduced them. Although that was nine years ago, I think Alan (still single) might not be completely over Rose – he often spends the wee hours of the morning liking her Facebook photos and posts while she sleeps.

'Two whole weeks, so I probably won't see you much.' Rose fishes a Chapstick out of her pocket and smears it over her lips. 'I'm going to force him into doing all the school runs while I sleep until midday. He can collect Grace on Mondays too. I know you're working.'

Then Jason returns, looking for juice and complaining that Grace isn't playing with him properly.

'She keeps doing things first!' he moans, throwing himself down on a chair. 'I wanted to jump in the ball pit first.'

Grace suddenly gallops over, thirsty and not giving a crap that Jason's telling tales on her. She knocks back orange juice from a blue plastic tumbler, before triumphantly declaring, 'You snooze, you lose, Jason!' and disappearing back into the fray. Jason responds with a wail and Rose cuddles him, trying to keep a straight face. When Jason finally slopes off towards the slides, Rose whispers, 'I like your kid. She doesn't take shit. Just like her mother, eh?' She winks.

*

Twenty minutes later, I'm ordering baked potatoes for the kids and wondering whether slushies are still as delicious as I remember them to be, when I hear my phone beep in my bag. It's Dylan.

Well? How did it go?

This man is so impatient.

Will text you latex.

Oh yeah? Kinky. Can't wait.

*LATER.

But you said latex.

Autocorrect fail. Now go away.

I switch my phone off and drop it back into my bag. I know Dylan is only desperate to know how my date with Tom went so he can gloat over how clever and right he is. Well, he can wait a bit longer.

At six we all head home. Grace finishes off her homework while I tidy her bombsite of a bedroom, making the bed around Heisenberg, who refuses to move. I open her desk drawer to throw some crayons in and find a picture of me, Peter and Grace from Grace's first Christmas. I'd forgotten about this photo. Peter's dad took it with the camera we'd just given him. We're all dressed up in party hats, sitting round my old dinner table, and we look happy. We look like a normal family. The longer I stare at the photograph, the more my heart hurts. To Grace it's just a photograph of me and her dad – she can't remember it any other way – but to me it's a reminder of hopes and dreams that came to nothing. I place it back where I found it and close the drawer.

I finally text Dylan back at 11.30 that evening, hoping he'll either be in bed asleep or in someone else's bed and too busy to reply. Of course I didn't mention Tom's cheesy outburst – I refuse to give him any ammunition.

Date went well and he wants to see me again. This will be date four – can I bloody organize it for once?

His reply is swift.

Read your 'bloody' book.

I sigh and grab it from my bag, flicking through the pages half-heartedly. I didn't fucking study this much when I did my degree.

> From date four you should be more open with your
> date. Share more of yourself but always leave him
> wanting more. Don't try to take the reins just yet.

BUT WHY? Why do I need to drag this nonsense out? I need clarification and, partly to annoy Dylan for making me mad at this hour, I call him. He answers sleepily.

'Hi, Dylan. Did I wake you? . . . Good. Now, date four – you say I can't ask him out yet, but why not? Why can't I?'

'It's midnight, Cat. THIS IS THE VERY REASON WHY THE BOOK SAYS NOT TO CALL MEN.'

'Oh, behave – that applies to men I want to date, not

authors who promised to help me after threatening to ruin my career.'

He's silent for a moment. 'Look, we – and by "*we*" I mean men – need to feel like we're in control. If *you* suggest somewhere shit to go, we'll agree, but we'll resent you for it and question your judgement.'

'The fact that I'm talking to you means my judgement has already been brought into question.'

'Oh, very mature, Cat. If you act like this on dates, it won't be long before he's tired of that noise coming from the hole under your nose.'

'At least I don't have a shower cap with bananas on it.'

'IT WAS A STUPID GIFT FROM MY SISTER, ALL RIGHT? I forgot it was in there.'

'Why are you shouting at me? And, what? You have siblings? Damn, I totally had you down as an only child. Possibly raised by wolves and—'

'I'm ending this call. Goodnight.'

'And—'

He hangs up before I can finish. I hate that. I have an overwhelming urge to rile him, so I wait almost an hour – until I'm sure he'll be asleep and unable to reply. Then I text: '*AND YOU WERE BORN OF A JACKAL.*'

I turn my phone off, because if he replies I'll be up all night trying to get the last word in. I know me.

*

On Friday morning I'm leaving with Grace for school when I meet the postman outside. We exchange pleasantries, I admire his moustache and he hands me my post, which consists of junk, a council-tax bill and a fancy white, card-sized envelope. I pause and look at it for a moment, wondering if I've managed to forget my own birthday.

'I KNOW WHAT THAT IS!' Grace shrieks, even though she's standing right beside me. 'OPEN IT!'

'Did you send me this, you lovely thing?' I start tearing open the envelope, which has small bells embossed on the back. Bells? Grace tugs on my jacket.

'No, Daddy sent it. Hurry up, Mum!'

They're wedding bells. Oh shit. I know exactly what this is. I don't want to open it. I want to pretend it contains spiders and anthrax and kill it with fire. I look down at Grace, who's bursting for me to see the invitation to her dad's wedding. I want to explain how weird and awkward this is for me and how her dad should have factored in how I'd feel before sending this, but I don't. Instead I beam back at her.

'We're going to be late for school; Grace, jump in the back seat. I'll open it in the car.'

I get into the driver's seat and start the engine, while Grace clicks her seat belt on. There's no way I can't open it, she's too excited. I gingerly ease the white card out of the envelope and my lap is suddenly showered in tiny silver stars. Grace squeals, 'I put them in!! I gave you extra.

Isn't it pretty? Mum, you're not looking – LOOK. AT. THE. CARD.'

I obey and feast my eyes on the smooth cardboard. The front has a subtle floral pattern, with the words 'Peter and Emma' and '21 November 2014' printed in plain black script. Inside it reads:

Mr Peter Anderson and Miss Emma Davies
request the pleasure of your company at their marriage
on Friday 21 November 2014 at 11 a.m.
Southside Parish Church, Newmill Road.
Dinner and dancing will follow at 7 p.m. in the Hilton Hotel.

At this very moment I am having all of the feelings. Sadness, jealousy, annoyance, loneliness, self-pity, hunger, ALL OF THEM.

I close the card and give Grace my best sunny smile. My heart is beating at a million miles an hour.

'Well, isn't that exciting? I'll get to see you in your flower-girl dress! And in November! So soon! Why is it so soon? Are you hot, Grace? I'm hot. Let's get to school!'

I open the driver's window and release the handbrake, aware that Grace is now looking at me like I'm psychotic.

'They got a cancellation. Are you OK, Mum? Dad didn't think you'd want to come, but I made him send you an invitation because I knew you'd be sad to miss it.'

I turn left at Queens Park, narrowly missing a magpie

in the road. 'Of course I want to come, darling! It's a big day for everyone. And you know how much I love getting dressed up. It'll be fun!'

Fun? My ex has just invited me to watch him get married. It'll be fucking humiliating. There's no way in hell I'm going. We pull up at the school gates just as the bell is ringing.

'See you at three, Mum. Love you!'

'Love you more, Grace. Have a great day.'

I watch her catch up to a small boy in a neon jacket and they walk into the playground together. As soon as she's out of sight, I place my head on the steering wheel and exhale. For ten minutes all I do is sit there and breathe.

'I don't understand why you're so upset.'

Helen hands me back the invitation and continues sipping her coffee, oblivious to my 'What the actual fuck?' facial expression.

'I mean, come on, Cat. You and Peter haven't been together for years, and you knew this was happening. Not too sure about a November wedding though. It'll be freezing.'

I rub my temples; my head is beginning to ache. I'm beginning to regret asking Helen over for a chat. 'So you don't think it's wildly inappropriate that he's invited me?'

'I do,' she agrees, 'but you're over-thinking it. Grace probably nagged him until he agreed to send an invite. You two have spent years hiding how much you loathe each other from Grace; how can you then expect Peter to explain why the mother she adores isn't welcome to such an important day? Or why you're refusing to share in a day that's so exciting for her? That would be cruel.'

I sit back and consider this. I'm so used to Peter being underhanded and shitty to me, I never considered he might just be trying to make Grace happy.

'I guess you're right. It's just going to be so hard watching him marry someone else—'

Helen throws her hands up in the air. 'Jesus, Cat, will you please just move the fuck on?' I'm shocked. Helen hardly ever swears. She picks up the invitation and waves it at me. 'LOOK! Peter has, the rest of the planet has, but you're STILL moping over a man who was never, ever right for you.'

I lean back on my couch, trying to avoid being poked in the eye by the invitation Helen's flapping around in my face. 'Maybe when I find someone—'

'You will NEVER find someone while you continue to act like a tortured character from a bloody Brontë novel.'

'You're being too hard on me. We had a child together. Peter was the love of my—'

'Don't you *dare* finish that sentence. There is no such thing as the love of your life, that's bullshit. There are only men you will love for varying amounts of time and with varying amounts of passion. Look forward to the next one instead of grieving over the last.'

She puts down the invitation and takes my hand. 'I am being hard on you because I don't want to see you end up like Mum. After Dad vanished, she closed herself off to the possibility of ever finding anyone again and we became her life. Only that wasn't fair on her, or us. Remember?'

I nod. After Helen went to university, mum coped because she still had me around. But five years later it was my turn, and she begged me not to move into student digs. Maybe I should have stayed, but I desperately needed to spread my wings: I left for Manchester. Helen and I visited as much as we could, but I could tell she was lonely. For instance, everything in the house was spotless – it wasn't the home of someone who had a life; it was the home of someone who had nothing else to do but clean.

'It's hard,' I sigh, my lip beginning to tremble. 'What if this is it? Just me and Grace until she moves out? Mum might have been able to cope with that, but I couldn't. I don't want this to be . . . it.'

I wipe away a tear before it begins its descent down my face and then reach in to hug my sister, who squeezes me back tightly. 'You'll be happy again, Cat, and when Grace comes home to visit, she'll come back to a home that's full of life, not one that's shrouded in memories. Don't ever let a man get the better of you – that's all Peter is. Just one man. Now, pull yourself together and make me a decent coffee – this stuff tastes like tar.'

I sniff and laugh at the same time, taking her half-full

cup with me to the kitchen. I feel exhausted but hopeful. Fuck today. Tomorrow will be better.

The Lowdown magazine – *Saturday 8 November 2014*

My choice or yours?

In the modern world, dating is a two-way street. Relationship decisions are made together and, in between all of this important and undoubtedly sexy decision-making, men and women have meaningful conversations, touch below the waistline and happily participate in all the fun things that are forbidden in *The Rules of Engagement*.

I'm not allowed to do any of this. The only decisions I get to make are what to wear on the date of his choice and, eventually, the best way to dispose of his body when I inevitably snap. But I promised to follow the rules until the bitter end, and I'm a woman of my word.

But an unexpected obstacle got in the way: Mr X was taking far too long to organize our third date and I was forced to move things along myself. Why? Because my deadline waits for no man; not even a handsome English one with a gym membership and stylish hair.

I'll admit – I did things I'm not proud of. With a little help from various people, I randomly appeared at his workplace wearing something low-cut and then pretended I had better things to do *other than* be there, even though I had actually spent the whole day plotting the situation. It wasn't my finest hour, but it worked. The following day we had lunch.

It was a very pleasant lunch, my chat was marginally more

interesting (his was certainly more revealing) and neither of us felt the need to overturn the table and have a full-on fist fight by the end of it. He isn't perfect, but then, neither am I.

Oh, did I mention that we kissed? Yes, our lips touched and saliva was exchanged, as was talk of another date. It's a good day to be me.

So what happens on date four? It seems I'm still not allowed to choose the venue or reveal anything about myself that might cause him to cry or vomit. Oh, and still no sex. Not even outside-the-clothes crotch rubbing is allowed at this stage. I hope this is killing him as much as it's killing me.

CHAPTER THIRTEEN

Back in the office today and I'm pleased to see Leanne back from her holiday looking slightly sunburned and sporting hair braids. She swoops on me when I walk in.

'You're here! I looked for you at the station this morning! I've just caught up on your column and I'm expecting you to buy me sweets to thank me for recommending this genius book. Tell me about your mystery man – I want details!'

'It isn't genius, Leanne, it's fucking torture.' I place my jacket over my chair and sigh as I sit down. 'And it's hard bloody work.'

Her head tilts to one side and she throws me a sympathetic look. 'I know. You have to make compromises. I remember when I first started seeing Charlie. I had to pretend that I didn't find *The Big Bang Theory* funny or watch clips from *Pitch Perfect* on a daily basis because he despised those things.'

'But *Pitch Perfect* is THE ultimate film!' I point out,

completely ignoring *The Big Bang Theory* – I'm with Charlie on that one. 'This is crazy. Why are we changing who we are for men?'

'Because you're all nuts?' mumbles Gordon, without even looking up.

'No, because Charlie was more important than amazingly funny female singers engaging in voice battles with hot geeky men. Now we've been together for two years, and he loves me enough to not care that I love them almost as much as I love him.'

I look over and see both Patrick and Gordon pretending to work but smirking like schoolboys.

'What I'm saying,' she continues, 'is that once he loves you he won't care that you're a bit off the wall. You just have to limit what he finds out until that happens.'

'Off the wall? Are you implying I'm weird?'

'Not at all!' she protests.

'Yes, she is,' Patrick mutters.

'Shut up, Patrick. All I'm saying is you're different and that's why we all love you . . . Don't say anything, Patrick!'

Patrick does as he's told, slinking out of the office with his coffee mug, tail between his tiny legs. He hates it when Leanne tells him off.

'So when's the next date? Has he called yet?' Gordon interjects. I glance round to see him tearing pages out of a newspaper. 'For our fourth date, I took the wife to a hotel in Aberdeen.'

'Against her wishes?'

He smirks and continues ripping. 'Not at all. Maybe your guy will do something grand. If he thinks he might get some action out of it, he probably will. I did.'

'Well, he hasn't called. Actually, come to think of it he's never called – just texted.'

'I used to call up Charlie on his home phone when he was at work and listen to his voice on the answering machine.'

Gordon and I both turn to look at Leanne, who's practically bent over backwards, fiddling with her contact lens. 'It helped. I got my fix without him knowing. Don't you just yearn to hear his voice when you're not with him?'

'Of course I do!' I lie. Leanne really is the type of woman Dylan wrote this book for; women I'd previously have argued don't exist. Until now. Truth is, I think about Tom all the time, but then again I also think about Jake from *Scandal* – but do I want to stalk either of their answering machines? Not particularly.

I leave the office at lunchtime to interview a terribly unfunny comedian who somehow won best newcomer at the Edinburgh Fringe. After about twenty minutes I literally can't take it any more, so I heartlessly pretend he was late for the interview and I have to go home early to pick Grace up from school.

When we get back to the flat, we meet Helen and her

suitcase in the hallway. Grace needs the bathroom so I hand her the keys and she goes inside.

'Helen, have you been evicted?'

She puts her hand on her hip and waits for me to remember why she has a suitcase. When Adam also appears, passport in hand, it clicks. 'Egypt! Damn, I thought that was next week!' I didn't. I'd totally forgotten they were even going.

'Well done, Cat,' Adam teases. 'Flight's at six, I cannot wait to fuck off out of here for a week.' He hands me their keys – 'For emergencies.'

'Now remember, an emergency is NOT using all of my hairspray and hair oil, Cat,' lectures Helen.

'That happened seven years ago, Helen, and it *was* an emergency. I had ridiculous frizz that summer.'

A quick kiss goodbye and they're off to sunny Sharm el-Sheikh, leaving me with no babysitters, but also with complete access to their well-stocked freezer.

If a week of 24/7 childcare wasn't enough, I had forgotten it's parents' night tomorrow – an hour of playing happy families with Peter while we discuss Grace's progress. The school have sent home several jotters for me to look through ahead of meeting with her teacher, Mrs Sharma. After dinner, Grace proudly presents me with her schoolwork to date: mostly textbooks I vaguely remember covering in old wallpaper at 1 a.m., filled with complicated maths problems like 3x3, and workbooks bursting with writing in a pencil Grace obviously couldn't be bothered to sharpen.

'Do you think you'll get a good report?' I ask her as I rummage through the cupboard in search of something to make for dinner. 'Or have you been terrorizing your teacher with blunt pencils and making mischief all year?'

She giggles. 'OF COURSE NOT. I like my teacher. She brought in a safari to show us. I tried it on.'

'You mean a sari?'

'Yes. It was gold. She's really nice. We used to have Mrs Hall two days a week but she left. I hated her; she used to shout at us all the time for no reason. Kelly called her "Mrs Hell".'

'I like Kelly.'

My mobile rings from the other side of the room and Grace runs over to get it. Before I can yell, 'Let me answer it!' she's swiped right and is shouting 'Hello!' unnecessarily loudly into the mouthpiece.

'Mum, it's a man called Tom. He wants to talk to you.'

She throws the phone at me before it's dawned who that might be. By the time it's in my hands, my brain has kicked in and I nervously move the handset to my ear.

'Hi! Hello.'

Grace returns to the couch and sits beside me. 'Mum, who's Tom?'

'He's my friend, Grace. Sorry, Tom, give me two seconds.'

I cover the mouthpiece. 'Gracey, go and play while I take this.'

'Why is your face red, Mum? IS TOM YOUR BOYFRIEND?'

'Stop it, Grace. Go and play.'

'BUT IS HE?'

Oh sweet Jesus. I firmly point in the direction of the hall and she bounces off to her room, singing, 'Mum's got a boyfriend, Mum's got a boyfriend!'

'Sorry, Tom, privacy is a little hard to come by these days.'

'Not a problem. So, am I your boyfriend?'

My already red face bursts into flames. 'Ha, well. Sorry about that. Y'know kids. Um.'

Oh, just fucking kill me.

'I'm just teasing. I was hoping we could have dinner on Wednesday? Your daughter goes to her dad's that night, right?'

Someone has been paying attention.

'She does. Yes, that would be nice. Did you have any-where in mind?'

To Tom I might sound unfazed by the fact we're having another date, but I'm doing a happy bum shuffle on the couch. I hope he takes me to that new Thai place in the West End.

'How about at home?'

YES! HE WANTS TO HAVE SEX.

'Sure. Your place?'

'Actually, I was thinking your place . . . I would have suggested here but the landlord is having the radiators replaced and it's a bit of a mess. Be nice to see where you live.'

Bollocks, that's less good. And wait, what number date is this again? Am I even ALLOWED to have sex yet?

'Sounds great,' I reply cheerily, slapping my forehead. 'You bring the wine and I'll cook. Say seven thirty?'

'Excellent. I'll see you then!'

He's already hung up, but I stay holding the phone to my ear. Why did I just agree to this? Can I trust myself not to jump him? Can I trust my cooking not to poison him? WHAT WILL I WEAR?

'GRACE, TWENTY MINUTES UNTIL YOUR BATH!' I shriek hysterically. Her head pops round the door. 'Mum, why are you shouting?'

'I don't know. Sorry. Quick question – what do I make for dinner that's nice?'

'Chicken teddy bears and sweetcorn, ham omelettes, sausages and mash.' She spins around and I hear her hop back into her room.

Chicken teddy bears? This is going to be a catastrophe. I jump up and scour through my bookcase, hoping a gourmet cookbook will have magically appeared in the last five minutes. Shit. It's Monday evening and I have a day and a half to become bloody Nigella. I rush through to the bathroom and start running Grace's bath. How the hell am I meant to pull this off? What would a *Rules of Engagement* girl do?

Dylan answers his phone almost immediately.

'What's up?' he asks breezily. 'I take it loverboy called?'

'Yes, and somehow I've agreed to him coming over to my house for dinner.'

'And this is a problem? Are you in the bath?'

'No, I'm running one for Grace and, YES, it's a problem. What if he expects something good?! Though I guess I could just order a Chinese and—'

'Don't get a takeaway, Cat. First, it tells him you didn't make any effort for him, and second, it lets him know you're a terrible cook.'

'I am not a terrible cook!'

'So cook him something then!'

'I can't, I'm terrible.' I hit my forehead against the bathroom mirror with a thud. It hurts more than I thought it would.

'Look, you have a kid; you must be able to cook something.'

'Hmm. *Cook* is a strong word. I can boil, steam and put things I bought in the oven. Does that count?'

'Can you make anything from scratch?'

'Toast?'

'Get your sister to cook for you.'

'Helen's on holiday.'

'You're screwed then.'

My head hits the mirror again. 'Dylan, I'll have you know that if I wasn't following your book, I'd be feeding him pizza and taking him to bed.'

I hear him sigh. 'Any girl can do that. The point of all of this is to prove you're *not* every other girl.'

'Hang on a minute.' I turn off the taps and call Grace through. She bursts into the bathroom naked, carrying a couple of dolls and a teapot. 'I'll be back in five, Grace, don't splash too much.'

I take my conversation into the living room. 'You still there?'

'Cat, what's your address?'

'Why?'

'Because I'm going to come over and help you.'

'But it's late. My daughter is here.'

'It's seven, Cat. And so what? Because you're a single mother, you're not allowed to have friends over?'

'Well, no, but—'

'Either I can come over and teach you how to make an amazing Bolognese from scratch, or you can buy store-bought food and hope he doesn't notice.'

'You think I'm too stupid to look up a recipe online?'

'Not at all, but I imagine that finding recipes isn't the problem or you'd be confidently cooking already . . .'

He's right. I once tried to make a Christmas log for the school fair and Grace refused to let me hand it in, telling me she'd rather die than hand in a cake that looked like a fruity poo. I grumpily concede and give him my address.

'OK, I'll be over in an hour.'

I put my phone in my pocket and rush through to Grace, who's happily still alive and splashing around in the bath.

'Grace, I've got a friend coming over in a little while, so I'd like you to go to bed early.'

'But it's not bedtime! I still have HOURS left.'

'Not hours, ONE hour. You can read or something until eight thirty.'

'Can I watch *Frozen*?'

'Fine, but please don't sing that Snowman song repeatedly.'

'Deal.'

I wash and condition her hair while she does the same with her dolls, tipping water from her teapot on to their tiny plastic heads. It takes a further fifteen minutes to do her teeth, get her nightdress on and prise her DVD from under the cat's arse. Once she's settled I close her bedroom door behind me.

'Mum, keep it open. Heisenberg might want out.'

I leave the door slightly ajar, then nip to the kitchen to tidy up. I don't need Dylan judging me for not having done the dishes for two days.

Right on schedule, I see him park in the street outside. 'Nice Jeep,' I mumble to myself. 'Paid for by the souls of single women, I expect.' I count to three and take a deep breath before I let him in.

'Hello!' he chirps, wiping his shoes on the doormat. 'Point me in the direction of the kitchen then.'

He drops two shopping bags on the kitchen table and slips off his jacket. 'Nice place, Cat. Different to what I imagined.'

'I'm scared to ask what you imagined,' I reply, peeking inside the bags. There are loads of ingredients inside: bottle of red, tinned tomatoes, cherry tomatoes, garlic, onions, some sort of green plant. I'm impressed.

He rolls up his sleeves and washes his hands. 'I imagined something a lot less colourful.'

I have no idea whether this is a dig at my beautiful apple-green kitchen or if he does actually like it. Either way, I don't care. He's here to cook, not remark on my fabulous home interior.

He takes all the ingredients out of the bag and then starts opening drawers at random, grabbing knives, saucepans and the chopping board.

'Where's your music?' he asks, opening a tin of tomatoes. 'You need music to cook.'

'Do you? Well, it's in the living room, but Grace is asleep; I don't want to wake her.'

He nods over to the kitchen door. 'You sure about that?'

I turn around and see Grace standing at the door in her red dressing grown. 'Mum, can I have a drink?'

'Yes, I'll bring it through. Go back to bed.'

She creeps over to the fridge beside me. 'Who is that?'

she whispers, pointing to the man who's frantically chopping an onion at my countertop. 'Is that Tom?'

I hand Grace some milk while Dylan sniggers. 'No, honey, this is Dylan. He's helping me make spaghetti Bolognese.'

'But it's bedtime. That's weird.'

'I know.'

Dylan stops chopping, wipes his hand on a tea towel and holds it out. 'I'm Dylan. You must be Cat's sister Helen. She never told me you were so small.'

Grace bursts out laughing and shakes his hand. 'You're silly. I'm not Helen, I'm Grace. This is my mum.'

Dylan grins at her. 'Very pleased to meet you. Your mum said she didn't know how to make spaghetti Bolognese for you and this upset me, so I rushed round to teach her how. Do you want to help?'

'No, it's late,' I interrupt. 'Grace has school tomorrow.'

'Oh pleeease, Mum!' she begs. 'Just for a minute?'

'Oh, all right, but just for a little while.'

I stand back and watch as Dylan lets Grace pour olive oil into the saucepan, which he heats up to fry diced bacon. Then she tears at the green plant (which turns out to be rosemary) while he chats to her about the fact that raw celery sucks, but cooked, it adds flavour to the meal. Her little cheeks are flushed with excitement and she's really paying attention. This man, in the space of ten minutes, seems to have completely charmed my eight-year-old.

I feel something brush past my leg and look down to see Heisenberg sitting at my feet, staring at Dylan. I don't like that look in his eye, but for once I'm not the enemy in the room. If Heisenberg wants to maul Dylan, it's unlikely I'll stop him.

'Grace, it's time to go to bed. The cat is wondering what you're doing out here.'

She hops off the kitchen chair and bends down to pat Heisenberg, who miaows at her. 'OK, fluffy face, I'm coming.'

Dylan puts down his wooden spoon and looks over. 'Cool cat. What's his name?'

'Heisenberg. He only likes me,' Grace replies. 'He doesn't even let Mum cuddle him, and her cuddles are the best.'

He walks over to Heisenberg and bends down. 'I'm sure your mum's cuddles are excellent, Grace, and your cat has the greatest name ever.' He offers his hand to Heisenberg, who gives it a sniff, then arches his back. I close my eyes and prepare for Dylan's imminent demise. Seconds later, Grace gives a little gasp and I open one eye to see Heisenberg practically dry-humping Dylan with happiness. He's purring like a power drill and wrapping his entire body around Dylan's leg. What kind of black magic is this?

'Bed, Grace. Let's go. Say goodnight to Dylan.'

I usher her out of the kitchen and down the hall to her bedroom.

'But, MUM, did you see that? He never likes ANYONE!'

'I think Dylan slipped him some food or something. Anyway, get to sleep; I'll see you for breakfast.'

As I make my way back to the kitchen, I pass Heisenberg in the hall. 'Traitor,' I whisper, but he completely blanks me, slipping round the door into Grace's room. I nip into the living room for a quick moment to myself. Grace wasn't supposed to meet Dylan – let alone like him – and I'm surprisingly jealous that my cat prefers this man to the person who buys his fucking food. I'm utterly confused.

Even with the door closed, the smells wafting from the kitchen are magnificent. I sigh, then push it open gently to find that Dylan has turned on the music player on his phone and is stirring in time to 'Scooby Snacks' by Fun Lovin' Criminals.

'This reminds me of school,' I remark, closing the door behind me. 'I went out with a boy called Gary Hughes – big dope smoker, terrible kisser, and this was playing the first time I ever got high with him.'

Dylan places a lid on the saucepan, lifts the bottle of red wine and pulls out a chair. He stands there for a moment, smiling. 'Quite the wild child, weren't you? I was in uni when this came out. I was dating Melanie Hawthorne – *great* kisser, but mediocre shag, bought me a ticket to their gig.'

'Lucky you. Were they good live?'

'No idea. She sold it when she found out I slept with her flatmate.'

'You're despicable.'

'Corkscrew?'

I point at the drawer under the microwave. 'I wasn't the one getting wasted in high school,' he continues, 'but yeah, not my finest hour.'

I take two wine glasses down from the shelf and sit at the table while he pours.

'It smells great, Dylan. You might be a cheating cad, but it seems you can cook.'

'My sister is a chef. I pay attention. Your daughter is great.' He lifts his glass and pours his wine directly into the Bolognese, before refilling it.

'Let me guess – not what you expected?'

He takes a sip of wine. 'I wasn't expecting anything. I'm just saying – she seems like a great kid. You're obviously a good mum.'

'Wow. Is that a compliment?'

'Just an observation.'

We drink our wine while Dylan's music app shuffles to Simon and Garfunkel and we listen in silence over the sound of the simmering saucepan. It's nice. For a moment I forget about the book and the reason we met and I enjoy just sitting in my apple-green kitchen with a pot of deliciousness simmering and a man whose playlist for the evening is making my heart less heavy. Dylan stands up and goes to inspect his culinary masterpiece and I admire how broad his shoulders are. I'd forgotten about that too.

He mumbles to himself, adding more salt, stirs again and then invites me over for a taste. I take the spoon from him and sample it, being careful not to burn my mouth.

'My God, that's divine. You're a genius. If you weren't here I'd be head first into that pot.'

'Thank you. Tastes better than that shit you buy in a jar, doesn't it?'

'It's delicious. That little kick of chilli is making my tongue tingle. Do I have it all over my face?'

Dylan runs his thumb just below my lip. 'You're good now.' He briefly sucks the sauce from the back of his thumb, and I find myself transfixed by his mouth. His perfectly pouty, heart-shaped mouth. I can't look away. Is this the same voodoo shit he used on Heisenberg? Dylan catches me staring and for a brief second we lock eyes. He grins.

'I'm sure he'll enjoy it too. Can I have my spoon back?'

'What? Who will? Oh yes, the spoon. Sure.'

He takes it and turns away, rinsing it under the sink. 'Tom.' He laughs. 'I'm sure *Tom* will enjoy the Bolognese. You do remember Tom, right?'

Fuck. I have forgotten about everything, including the reason Dylan is in my kitchen. Did we just have a moment? Is Dylan even capable of having a moment?

'Oh yes, of course. He'll love it.' I sit back down and proceed to inhale my wine.

Dylan turns off the hob and the music on his phone.

'Just refrigerate that, and heat it up on Wednesday. There's spaghetti in the small bag.'

I'm barely listening to him. All I can think is, *Goddammit, if he'd tried, I would have let him kiss me.* I need to snap out of this.

'Thanks. Shall we take our glasses through to the living room?' My suggestion is met with a nod and he follows me out. He takes a look around as I turn on some of my music, keeping the volume at a respectable level.

'What colour is that wall? Turquoise?'

'Teal.'

'Nice . . . and so is this couch. I always wanted a corner one, but it'd look odd in my living room.'

As he sits down, he spots his book on the coffee table. 'Glad to see you haven't binned it then.'

'How could I?' I reply. 'You'd have me fired. Or shot.'

'Still think it's bullshit?'

'Does it matter?'

He pauses for a moment. 'Probably not.'

I lift the book and look at its glossy black cover with his pseudonym in gold lettering. 'Why didn't you use your real name?'

'I could ask you the same question, Glasgow Girl.'

I smile. 'It's just easier. Some of the stuff I write could embarrass people who are close to me.'

He runs his hand through his hair and leans forward. 'Sometimes I wish I'd never written it. Don't get me wrong

– I stand by my book – but I guess I just didn't want to be known forever as that guy who writes about dating. I wanted to save my real name for my serious writing.'

Fucking hell, we're actually having a genuine conversation. I offer him more wine, but he covers his glass. 'I'm driving, remember.'

I pour the rest of the bottle into my glass. 'So, what happened?'

'In a nutshell, I never got round to writing another book. Turns out that being financially secure killed my creativity.'

'But you have the Filmhouse now. That must be interesting.'

'Oh, that was purely an investment. I'm never there. Adrian handles everything. Although I do insist we run a horror night every month. We're showing *Carrie* and *The Shining* as a double bill in a couple of weeks.'

'No way! I love Stephen King. I'll totally come to that.'

'You like King? Bullshit.'

I point to the entire row of Stephen King novels in my bookcase. 'Huge fan.'

He shakes his head. 'You continue to surprise me. Don't pretty, quirky girls like chick-lit and rom-coms?'

'Jesus, stop pigeonholing me!'

'Sorry, force of habit.' He looks embarrassed. 'Are you looking forward to Wednesday?'

'I think so.' I swirl the wine around in my glass before

finishing the remainder in one gulp. 'If he's coming here he'll be hoping to have sex, won't he?'

'Cat, men go to the supermarket hoping they'll have sex. It's what we do.'

'And I definitely can't?'

'Well, you can of course, but you'd be breaking the rules. I think we've established this.'

Damn him. Now I'm back in his flat, watching him strip. I drag my thoughts back to Tom.

'Well, that's unfair, because Tom is very attractive.'

'Surely you can resist his great and powerful dentist's charm for one more date?' he mocks. 'How hot can he be, for God's sake?'

'Very. He's bonfire hot. But following the rules is diffi-cult, you know? It's not just the sex thing, it's . . .'

'What?'

'It's THIS stuff. I won't get to do any of *this*. You know, have a proper conversation. Have a laugh. Swear! I'll be too busy being this fucking reserved, polite monster you've created.'

'You're such a drama queen. Just keep going with the book and you'll be fine. I know you underestimate it, but you also underestimate yourself. To be honest, I'm surprised you're single.'

Fuck me, was that another compliment? As my brain scrambles to make sense of this, I feel my face grow hot.

'And why are *you* single?'

'I don't like complications. And I'm terribly picky.' He smiles confidently at me, but I suspect it's partly bullshit. I'm pretty sure that behind his good looks and cocky bravado lies a man who, at some point in his adult life, has had his heart well and truly broken.

'Who was she?' I ask.

'Who?'

'You know who I mean. The ex. Your cynicism towards dating and women has to come from somewhere.'

He stays silent, likely hoping that I'll just shut up. But I don't.

'Oh, come on, you know almost everything about my dating life. Why—'

'Anna. Her name was Anna.' His body language has gone from flirtatious to fuck off. 'She left me six months before I wrote the book. I was gutted of course, but I was able to recognize the mistakes I'd made and how I'd ignored a lot of her bullshit, thinking it didn't matter because I loved her.'

'Bullshit like calling you constantly and over-sharing?'

'Exactly.'

'But that was just one woman –'

He throws his head back and sighs. 'But it only takes one woman to fuck your life up. You need to do things differently or it'll just happen over and over again. We're told that being honest and vulnerable with someone who has the ability to rip out your fucking heart is a good thing! It isn't. Believe it or not, when I wrote this book I actually wanted to save women some of the misery that goes along with dating. Give them realistic expectations. We don't need to be inside your head to be with you. We don't need to know every intimate detail about you, because after you've gone we still carry that around like you're still here.'

He stares at his empty glass and we sit in silence. I don't know if I want to hug him or shake him but I don't push him any further; instead I choose to call it a night.

Unlike the last time I left his flat, there's no sexual tension at the doorway – I thank him for coming over and he leaves quietly, wishing me luck for Wednesday and declining my offer to pay for the food he brought.

Maybe his Anna is my Peter? Whoever she was, she really did a number on him, but unlike Dylan, I haven't given up hope of finding someone again. It's clear he has.

If Peter and I were still together, only one of us would attend parents' evening, the other staying at home to take care of Grace. It's what families do. But as we're not together, neither of us wants to be the parent that doesn't make an appearance on the one night dedicated to parents. It's a matter of fucking principle. What if the teacher says something cool about Grace and the other one forgets to relay this important information? What would people we couldn't give a shit about think of us? Even after three years, neither of us will budge, meaning Grace has to come with us while we have the privilege of being alone with her teacher for a whole ten minutes.

Peter is already there when Grace and I arrive and she spots him first, charging towards him like a very tiny bull. I take a little longer. She leads us in to the gym, where there are the other children forced to return to school. Grace doesn't seem to mind, immediately ditching us to go to the library with some lanky child called Patsy or Parsley or something beginning with P.

Peter and I sit on the plastic chairs beside the P4 sign, where her teacher is finishing up with a set of parents both wearing identical black parka jackets. We're only there for a few minutes before she calls us over.

Mrs Sharma is a jolly woman in her fifties who bleeds enthusiasm and takes great delight in telling us that there isn't much to say about Grace. 'She's a pleasure to have in my class. I'm sure you saw from her work jotters that she's coping well with the curriculum and I don't have any concerns. She's a credit to you!'

I can feel Peter's 'I didn't see her jotters' glare boring a hole into the side of my skull, but I ignore it. If he really wants to see them, I'm sure Happy Sharma will oblige him. She continues talking.

'Grace was just telling the class how she was making spaghetti Bolognese with your friend last night. She said he was quite the hit with her little cat too!'

Peter's skull-drilling resumes with more force than before. I shift uncomfortably in my seat. Time to go. 'Oh yes! Well, thanks very much for seeing us, Mrs Sharma, we're thrilled that Grace is doing so well.'

Peter is able to hold in his burst of interrogation for six seconds. A record for him.

'Cat, who was teaching Grace to make spag bol?'

'Just a friend of mine.'

'If you're seeing someone who's going to be around my daughter, I have a right to know who he is!'

I pull him into a classroom off the main corridor. I'm livid and we need to finish this before Grace gets back.

'Two things, Peter. Number one – you had Emma spending time with Grace before I knew anything about her. And number two – you don't "have a right" to know anything about my private life. What do you want? A checklist of people who might visit my house? You'll just have to trust that I'm making good decisions for my daughter. Why do you have to be like this? Grow the fuck up.'

I don't give him time to respond – I'm already stomping towards the library to collect Grace. I spot her sitting alone on a red beanbag, engrossed in a book about dinosaurs. I hear Peter behind me, the sound of his cloven hooves instantly recognizable. I take a deep breath and smile.

'Grace! Time to go, sweetheart!'

'AT LAST!' She slides the book back into the shelf and jumps up. 'Did you see my teacher?'

Peter chimes in. 'We did. Your mum and I are very proud. Emma will be too.'

Ugh. I'm aware that clubbing the smug bastard you share a child with to death with a dinosaur book is probably frowned upon, but it doesn't stop me imagining the sense of joy I'd feel afterwards.

Grace skips ahead of us towards the car and I walk quickly behind her, determined to stay at least five feet away from Peter and his potential random acts of interrogation. We get to my car and she hugs him goodbye. As I close the passenger door he places a hand on my arm.

'I'm sorry, Cat. You're right; I do trust your judgement. I just worry about who's around Grace. I can't help it.'

'Peter, if I do get involved with anyone and they become a part of Grace's life, then you'll know about it. Grace is a happy, clever girl and that's because somehow we're managing to give her a stable normal childhood. By implying that I'd do anything to fuck with that is insulting.'

'Fair enough – I said I'm sorry. I'll see her tomorrow when you drop her round.'

'Actually, can you pick her up after work? My car is going in for a service in the afternoon and I won't get it back until Thursday.' Complete lie but I could use the extra time to get ready for my date.

'OK, but it'll be six before I'm there. See you then.' He gives a final wave to Grace, then walks off down the street to his car.

Perfect. I make a mental note to park my car somewhere else tomorrow and finally start to get excited about date number four.

CHAPTER FOURTEEN

I'm supposed to be working, but I've just spent the past three hours cleaning my flat. Generally if I'm having guests round I'll just have a quick surface tidy, but according to *The Rules of Engagement*, I should ensure that my flat is free from any signs that I might be a bunny boiler.

> *Don't leave your shit lying around. It's off-putting.*
> *This means no time-of-the-month undies hanging in*
> *the bathroom, no romance novels or 'How to trap*
> *a man' magazines lying in plain sight.*

I have to say I'm finding the whole experience of consulting the book a bit weird after Dylan's 'confession' . . .

In order to keep up my car lie, I nip to the shops to collect a few bits and pieces and then craftily park in the street behind my house. I've asked Rose's husband Rob to drop Grace home as a favour. My somewhat slapdash plan seems to be working.

I tell Grace I'll buy her anything she wants from the toy shop if she promises not to wreck my beautifully clean house before her dad picks her up. She agrees as long as that something is an overpriced monster doll. I've bought fresh flowers for the living room and I'm burning a candle that is supposed to smell like cookies. I'm not convinced, and neither is Grace: 'I don't like it, Mum. It smells like a dead biscuit.' I snuff it out and burn some incense instead.

I figure that even though I'm not sleeping with Tom this evening, there still might be a freak accident in which all my clothes fall off, so I'm not taking any chances. I shave myself into oblivion, leaving only the hair on my head and a landing strip intact.

I've only managed to dry half my hair when the buzzer goes at 6.35 p.m. Peter. Grace skips down the hall to answer it, while I mouth the words 'about fucking time'. I grab my less-than-sexy dressing gown as I too head for the door. Grace doesn't even ask who it is; she just buzzes them in and slides past me like Tom Cruise in *Risky Business*. I make a mental note to have words with her later about letting random psychos into the flat, and then brace myself for Peter's inevitable comments on my 'outfit'. I hold my dressing gown closed with one hand and open the door.

'Dylan?!'

He's standing there holding a tub of parmesan cheese and a giant pepper mill.

'Hi, Cat; I noticed the other night that you were missing these. You can't have a good spag bol without parmesan and freshly ground black pepper.'

He's waiting for me to invite him in, but I have no words. I also have no pants on. I clutch my dressing gown tightly and move to the left to let him by.

'I don't mean to be rude, Dylan, but Peter's due any minute to collect Grace and I'm running late and, GRACE, STOP SLIDING IN YOUR SOCKS AND GET YOUR SHOES ON.'

'You seem a tad stressed. Look, go and finish getting ready and I'll sort the food out. Will that help? You won't even know I'm here.'

'Why are you doing this?' I ask, genuinely confused. 'What, are we mates now?'

'Maybe,' he says, considering. 'But I think the most obvious reason is that I want a look at this Tom guy.'

'No. No way!' I panic. 'You have to leave before he gets here.'

'You're wasting valuable drying time arguing with me, Cat. Unless your hair is meant to look like that?'

'Fine! Help if you want to.' I throw my arms up in the air and head back into my bedroom; he carries on down the hall towards the kitchen. 'GRACE! Come and sit in here with me until your dad comes.'

'But why?' she moans from the living room. 'I'm watching *Adventure Time*.'

'Because your mother doesn't trust me not to teach you swear words!' Dylan yells from the kitchen.

Grace slopes through and glowers at me for the whole time it takes to dry my hair, but I can live with that. I decide on my blue lace top and skinny jeans; sexy but still casual. I appease a disgruntled Grace by letting her play with my make-up while I do my own face. Finally Peter rings the buzzer (forty minutes late) and Grace is free to leave my evil clutches. At least this time I'm dressed when I open the door. I can hear Dylan moving around in the next room.

'Hi, Cat, is Grace ready?'

'Yes, she's just grabbing her bag.' I'd normally invite him in to wait, but no fucking way after his reaction on parents' night. 'She hasn't had dinner; she wanted to eat with you.'

Grace pushes past me, carrying her schoolbag and a cuddly tiger. 'Let's go, Dad! See you tomorrow, Mum!'

I wave her off and stare down the hall towards the kitchen. One down, one to go.

Determined to be firm with Dylan, I throw open the kitchen door, ready to tell him to go home . . . but am surprised to find myself stuck to the spot, grinning like an idiot.

In the time it's taken me to get ready, he's prepared a salad and set the table in a way that makes my cheap plates look almost classy. He's taken the small blue tea-light holders from the living room and placed them in the centre of the table, and now he's scooping the Bolognese into a pot, ready to be reheated. He has his back to me, but he knows I'm there. 'OK, Cat. You're all set. Do your spaghetti ten mins before you eat.'

He lifts the salad bowl and places it between the tea lights as a final touch. 'Not bad, eh?'

'I'm speechless,' I reply. 'And very grateful. Why are you staring at me?'

He shakes his head, 'Am I? Sorry. It's just those jeans. Damn.'

'Thank you! I'm glad they're having such an impact on you. Hopefully Tom will – oh shit, what time is it?'

I look at the kitchen clock. 7.15. There's still time to get Dylan out of here before –

The sound of the buzzer makes me jump. He's early. WHY IS HE EARLY? Dylan begins laughing. 'Ha ha, oh no, Cat, it's too late. Here's here! Now I get to meet loverboy. However will you explain me? Should I stay for dinner? Maybe he won't notice.'

My heart is in my mouth. The buzzer goes again. Twice.

'Stay in here. I need to answer the door. AND STOP LAUGHING.'

I gallop down the hall and grab the handset. 'Hello? Hi, Tom, I'll let you in.'

I try to calm myself down. Maybe I can sneak Dylan out while Tom is in the living room. It's worth a shot.

Seconds later Tom knocks on the door. When I answer it I give him my best smile. He's wearing a dark blue suit and carrying flowers and wine. He's like a fucking advert for perfection. He steps inside – men who look like Tom don't need an invitation.

'You look nice, Cat.' He hands me the flowers and then bends in and kisses me on the cheek. 'I feel a little over-dressed, but I came straight from a meeting.'

'You're beautiful.' Oh shit shit shit. I'm flustered.

'I mean, they're beautiful!' I back-pedal. 'The flowers – and you look great too. Come through to the living room and I'll put these in some water.'

He follows me down the hall. Hopefully he's looking at my arse and not thinking about the fact I'm a gibbering loon. I take his jacket and offer him some wine. 'Dinner won't be too long so—'

I'm interrupted by a loud clanging noise from the kitchen. Then another. My heart sinks. What the hell is he doing? Tom is looking at me, waiting for an explanation, but I haven't had time to invent one yet so I mumble, 'Give me a minute, will you?' and walk to the kitchen as calmly as I can. Dylan is already coming out. He stops for a moment and winks at me. 'All done, Cat!' he announces loudly. 'Should be working fine now.' He breezes past me and straight into the living room. I rush in behind him.

He sees Tom and stops in his tracks. He doesn't look quite so cocky any more.

'Oh! Sorry for interrupting. I'm Dylan – upstairs neighbour.'

Tom stands up to greet him. 'Tom Ward. Pleasure.'

They're both just staring at each other. Are they sizing each other up? Fuck me, this is awkward. I step in. 'The light bulbs in the kitchen blew. Dylan was kind enough to change them for me. I mean, I know how to change a light bulb; I'm just too damn short for these high ceilings.'

It might not be a great explanation, but it's better than the truth. The testosterone in the air is threatening to suffocate us all, so I grab Dylan by the arm. 'So, thanks very much, Dylan. Let me show you out. Tom, make yourself at home.'

'Nice to meet you, Tom,' Dylan says, following me out. I close the living-room door and we hastily move to the front door.

'Nice save, Cat. I was going to go with a blocked sink, but I liked that better. Oh, the sauce is heating up on the hob as we speak.'

'I'm about to have a breakdown here. Can you please go?'

I open the front door, but he still isn't leaving. Instead he whispers, 'This guy? You're sure this guy is your type? Yeah, he's good looking but—'

'Don't you do that!' I interrupt. 'Don't try and fuck with me. There is NOTHING wrong with him. Of course he's my type – did you see him?! Now let me follow your stupid rules and see where this goes.'

He takes the hint and steps outside. 'You know what I was saying about women not being worth the hass—'

'Dylan. Can we talk later? I don't want to leave Tom on his own.'

'Oh. Right. Later then.'

I slam the door and return to the living room, where Tom is still sitting in the same position. 'Sorry about that. I'd normally ask Adam, but they're on holiday.'

Oh, shut up, Cat, he doesn't need this much detail. 'Anyway, as I was saying, let me get you some wine.'

I turn on my mp3 player and grab some glasses and a corkscrew from the kitchen. To my horror, I return to hear Lady Gaga singing 'Applause'. I love this song, but he doesn't need to know that yet. He gives me a 'So this is an unexpected song choice' look.

'I'm sorry. My daughter has a lot of her music on here too. Let me just change that.' I quickly scroll through, find George Ezra's album and press play. First disaster of the evening averted, although, quite frankly, if Tom doesn't like this he can leave.

'Dinner smells good,' he comments, uncorking the red wine he's brought. 'What are we having?'

'Oh, just a spag bol I knocked up. From scratch.'

'Impressive. You like to cook?'

Fuck no.

'When I have the time. I find it very relaxing.' I'm a pro at *The Rules of Engagement* now. 'Let me just put the spaghetti on. Won't be a sec.'

I'm standing reading the spaghetti packet when Tom appears. 'Can I help with anything?'

Why yes. How in the love of fuck does one actually cook spaghetti?

'Oh no, I'm fine. Thanks, Tom.' He sits at the kitchen table instead. Oh fuck me, he's going to watch. I need to pretend I know what I'm doing.

The water in the pot is already boiling so I carefully lower the spaghetti in, but my pot is too small and I'm forced to try to snap them into submission. I press nine minutes on my digital timer.

'Your place is very nice,' Tom remarks. 'Different to your sister's. Yours is much more . . . fun.'

I politely laugh. 'Yes, well, Helen's house is more sophisticated than mine, but I have an eight-year-old. I like to make it fun for her.'

This is only kind of true. Fact is, I've been living like this since I left home. Helen's house is for grown-ups; everything is white and wood and it all matches. Mine is a bit chaotic, but fairy lights, mood cubes and colourful walls make me happy. I need colour in my life.

Spaghetti finally submerged, I taste the sauce – it's warm, and just as delicious as when Dylan first made it. I lower the heat and get the serving bowls down from the cupboard while Tom tells me about the workmen who are currently invading his house.

'I swear, none of them can whistle, yet they all seem insistent on doing it.'

'Are they seven tiny men?' I ask, giggling at my own joke. Tom laughs, but the look on his face tells me he doesn't quite get it.

The timer goes off and I look down at my spaghetti. I read somewhere that you're supposed to throw a piece against the wall to check it's cooked, so I carefully fish out a short strand and fling it against the splashback. It sticks! I am now entirely proficient in the art of pasta cooking and flinging. I want to point at the wall and shout, 'LOOK AT THAT BAD BOY!' but even I know that would be weird.

Despite the fact that I'm still struggling to hide my crazy, dinner is perfect. Tom compliments me profusely on my sauce, and because I have no idea what is actually in it, I tell him it's my great-grandmother's recipe and I've been sworn to secrecy. It's officially the lamest secret anyone has ever pretended to keep, but he doesn't question it. For dessert I offer Tom some Häagen-Dazs ice cream, and I'm glad when he refuses because I had planned on eating it by myself at some point later. Instead we have cheese and crackers before taking our coffee through to the living room, where the George Ezra album has finished. Tom sits on the couch and I join him.

Normally I'd be getting nervous around now because,

with dinner out of the way, it'd be time for more wine, flirting, and then desperate kissing followed by clumsy sex. But I feel fine – actually, I feel in control. Unbeknownst to Tom, sex isn't on the cards this evening, so the flirting will be minimal and I know exactly how this is going to end; him in a taxi and me seductively spooning Häagen-Dazs into my mouth. There are no butterflies, no buckling anticipation, just me and a handsome guy, sitting an appropriate distance from each other on a couch. However, I really need to pee.

On the other hand, it seems that Tom is fully in the moment.

'I find you extremely attractive, Catriona,' he purrs, moving in closer to me. 'You're exactly my kind of woman. I think we really have a connection.'

Oh, please stop being so bloody corny! It's distracting me from your perfect face.

He strokes my hair. 'I'm going to kiss you now.'

I close my eyes and feel his lips touch mine. One of his hands is resting lightly on my knee and the other on the side of my face. It's very sweet, and I can feel his kissing becoming more urgent, but I'm distracted and the only urgency I feel is coming from my bladder. If I don't pee soon, I'm going to wet myself. I wrench my mouth away from his and open my eyes.

'Everything OK?'

'I need the loo. Back in a sec.'

I hastily make my way to the bathroom, praying that I don't dribble on to the expensive knickers I've worn especially for this evening. I lock the door and make it to the toilet without incident, loudly breathing a sigh of relief which echoes over the tiles. The flat is silent. Bollocks, I should have put some more music on. Oh God, the house is too quiet and Tom is going to hear me pee. We've only been on three dates – he doesn't need to hear my bodily functions this early in the game.

I reach across and turn on the taps in the hope that the sound of running water will drown out the sound of me pissing like a gin-drinking racehorse. I hear him call from the living room:

'What's taking so long? Are you freshening up?'

Perfect, he thinks I'm in here flannelling my foof, and I'm *still* peeing. No normal person takes this long to use the toilet . . . unless it's a number two. ARGH, this is getting worse. I finish, flush, turn off the taps and throw open the bathroom door dramatically. The sight of Tom standing there makes me yelp in surprise.

'My turn.'

Oh God, he's totally going to wash his bits now because he thinks I have. He brushes past me and closes the door while I return to the living room, totally ashamed of my unforeseen neurosis. I have turned into a clandestine urinator and I'm not happy.

After a much shorter amount of time, Tom strides

confidently back into the living room and sinks back on to the couch beside me. This time he kisses me without announcing it first.

'Let's take this to the bedroom, Cat.' He starts kissing my neck.

Oh God, here we go. Time to pretend I'm not in the mood to find out if his body is as toned as I suspect it is. I could claim I have my period, but the book states I must not mention any kind of bodily function, so instead I tell the truth. Well, kind of.

'I want to, Tom, I really do, but I have a personal rule: no sex until the fifth date.'

He moves his lips away from my neck. 'Really? Five?'

'Yes,' I insist, 'but I do like you, Tom.'

'Five?' he repeats, seemingly stunned by my revelation.

I place my hand on his. 'I just need to be sure of someone before I sleep with them. Like, *really* sure.'

He looks deep into my eyes. 'I respect that, Cat. You're not driven by emotion or lust. That's admirable.'

Well, maybe it would be if I actually felt that way.

'On the bright side,' he continues, adjusting his trousers, 'the next date will be our fifth. When are you free?'

Keen!

'Saturday. Grace will be at her dad's again.'

'Great, come over to mine. I can't cook like you can, but I'm a master at ordering takeaway.'

I start to laugh. I can't help myself.

'What's so funny?'

'Nothing. Nothing at all. Saturday sounds great.'

He takes my hand. 'You know, you never answered my question the other day. Am I your boyfriend?'

Awkward. I feel like I'm in an episode of *Saved by the Bell*. I lean in and kiss him deeply, which is technically against the rules, but I'm stalling while I think of a suitable answer. Am I even allowed to answer that question? Isn't it too soon to be talking about boyfriends anyway? Eventually I reply, 'Does that answer your question?'

'It does. I'll see *you* on Saturday.'

After I show Tom out, I text Dylan.

Dinner was a success. Fifth date on Saturday. Looks like you were right. Not about everything but I'm starting to get it now x

I wait for a reply that never comes.

The Lowdown magazine – *Saturday 15 November 2014*

Glasgow Girl's home is no longer a man-free zone

I was expecting something different for my fourth date with Mr X. A movie perhaps? An art gallery? Maybe the opera? Possibly a dirty weekend where we use baby oil, owl masks and a safe word, I'm not sure. What I wasn't expecting was to have him over for dinner at my place, but that is exactly what happened.

The first hurdle was feeding him. According to my daughter, my culinary skills are limited to processed meat shaped like animals and the opening of tins, but I was assured by someone who is very familiar with *The Rules of Engagement* that anything less than a meal home-cooked from scratch would be a disaster: a real man knows home-made from store-bought. So I did what any self-respecting killer of cuisine would do – I got someone else to make it for me.

Next I cleaned my flat, getting rid of anything that would give the impression I'm a normal, messy human being. The book says: *At some point he might think about living with you, so it's best to throw away anything that might make him reconsider.*

Of course I felt sad about having to get rid of both my home-made wedding altar AND all of my friends, but I chose to follow these rules so I guess I can't complain.

The food went down well, and in general the date was going smoothly until he suggested we have sex. All readers of *The Rules of Engagement* will know that sex *ist completely verboten* before the fifth date. It wasn't easy, but I managed to decline and, like the gentleman he is, Mr X respected my decision. In hindsight, I think the only reason he was so cool about it is that our next date will be our fifth; otherwise I fear I might have witnessed a grown man begging.

The author states at the beginning of the book that if you follow his rules *you'll be in control of your own dating life*, and I didn't really believe him . . . until now. Mr X might have decided *what* we were doing on our date, but I was the one calling the shots in all other respects. I guess, on reflection, the only thing missing for me was the excitement of wondering what will happen next. Following the rules means there can't ever really be a thrill of the unknown – the where and how of everything is already prescribed.

The fifth date will take place at his house tonight (he's buying me a takeaway, ahem), and if you think I'm going to kiss and tell, you're absolutely right.

It's showtime, baby.

CHAPTER FIFTEEN

Rule 6 – Don't Sleep with Him Straight Away.
Sex isn't the gateway to happiness or the filler for
your emotional void; it's just sex.

Condescending nonsense. I throw down the book and pick
up my phone:

Dylan: every woman already knows that the gateway to
happiness is not sex but killer heels that don't cripple your
feet. Look, I know you're either dead or ignoring me, but
I thought I'd let you know that next week will be my last
column following your rules. So we'll both be off the hook. I
think I'm officially dating Tom now, so much as it pains me
to say this – it worked.

I press Send on no doubt my fifth unanswered text to
Dylan, place my phone under my pillow and roll over
in bed. It's half past eight on Saturday morning, and for

once Grace is still asleep but I'm wide awake. I listen to the heavy rain battering off my bedroom window like a million angry fists and try to ignore the feeling that is gnawing away in the pit of my stomach. I'm not sure whether it's hunger, or nerves about this evening, or even annoyance that Dylan seems to have cut me off with no explanation. Whatever it is, I don't like it. In some weird way, I do sort of miss him.

The rain doesn't let up all day so Grace and I spend the afternoon playing board games and eating toast and cheese with pickle before she has leave for Peter's house. I can tell she's thrilled to spend so much time with me and I feel the same. Everything has become so hectic lately, it's nice to just sit quietly with her and remember how delightfully simple things can be.

At three she pulls on her shiny yellow wellington boots and hunts through the hall cupboard looking for her bumblebee umbrella while I hang my one and only little black dress on the back of my bedroom door to de-wrinkle. It's my secret weapon: not too tight but clingy in all the right places. I'll be completely overdressed for a takeaway, but then again, I don't intend to stay dressed for all that long.

The puddle count outside is impressive. I'm wearing my old Converse so I skip over them like a baby deer while Grace plunges into every one with great delight, spinning her umbrella as she splashes.

Windscreen wipers on full, we drive slowly through the

Southside, past seas of umbrellas and unhappy wet faces. Grace's bright idea to play I Spy is quickly cut short when I keep driving past things she's spied.

'No, the answer was "dog", Mum.'

'Where's the dog?'

'Back there. Turn around – you might still see him!'

'I'm driving, Grace.'

'This is rubbish.'

At long last we arrive at Peter's house and I move Grace from the car to the front door as swiftly as possible. Peter, who looks like he's been in bed all day, helps her take off her wellies at the front door.

'Go and get dry,' he says, shaking her umbrella danger-ously close to me. 'I'll be there in a sec.'

'Bye, Grace! Hi, Peter, nothing to report,' I say, getting wetter by the minute. 'I'll see her tomorrow.'

'The wedding is next week and you haven't RSVP'd. We were just wondering if you were coming and if you were bringing anyone. You know, to get an idea of the numbers.'

NEXT WEEK? That can't be right, surely.

'Yes. To both,' I reply, knowing I can't go alone, but wondering who to bring. Peter and Kerry hate each other. Helen maybe? Tom? A big drop of rain targets the back of my neck and I shiver. 'I'm getting soaked here, Peter. I need to run. I'll see you later.'

I can tell he wants to chat, but I'm off like a shot back to the car. I have a date to get ready for.

Forty minutes before I'm due to leave for Tom's house, the elusive Dylan turns up at my door, looking unkempt and mischievous.

'Dylan? What are you doing here? Why have you been ignoring my texts?'

'Sorry, MUM. Been busy,' he replies, squeezing past me. 'And you practically drop-kicked me out of your house last time . . . but since your last column is coming up, I thought I'd give you a final pep talk. Nice dress.'

I close the door behind him. He's already making himself at home. 'Thanks all the same, Dylan, but I'm sure I'll be fine. Don't hang your coat on the door handle – I do have hooks, you know.'

He hands it over. 'There are things you need to consider. I myself have never had sex with a dentist, but what if it's all too dentisty? What if he makes you open your mouth and say, "AHHHHHHH"?'

'Shut up.' I try not to laugh.

'Oh, and the most important thing to consider: what if he has a small knob? I've heard that's quite common with dentists. Well, dentists and also men who aren't me. Make me a cuppa, will you? I'm freezing.'

Before I can reply, he's striding up the hall towards the kitchen, asking if I have anything to eat. I'm left holding his jacket. He munches on some biscuits he's found in the cupboard while I organize the tea. I can tell he's waiting for a response. 'So, what do you think, Cat?'

'Are you trying to make me anxious, Dylan? Cos it's working.'

He stops munching. 'Why are you anxious?'

'Ugh, I don't know. Something just doesn't feel right.' I stare blankly at the kettle while it boils.

He brushes biscuit crumbs from the table into his hand and disposes of them in the bin. 'Is there something you're not telling me? Did he get weird with you? What did he do?'

'Nothing! This isn't his fault. I'm just not being fair to him. Or me.' I stick two teabags in the pot and pour in the water. 'Sugar?'

'Um, one,' he replies. 'You're over-thinking this again. You like him – he likes you; what's the problem?'

I thump a mug down on the worktop. 'He likes me? How can he like me? He doesn't know me! He knows "Cat", the woman who doesn't have any fucking discernible personality. He doesn't know that I read horror in bed, that I can't cook for shit and that I'm—'

'Taking ages to make the tea?'

'Fuck the tea, I'm serious! He doesn't know me, Dylan! He thinks I'm sensible and reserved. ME!! I talk to myself! I shout at the television! I cry like a baby when I listen to "Wichita Lineman" and I can't hear "Icky Thump" without getting the horn.'

He nods. '"Icky Thump" is a dirty, dirty track.'

'It really is, isn't it? Now, what was I saying?'

'That you're weird and he isn't.' He starts on his second biscuit.

I carry the teapot over to the table and sit down with a groan. 'You just don't get it.'

He pauses. 'I don't actually. You're going out with a good-looking bloke, decent job, who's probably boring as fuck but who wants to spend time listening to you and having sex with you, but you're unsure because you might not get to shout at the TV in front of him? There must be more to it than that?'

'There isn't, and you're making me sound shallow,' I reply, pouring the tea. 'It's not as simple as that. If I had to choose between a lifetime of controlled happiness or a lifetime of being myself, I'd choose the latter.'

'If it helps, there's a chapter on what do when you break up with—'

'Oh, shut up about your bloody book.'

'That's harsh.'

'Don't look at me like that! You created this whole sorry mess. You and Leanne.'

'Who's Leanne?'

'One of your devotees. Between the pair of you, I've successfully pursued someone who has no idea what I'm actually like.'

He puts his mug down, pushes out his chair and stands up. 'You can't blame me or my book, Cat. Remember, I didn't choose Tom for you. You were the one who agreed to go out with him in the first place.'

'You're right; I did agree to go out with him. I really liked him, but that was before—'

'Before what?'

'Nothing. It doesn't matter.'

'Oh for fuck's sake, just tell me!'

'Before I met you.'

We both take a second to let my words sink in. As he stares at me I begin to wonder if it's possible to kill yourself with a teapot. The longer he remains silent, the more frustrated I become. I might as well say the rest:

'Do you know what I hate the most, Dylan? Of all the things I've kept from Tom, the biggest one is that when I'm not with him I'm thinking about YOU, and even when I AM with him, you're still in my head! One minute you're teaching Grace to cook, the next you won't even reply to my texts and now you're over here, uninvited, AGAIN. What is it you want?'

He gets to his feet. 'I think I should leave.' His voice is soft and calm. 'I shouldn't have come here –'

I stand up and block his way. 'So why did you? Answer me, Dylan. Why all of this? Why are you here?'

'Because, Cat, you make it fucking impossible for me to want to be anywhere else!' He grabs my face with both hands and he kisses me hard. Jesus, it's a good kiss. I don't know what it means, but –

It's the kind of kiss that will ruin me forever.

CHAPTER SIXTEEN

'And then what happened?!'

I can hear the anticipation in Kerry's voice as I lock my front door and make my way to the waiting taxi. 'Then nothing. He pulled away, said he was sorry and left.'

'He left? But he said nice things! He kissed you! What was he sorry for? Did he say anything else? I HAVE SO MANY QUESTIONS.'

I open the taxi door and clamber inside. 'Arlington Avenue, please. You still there, Kerry?'

'Hang on, are you in a taxi? Why are you in a . . .? You're not still meeting Tom, are you?'

'Yep.'

'Are you insane?! But you're not sure about Tom! You just told Dylan you liked him!!'

'I do, I guess, but it doesn't mean I don't like Tom too. At least he seems genuine. That kiss with Dylan was . . . a momentary lapse in judgement. I was frustrated. You know how I get when I'm frustrated.'

'Aroused?'

'No. Emotional. Now I'm just confused.'

'Maybe you should call Dylan or—'

'Call him? HE PASSIONATELY KISSES ME AND THEN BOLTS FROM MY FLAT. I DO STILL HAVE A SMALL SHRED OF DIGNITY LEFT!' I see the driver's eyes staring at me in the mirror so I lower my voice. 'I feel so stupid. I want nothing more to do with that man.'

'OK, understandable, but are you sure seeing Tom is a good idea? I could come over instead?'

'I didn't put on my best underwear to spend the evening in with you, Kerry. I'm going to have a nice dinner, with a nice man, who hopefully has enough booze and sexual prowess to make me forget I ever met Dylan fucking Morrison.'

'OK, Cat,' she replies, clearly aware that my mind has been made up. 'Call me if you need me.'

I hang up, check my make-up in my little gold compact and tell myself that everything will be fine. I focus on ignoring the aftershock of Dylan's kiss, which is still coursing through my body.

Arlington Avenue is about as middle-class suburban as you can get. Thirty white houses all sitting merrily in a row, each one slightly hidden by a large, perfectly pruned hedge. Tom rents number eighteen, which is the last bungalow at the top of the cul-de-sac. Through the rain-splattered window, I spot his BMW and ask the taxi driver to stop. I pay, take a deep breath and dart quickly to his front door.

He greets me wearing jeans and a black V-neck T-shirt that hugs his chest.

'Come in, Cat. It's lovely to see you. Weather's been awful, eh?' He takes my coat and I see his eyes scanning my little black dress. Half of me wants him to just slam the door shut, throw me on the hall floor and shag Dylan clean out of my system, but the other half is really fucking famished.

He leads me down a short hallway and into his cream-accented living room, which is dimly lit and welcoming. There's a real flame electric fire mounted on the wall and champagne in an ice bucket on the table with two glasses. At the back of the living room I spot French windows leading out into a conservatory. I knew it! I'm totally having a proper snoop later.

'Make yourself at home, Cat. I've ordered Chinese; it should be here in half an hour. Can I get you a drink?'

'Please. Your home is beautiful, Tom. Good find.'

'Yeah, I like it here. I prefer living a bit outside the city these days. Must be my age. Not sure how long I'll rent, but I'm happy for now.'

He pops the champagne cork without flinching – a skill I've always admired in a man – and we toast to a 'lovely evening', which of course is code for 'please let the sex be good'.

Even though this is our fifth date, it still feels like we're mostly communicating via small talk. By my fifth date with Peter, I knew that he'd been bullied at school, had a moon-shaped birthmark on his hip, took two sugars in his tea and could do a really funny impersonation of Alan Rickman. Conversely, I feel like Tom and I are still floating on the surface – neither of us attempting to dive a bit deeper. I have my obvious reasons for doing this, but either he's also holding back or that's just the way he is.

I hear my phone beeping in my bag, but I don't check it until Tom leaves the room to answer the door to the delivery driver. Even though I've just fervently kissed another man in my hallway, I do have a modicum of dating etiquette left. It's a text from Peter:

Grace had some dry skin on her shins but we've dealt with it.

'*We've dealt with it.*' I picture him and Emma both dressed in hospital scrubs, smearing Vaseline on to a small patch of dry skin, commending each other on their quick, incisive action.

Excellent news, Peter. Glad you were able to save the leg. Teamwork for the win!

I slip my phone back in my bag and take a huge gulp of champagne. Tom closes the front door and I hear the rustle of carrier bags. 'I'll just get the table ready,' he calls. 'Won't be long.' I have a brief mental image of Dylan letting Grace stir the Bolognese in my kitchen.

What am I doing? Here I am, in a beautiful house, with a super-hot man, drinking champagne and allowing myself to be infuriated by the memory of a fucking mediocre writer who has no idea how to treat women. Fuck him and fuck his book. It's game over.

I mosey around Tom's living room while I wait for dinner, spotting a large pile of neatly stacked magazines beside the television. Hoping I haven't stumbled on his porn collection, I have a peek and wish that were actually the case. Tom appears to have subscriptions to both the *Classic Car Club* and *Golf Monthly*, and he hasn't had the good sense to hide them under his mattress.

'I see you've found my weakness.'

'FUCK, you scared me, Tom!' I yelp, staggering backwards. He reaches out to steady me and laughs. 'Sorry. It's these carpets, they muffle footsteps. It's so strange – hearing you swear like that! Kathryn, my ex, used to make me put a quid in the swear jar every time I did.'

I'm starting to feel I know this Kathryn woman more intimately than I know Tom . . . 'Oh, sorry, I try not to do it very often,' I lie, but in my head I'm running through the entire alphabet of swear words.

I follow him through to the kitchen, which is about twice the size of mine and sports a large wooden white table in the centre, on which Tom has laid out our Chinese meal: sweet-and-sour something, Kung Po chicken, Peking duck, rice and prawn crackers. I think back to when I met Dylan at Yen . . . This time I intend to demolish that Kung Po.

Stop. Thinking. About. Dylan.

'I thought Chinese would be a safe bet – not everyone likes spicy food,' Tom says, setting the cutlery down. 'Please, sit.'

We sit across from each other and, despite being famished, I do my very best not to hoover up everything in ten seconds, like I would at home. I also – small victories – succeed in not spilling anything down my dress. Tom, on the other hand, manages to get sticky sauce on his shirt.

'How embarrassing,' he says, wiping it away with his napkin. 'I'm not usually this uncoordinated.'

He finds THIS embarrassing? Between me and Grace, this is an hourly occurrence. 'Don't be silly,' I reply. 'I have an eight-year-old; I've seen worse.'

'Sometimes I forget you're a mum.'

'Sorry?'

'I mean, it's fine that you are, I'm just grateful you don't go on and on about your child like some women I know. I think that's one of the things I like best about you – you keep that side of your life private.'

His words sting – that side of my life is the most important part. I feel uneasy, like I've somehow betrayed Grace. I can't even really blame him – in following these rules

I've told him nearly nothing about her. I'm not allowed to. The feeling stays with me through the remainder of the meal and, hard as I try to ignore it, I can't.

'These wine glasses are beautiful,' I deflect. 'You have good taste.'

'Thank you. I got custody of them in the divorce. If I recall, they were a present from Kathryn's parents.'

And there she is again.

We finish dinner and I excuse myself to use the bathroom. I need time to think.

I'm sure his bathroom is as charming as the rest of his house, but I barely notice anything as I sit down on the closed toilet seat to decide whether a night of sex is actually going to change the fact that I'm starting to feel I might not be really all that compatible with Tom and his omnipresent ex-wife, Kathryn.

Tom's in the living room, casually lounging on his chesterfield sofa when I return. He motions for me to sit down, stroking the seat beside him. 'Come here, cutie.'

Coffin: meet the last nail.

'Please don't call me that. It's kind of cheesy.'

He looks surprised. 'Oh. Sorry. I thought you liked that.'

'Not particularly.'

'Is there something bothering you, Cat?'

'I need to apologize to you, Tom,' I say, sliding on to the couch beside him. 'I've been trying to be someone I'm not, and you deserve better than that.'

'I don't understand.' He looks completely baffled and I don't blame him.

'I use swear words, Tom. All the time, well, except around Grace, of course – whom, by the way, I frequently discuss with people I'm close to because she's the most important person in my life. I write about sex and dating and romance and I think my ex is a massive bastard and I also think you talk about your ex way too much, which is odd . . . and what I really want to know more than anything is, have you ever fucked anyone in your dentist chair?'

'My chair? No. Cat, have you taken something?'

'Oh, and I lie!' I exclaim happily. 'Not usually, but with you I have lied about loads of stuff. Like my neighbour, Dylan – he isn't really my neighbour; he's the man who made the meal I pretended to cook and also a man I slept with a while ago because I DO have sex before the fifth date – that was bullshit too, but I wanted you to stay interested in me and – Jesus, Tom – you've gone as white as a sheet.'

I realize I'm being a bit unkind, but now that I've told him I feel a rush of relief. I reach over and drink the rest of my champagne while Tom tries to process what he's just heard.

'Is there anything else?'

'Don't think so. I'm sorry, Tom, I really do like you, but as much as I've been dying to see you without any clothes on, I'm going to walk to the main road and flag down a taxi now.'

I grab my bag and walk into the hall, taking my coat from the mahogany coat stand. As I pull it on, I hear him say, 'It's pouring down. You don't have to go.'

He's standing at the living-room door with his arms folded across his chest, looking marginally less scared than he was two minutes ago.

'I do,' I reply. 'You're really great, Tom. I'm sorry about all of this; I just followed some bad advice.'

I step into the rain and begin walking up the street towards the main road, breathing a huge sigh of relief. One more column and I can put all of this behind me. Glasgow Girl is back to square one.

CHAPTER SEVENTEEN

For the purposes of 'cheering me up', Kerry has the bright idea that we should eat lunch in the park – if you can call two limp tuna sandwiches and a sharing bag of pretzels lunch. It's a cold and drizzly Sunday, but I welcome the opportunity to get her insight on my evening.

'I must admit I'm surprised.' Kerry breaks off a piece of her sandwich and throws it towards a small duck that's been patiently eyeballing her for the past few minutes. 'After we spoke, I totally thought you'd have shagged Tom, not dumped him. You seemed so determined.'

'It was the right thing to do.' I gesture towards the pond. 'That fat one over there is an arsehole. Did you see him try and steal the wee one's bread? YOU'VE HAD ENOUGH BREAD, BEAKFACE.'

'So what happens now?'

'No idea, except that I now have to write a column entitled "I dumped Mr X because I have a fucking conscience" or something. Natasha won't be pleased. I think she was expecting a more electrifying conclusion to the whole thing. We all were.'

'You could always write about Dylan . . .'

'Ha, and say what? "I momentarily lost my mind because this random guy was nice to my kid and my cat didn't hate him"?'

'Heisenberg liked him? Wow.'

'Don't be impressed, my cat is perverse. He'd probably take a shine to Hitler.'

She stuffs her wrappers into the rotting grey bin beside our bench. 'But he *did* kiss you. He told you he can't stay away from you. Aren't you curious to hear what else he has to say?'

'By which you mean you're curious.'

'Yes! But you must be too.'

'I'm not. I'm fed up of hearing what he has to say. I've read his book. He goes on and on about how men will pursue women if they're into them. Nowhere does he write that they will shag you, manipulate you, then assist you in wooing another man before kissing you passionately and fucking off immediately after. You can't just kiss a girl like *that* and then leave! Those kinds of kisses are supposed to mean something.'

'You really liked him, didn't you?'

I nod and throw a pretzel at the mean duck. 'Doesn't matter now. He's a professional player. Everything is a game to him. At least Tom wasn't like that.'

'And you're sure Tom is a definite no-go?'

'He likes golf and classic cars, Kerry. I will never believe that these are acceptable hobbies for anyone to have.'

'Golf?' She gives a little shudder. 'Enough said.'

Eventually we submit to the cold afternoon air and leave our little bench, walking quickly towards Kerry's red Mini in the rapidly emptying car park. She turns on the heater to thaw out our stinging faces and suggests we stop for a takeaway coffee on the way home.

'They're doing that pumpkin coffee crap now,' she says, clicking her seat belt in. 'It's "in season". It's also hipster bullshit, but I really want to try it. I'll probably hate it.'

She does hate it, and I end up returning to the flat with a milky tea and three-quarters of a skinny pumpkin-spice latte, which has been sworn at repeatedly by my pissed-off best friend. Grace arrives back at half past five, wrapped up in a fluffy hat and matching gloves, with a rosy face just made for kissing. Peter doesn't get out of the car, presumably sulking about my text reply.

'I tried on two dresses for the wedding, Mum! One was pink and had little beads on it and the other was purple and had a massive sticky-out skirt. I liked that best. I could swish in it.'

'Swishing is important,' I agree. 'Sounds like you had a great weekend.'

'I'd give it eighty-nine per cent. It lost points because Netflix wasn't working.'

'Take your stuff off and I'll make dinner. What do you fancy?'

'That spaghetti stuff Dylan made. Can we have that?' She throws her hat on the floor, causing Heisenberg to arch himself into something resembling a hissing croquet hoop.

'Another day, honey. I'm not sure of all the ingredients and—'

'Phone Dylan, then. Maybe he can come and make it for us again? Do you remember when he was making the celery talk? He's funny.'

My heart sinks. Right about now I expect a Parent of the Year award to plummet down on me from the sky and cause considerable bleeding from my stupid inconsiderate head. 'He's working away just now, Grace, but we'll arrange it when he comes back.'

Happy with my excuse, she darts into the living room to see if Netflix is up and running again, leaving me to pull together a lame dinner of fish, oven chips and microwaved beans. It's hardly haute cuisine, but it'll have to do.

It's half past ten before I sit down again, having organized Grace's school clothes, made her packed lunch, washed the dishes, bathed her and finally insisted she go the fuck to bed. I'm exhausted, but my brain is far from sleepy. I need to come up with something for my article this week that doesn't make it look like I just gave up on *The Rules of Engagement*. I could say Tom turned out to be a massive racist . . . no, that's just mean. Maybe I can lie and say that Tom dumped me? Being dumped is far more interesting that taking the moral high ground, right? But then that implies that the rules don't work . . . What if Tom dumped me to get back with his ex-wife? That could work. Who am I to stand in the way of true love . . .?

Reluctantly I pick up *The Rules of Engagement* and search for advice on being dumped. As I suspected, it's an onwards-and-upwards approach, designed for people with no emotional inner life. From what I gather, I must not walk around with a face like the Wailing Wall. He then goes on to talk about some of the emotions a lady might experience and I make my own notes underneath each point:

Sadness – (*Why didn't he love me? I'm totally loveable.*)

Anger – (*Who does he think he is? He's a fucking dead man walking.*)

Crazy – (*If I can't date him any more, I'm going to cut my hair off with this spoon.*)

Vengeful – (*I'm going to buy him a dog and then STEAL the dog and then I'll have a dog and HE'LL HAVE NOTHING LEFT.*)

Denial – (*He'll be back. I'll just eat everything until that happens.*)

Dylan says the most important point is to have self-respect.
I must not become a weeping chick-flick cliché. I must not
beg for him to come back because I will inevitably cry, and
not just a single Sinead O'Connor solitary tear. No, it will
be massive showers of salty despair, streaming down my
face, soaking through the baggy T-shirt I've been wearing
since I stopped caring about my appearance. Women who
stop caring how they look will eventually shrivel up and
die, while their ex-boyfriend is probably off in Cannes,
shagging someone better on a yacht. Unsurprisingly it
doesn't mention how to react when a man gives you a
kiss that still haunts you and then fucks off out of your
life forever.

If Tom had actually dumped me, this chapter would be
no help at all. Still, at least I have something to work with
for Saturday's column. I close *The Rules of Engagement* and
throw it in the bin.

Helen and Adam are back from their holiday, looking
suitably rested and pleased to see Grace when I drop her
off before school.

'Did you bring me something?' Grace asks first thing.

'Yup. Go inside and see what Uncle Adam has for you.'

Grace kisses me and then vanishes into the flat, giving
Helen exactly sixty-seven seconds to interrogate me before
I have to leave for work.

'How's it going with Tom?'

There is no way I'm getting into this before work. 'Fine, Helen. I'll fill you in later. I really need to go.'

'Just fine? Have you seen him this week?'

'I really have to go. Later. I promise.'

I trot off down the hall as she yells after me, 'I BOUGHT YOU SOME RASPBERRY VODKA. YOU'RE NOT GETTING IT UNTIL YOU SPILL THE BEANS.'

Bollocks, I love raspberry vodka. She's so unfair. She's going to lose her shit when she finds out I dumped Tom. With the week I've had, I really wish it was acceptable to start drinking on the train to work.

'What is that awful smell?' I've only been in the office for two minutes and I'm opening windows and looking for signs of a dead animal. Great start to Monday. I look at Leanne, who's spraying everything with cheap air freshener she borrowed from the staff toilets.

'I have no idea, but these cleaners need to be sacked.' There's something different about her today . . . her face . . . Oh, I see what it is. Jesus wept.

'Leanne, what's going on with your eyebrows?'

Leanne furrows her forehead and looks up in a failed attempt to see her own brows. 'I got them done on Saturday – "High Definition" brows. I love them.'

They look as if they've been drawn on with a Sharpie, but I don't have the heart to tell her. The woman's just tried to see her own forehead without a mirror after all; it would be like kicking a really stupid puppy.

Leanne and I are the only ones in the office today. Patrick has the week off, Gordon is in Edinburgh all day and Natasha is at some conference in Perth. I'm extremely happy about this; the fewer people ask me about date five, the better. Leanne predictably tries to prise it out of me, but her high-definition face is getting nowhere:

'You'll have to wait until Saturday!'

'Exciting! Shame it's your last one. You'll have to come up with some brand-new ideas again.'

'This one wasn't my fucking idea in the first place,' I snap. Oh good, now Leanne has a colossal pout to go with her drawn-on brows. 'Sorry, I'm just a bit stressed. I didn't mean to bite your head off.'

Pout gone, Leanne offers to make me some tea and toddles off to the kitchen while I go through my emails and get organized for the day. The foul smell can't be ignored and seems to be coming from Patrick's desk. Eventually I'm forced to investigate. Thirty seconds later I'm carrying half a Tupperware of rotten kale down the stairs and disposing of it in the bin across the street. I then write a note for Patrick:

You didn't look after your kale and it died. I'm very sorry for your loss.

Also, WHO THE FUCK BRINGS KALE INTO WORK?

You owe me two new nostrils.

'I'll buy some baking soda at lunchtime,' I say to Leanne, taping the note to Patrick's monitor. 'It should soak up some of the smell.'

'I remember Patrick eating a kale salad last week. Baking soda? How do you know these things?'

'I have a kid and a cat,' I reply, riffling through the weekend papers. 'At some point they have both shat somewhere unexpected and left it for me to find. Also, Grace spills milk. Secretly and often.'

She smiles. 'I admire you. I can barely look after myself, never mind a kid. How the heck do you stay sane?'

'Grace is both the cause and the cure,' I reply. 'You'll understand when you grow one of your own.' I thank her for the tea and take my first call of the day – from a young PR woman called Penny who keeps pronouncing my name 'Cat-ree-*oh*-nah'.

'Sorry – Penny? It's actually pronounced "Ka-*treen*-a".'

'Are you sure?'

'Am I sure that's how my name is pronounced? Yes. Quiet sure.'

'Hmm. Weird, but OK.'

Needless to say the call ends there and I move on with my life, while Leanne greets the postman.

'One here for you, CAT-REE-*OH*-NA,' she mocks, tossing me a small white envelope.

'Yes, very funny.' I tear open the side and pull out an A5 piece of red card. The scrawled black handwriting reads:

Where: Filmhouse.
When: Friday 21 November 2014.
Time: Midnight.
D x

I turn it over but the other side is blank. That's it. I don't ask Leanne if she also got one – this is clearly for me alone, not a press invitation like last time. It's also Peter's wedding reception that night and I've promised Grace and told Peter I'll go. Can I manage both? Do I even *want* to see him?

'Everything all right?' asks Leanne, clearly concerned by my expression.

'Oh yes. I just remembered I have Peter's wedding on Friday night and I, um . . . haven't bought them a gift.' This is a lie.

'Debenhams have thirty per cent off just now,' she replies, 'I'm sure you can get them something there. It must be hard to see your ex so happy, but it'll be your turn one day!'

I'm actually giving them a hideous vase Helen gave me for Christmas last year, but I thank Leanne for her helpful suggestion, ignore her hopes for my future and get back to work.

Rose has picked up Grace so I head to her house after a day of mostly coffees and procrastination. The kids play in the living room while Rose and I chat in the kitchen. I fill her in on everything that's been happening since we last met.

'That Dylan guy sounds like a puzzle!' she says. 'He sounds like an enigma . . . wrapped in a mystery, wrapped in a wanker.' She switches on the kettle, then opens a box of biscuits and places them in front of me. 'And how are you feeling about Peter's wedding? For what it's worth, I think you're doing a good thing.'

'I'm feeling . . . all right about it actually.' I stare into the box, deciding on my first of many shortbread fingers. 'It's funny, since I've been involved in the whole Dylan/ Tom fiasco, Peter's wedding has hardly crossed my mind. In fact Peter has hardly crossed my mind full stop.'

'That's because he's no longer the last man you had feelings for. It's funny how a new romance will put an old one in perspective, eh?'

I grin. 'He wants me to meet him, you know? Dylan. He sent me a mysterious note . . .'

'Mysterious? Hang ON.' She sticks her head round the kitchen door. 'JASON, WILL YOU STOP PLAYING WITH THAT KEYBOARD? IT'S TOO NOISY.'

She walks over to the kitchen drawers, shaking her head. 'I'm sorry I ever bought that bloody thing. I'd hide it but he loves it. Every time he plays it, it sounds like Jean-Michel Jarre is having a stroke . . . Sorry, you were saying – Dylan wants to meet up?'

'Yes. On Friday, at midnight. What should I do? Meet him after the reception or just ignore him?'

'I take it Grace is staying at the hotel?'

'Yes, they've booked rooms for the night. She's kipping in with Peter's dreadful Aunt Victoria.'

'Then go! You've nothing stopping you,' Rose says, removing cups from the dishwasher. 'Go and see what he wants.'

'But he's behaved so badly!' I object. 'He's so rude to me! Do I really need someone like that in my life?'

'Listen, I thought Rob was an arrogant sod when I first met him, but it was all bravado. Now I think he's the most humble, lovely man I've ever known. If you have a feeling about this Dylan guy, then see where it goes. You have nothing to lose.'

'Except my sanity.'

'Sanity is overrated. Just meet him.'

'And my dignity.'

'JUST MEET HIM.'

'I WILL THEN.' I stuff another biscuit into my mouth before I change my mind.

'You're doing the right thing, and if I don't see you before Friday, good luck at Peter's wedding. I hope it all goes smoothly. Whatever happens with this other guy, just be thankful that you're not the woman getting hitched to that lolloping clown.'

Lolloping. This makes me laugh more than it should.

*

Grace has only been in bed fifteen minutes when Helen knocks on the door. She's brought with her a litre of vodka and a stern look.

'Can you recommend a new dentist?'

Shit. She knows. 'Don't be so melodramatic. I was going to tell you tonight. How did you find out?'

She steps on my toe as she walks past me. 'I called Tom to invite him to dinner again, and he told me that it might be awkward because you weren't seeing each other any more. Actually, he said that you weren't really his type and he'd tried to let you down gently. He hopes you aren't too cut up about it.'

He dumped *me*? I smile. Good for him. I deserved that.

'I'm fine, Helen. Life goes on and I—'

'But then he said that he was never comfortable being with one of those single-mother types, so I told him to go fuck himself. So back to my original question – can you recommend a new dentist?'

I give Helen a massive hug and she whispers, 'It's obvious you broke it off, and I'm glad you did. Saving face is one thing, but how dare he look down his nose at you. You do an amazing job.'

She steps back and hands me my vodka. 'Have one on me. I'll see you for the wedding on Friday. I'm just going to wear that cream trouser suit I got in Fraser's sale. What are you wearing?'

'Baby-blue Jackie O suit for ceremony and my maroon swing dress with the little straps for the reception.'

I wait for her to launch into why my choice of outfits is unsuitable, but instead she says, 'You'll look wonderful. I'll see you on Friday.'

She kisses me on the cheek and goes back across the hall, leaving me and my raspberry vodka to become better acquainted. I pour myself a small one, mix it with lemonade, then settle down to write my final rules column. There won't be time later in the week, and I just want to get it down and move on.

The Lowdown magazine – *Saturday 22 November 2014*

I Followed the Rules
What happens when it all goes tits up?

It's been a bumpy ride. From supermarket stalking to spaghetti throwing, I've followed the rules in the hope that Mr X just might be *the one*. But when *the one* still harbours feelings for someone else, not even the mighty rule book can help. Yes, readers, it's over.

On the eve of the wedding Grace packs her tiny little bag with all manner of non-wedding related nonsense, like tiny plastic farm animals and stickers. She's excitedly gibbering on about how she has the important job of scattering rose petals and remembering not to run or dance down the aisle, while I watch for Peter at the window. It all feels very surreal.

'We're staying in the hotel for TWO nights, Mum! I'm going to sleep in Great Aunt Victoria's room. Someone is going to do our hair in the morning.'

'I can't wait to see how you look!' I kiss her face and secretly hope that she ignores Peter's instructions not to dance or run. I hope she fucking hoofs it down the aisle, finishing in a small Charleston or can-can.

The buzzer goes and I let Peter in. He's flustered but in good spirits.

'All set then?' I ask, making an effort at dull yet appropriate conversation.

'Yes. We'll see you at the church tomorrow morning?'

'Of course. Wouldn't miss it, and I'll pop along to the reception in the evening.'

He isn't listening; I know Peter: his brain is wondering how he's going to cope with his parents for two days and whether the hotel room has a well-stocked minibar. Anything I'm saying is just noise.

'Let's go, Dad!' Grace slinks under my arm and out into the hall. 'See you tomorrow, Mum. It's going to be so AMAZING.' And with a tiny squeal she's off down the hall towards the front door.

'See you tomorrow! And good luck, Peter.'

'Thanks. Have a good night.'

I close the door and lean against it for a second. I'm

not sure Helen is the wisest choice of partner, given her need to say everything that comes into her head, but I'm grateful not to be going alone . . . I'll turn up in my best church outfit, smile and wish them well. It all feels a bit unreal, but for the first time, I realize I don't feel upset about it. At last we're all finally moving on.

CHAPTER EIGHTEEN

The wedding. We arrived seven minutes ago and I'm already wearing shoes that aren't mine. The right heel of my planned *comfortable* footwear got wedged in a drain and snapped off as I was getting out of the car, so I've been ordered to put on my sister Helen's silver stiletto hoof-destroyers, which are too narrow for my huge flat feet. I would have been happy going barefoot, but apparently no sister of hers is '*walking around like a bloody hippy*', so I get her new Kurt Geigers and she's run off to her car for her ballet pumps while I hide around the side of the church.

As I watch Helen tiptoe over to her car, a taxi pulls up. A pretty brunette I don't recognize swings her legs out, knees together, expertly ensuring that her pastel pink miniskirt doesn't ride up and reveal her Spanx, followed by her stubble-faced partner who looks like he'd rather be anywhere else than stuck at a wedding on a Friday morning. Behind them I see Peter's friends Jay and Lonna walking up the car park, followed by a small group of women who've chosen to wear black. I predict they'll be sitting on Emma's side of the aisle.

I hate weddings. I've been to six weddings in the past seven years and the only pleasurable part is purposely finding really shit wedding gifts, like religious-themed salt and pepper shakers or 'his 'n' hers' hot-water bottles in the shape of genitalia. I always try to convince myself I'm going to enjoy it, but it's always the same old story: I spend the evening floating between tables of couples who are in various drunken stages of loved-upness and who feel compelled to tell me that 'it'll be my turn one day'. Sometimes I laugh and smile politely, and sometimes I tell them to shut the fuck up, but every time my heart gives a tiny painful yelp, reminding me that once upon a time I also believed this. This then leads to mild depression, soothed only by ludicrous amounts of buffet finger food, all while wearing a misjudged skirt that doesn't allow for carbohydrate-induced mid-section bloating

But this wedding will be different. It's Peter's wedding. Today I will watch the father of my child, the 'love of my life', marry someone who isn't me . . . and I'm surprisingly OK with this. Better than I thought I'd be anyway. I just want it to be over.

My attention is again drawn to the street, where I spy two wedding cars in the distance, waiting at the traffic lights. I wave frantically at Helen to hurry up; I'm certain the last thing Emma wants to see when she steps out of the car is her future husband's ex-girlfriend hobbling around the entrance to the church in unreasonably high shoes. Grace will be in the car too – I don't want to distract her.

Helen pirouettes through the car park in her ballet pumps and helps me inside before we're spotted. We find seats three rows from the back behind two middle-aged women wearing identical silly hats, which makes Helen snigger so hard she makes the whole pew shake.

I nudge her. 'Stop giggling.'

'It's too late. I'm gone. Save yourself.'

I move my head to the right and spy Peter standing at the altar. He's dressed in grey and purple and he looks understandably nervous. He sees me and gives me a quick wave, gesturing to his suit for my approval. I'm unexpectedly touched, but before I can give him a thumbs-up the doors behind me open, everyone stands and the music starts.

I turn to look at Helen, who winks at me. She leans in and whispers, 'Here we go.' I take a deep breath.

Here we fucking go indeed.

'Congratulations, I'm so happy for you both.'

I unhinge my smile and sigh. No. That sounds forced. It has to be more natural. I shake it off and grin at myself in the ladies' room mirror again.

'Congratulations! Let's hope you don't fuck this one up, eh, Peter?'

Nope. Jesus, the lighting in here makes me look about seventy. I try it without a grin – sombre yet meaningful, lowering my head like Princess Di used to do. 'I hope you'll have a wonderful life together . . . IN HELL.'

Oh for fuck's sake. Why is this so difficult? Throughout the wedding ceremony I was fine. No crying when they said, '*I do*,' minimal laughter when Emma, her three bridesmaids and Grace walked down the aisle to 'Somewhere Over the (fucking) Rainbow', and I smiled winningly when Grace waved at me twice during the ceremony. I really do hope they have a wonderful life together . . . yet I'm struggling to say it with any sort of sincerity because although I hope they're happy, I'm more concerned about what's waiting for me, not for the rest of my life but when I meet Dylan later.

The bathroom door swings open, momentarily letting the sound of laughter and music from the wedding reception float in before it closes again.

'MUM!'

Grace, in her purple swishy dress, runs towards me at full speed, throwing her arms around my waist, her head colliding with my chest. 'I've been dancing with Dad for ages. What's taking you so long?'

'Oh, you look so pretty, Gracey! Let me see you properly.'

She steps back and twirls around excitedly. I can tell that, despite it being Peter's wedding, she's been the centre of attention all day.

'Mum, I need to go to the toilet. Wait for me?'

She disappears into a cubicle and I finish reapplying my lipstick. As Grace emerges with her skirt tucked into her pants, I adjust the straps on my maroon dress and sneak one final look, feeling ready to take on whatever awaits me at the reception.

Grace washes her hands while I pull her dress down, hiding her tiny white pants. She leads me out of the bathroom and we walk hand in hand through the small lobby and into the main hall. I immediately spot Emma, still in her wedding dress and dancing with a tiny boy in a kilt. Peter is a little harder to locate, but Grace soon spots him talking to his mate Ryan towards the back of the hall. I feel awkward, as if I have no right to be here.

Grace skips over to Peter and he waves to me as I follow slowly behind. 'Hi, Grace! Listen, your grandpa was looking for you for a dance. Why don't you find him while I talk to your mum?'

We both watch her speed off towards Peter's dad.

'Has today been grim for you?'

I laugh. 'No. Not at all! The ceremony was beautiful. I appreciate the invite. I really am happy for you both.'

Nailed it.

He places his hand on my arm. 'Only, I'm not sure I'd have been able to watch you marry someone else. I know it must have been tough.'

'Oh, well, surprisingly it wasn't,' I reply, wondering where this is going. 'We were a lifetime ago, Peter.'

'I regret a lot,' he continues. 'And I've behaved badly at times. I want you to know that, despite everything, I think Grace has a fantastic mum and that you're a wonderful person.'

'But . . .?'

'No buts. That's all I wanted to say.'

As he hugs me, I'm dumbfounded. It seems that marrying Emma has turned Peter into a reflective, decent – albeit slightly tipsy – human being. This might turn out to be the best wedding yet and finally, *finally*, I really do feel happy for them.

As the evening goes on, Peter's elderly parents approach me with a mixture of caution and contempt – they still view me as the heartless witch who chose not to stay in a doomed relationship – but I just smile sweetly and give zero fucks. Emma is gracious and brings me a glass of champagne, thanking me for attending and being so cool about the whole thing. Ha, if only she knew.

By eleven, Grace is practically asleep on her feet and doesn't complain too much when her Great Aunt takes her up to the hotel room, which is also my cue to leave. Peter walks me out to the taxi and we hug again briefly before he goes back to his wedding guests and his new wife, and I make my way to the Filmhouse.

CHAPTER NINETEEN

The outside of the Filmhouse looks very different at midnight. Without its brightly lit exterior display, the old grey facade appears cold and uninviting. Menacing even. The fact that it's in Glasgow doesn't help matters. Even friendlier cities can turn on their residents when the sun goes down.

I try the front door but it's locked, and I briefly wonder if he's stood me up. However, my question is soon answered when the side door opens in the alley that runs alongside.

'Over here!' Dylan shouts, beckoning me in. Confused but intrigued, I hurry to join him.

'What am I doing here?' I ask as he closes the door behind me. He's unshaven and seems nervous.

He strokes the stubble on his chin. 'I wasn't sure you'd come. I thought I'd better explain myself after the other night . . . Just straight through there, Cat.'

'And you couldn't do that over the phone?' I walk through a small storage area, which takes me into the main lobby. It's dark, but there are candles lighting up the floor all the way to Screen 2.

'If I'd called, I wouldn't have been able to do this.'

I get a little shiver down my spine. This massive fire hazard has been secretly set up, just to impress me. And it's working.

'Did you get dressed up for me?'

'Don't flatter yourself; I've just come from my ex's wedding reception.'

'Oh shit.'

'Nah, it wasn't too bad.'

'Good. Well, if you'd like to make your way to Screen 2, the film will be starting shortly.'

'Film? But I thought you wanted to talk?'

'We can do both. It's my cinema.'

He leads me down the hall, following the candles, which stop outside the door. Dylan opens for it me and I go in first. Inside it's dimly lit with soft music playing. On the screen I read:

Stanley Kubrick's *The Shining*.

Running time: 146 minutes.

'You brought me here to scare me?'

He laughs. 'It's a good first-date movie.'

'Oh, so this is a date, eh?' I ask, making my way towards the rows of seats. Truth is, this is the most romantic thing anyone has ever done for me AND I'm wearing a splendid first-date dress. It's just a shame it's with the heartless kitchen absconder.

Dylan leads me to Row G, where he's laid out some drinks and snacks. 'When does the movie start?' I ask, sitting down and eyeing up the popcorn. I don't really know what's happening, but I seem to be going along with it, more so now that there are snacks. 'I hope you're paying the projectionist overtime.'

'No projectionist – everything is digital these days. The film will start soon but—'

'Hang on . . . is that Johnny Cash I can hear? It bloody is! Are you playing country for me?'

'Well, yes, but that's not—'

'I LOVE this song. It's so—'

'CAT! Can we talk? Please. I need to say this now.'

Oh my. I shush and casually throw some popcorn into my mouth.

'That night I left you in the kitchen . . . Listening to you speak with such passion about all the things Tom doesn't know about you . . . it suddenly dawned on me that I wanted to be the one who got to know all those things. I didn't want it to be Tom. You were my game-changer and I was too stupid to see it.'

'Your what? I don't understand. You're not making sense.'

Dylan reaches under his seat and hands me his iPad. 'I'm not being very articulate. Maybe this will help.'

It's logged on to the *Tribune*'s website. 'Click on your column.'

'What? My column? How will that help?'

'Just read it.'

'But I know what it says.'

He clicks on it for me. 'Just. Read. It.'

'Fine.' I hold up the iPad, feeling incredibly foolish.

We apologize but there will be no column from Glasgow Girl this week. Instead we have a special guest post from Guy Wright, author of The Rules of Engagement.

I stare at the screen in disbelief. What the fuck? I'm scared to read on, but my eyes have already continued without my consent . . .

When I wrote *The Rules of Engagement*, I made sure I covered every dating eventuality; what to say, what to wear, when to have sex, how to handle break-ups, but there was one question I never thought to ask myself, something I never even considered until now – what happens if you meet someone to whom the rules don't apply?

Let me be clear; this would be an extremely rare, freak occurrence: like frogs falling out of the sky, lightning striking the same person twice or Britain having warm weather on a Bank Holiday weekend but, like all of those events, it can happen.

So, in keeping with the book and the current theme of this blog,

I'd like to add an additional rule. It might seem a tad cryptic at first, but stay with me.

Rule 11 – The Game Changer

Throughout this book I've given advice on how to meet men, how to keep them interested and make sure they stay that way. But what if, without even trying, you've managed to turn an ordinary, emotionally bereft man into a smitten shell of his former self? And what if he hadn't told you this? How would you know?

Luckily, there are signs and signals you can look out for:

- He thinks it's charming that you can't cook.
- He'll admit that you're funnier than he is.
- He doesn't care that you like crappy country music.
- He can tell you're an amazing mum by the fact that your kid isn't a pain in the arse.
- He's sorry about the way you two met, but he's not sorry that he took you home. Not for one second.
- He f*cked up and has spent the last week kicking himself, and hoping he hasn't completely blown it.

And if all else fails:

- He hijacks your column and publicly declares that he's in love with you.

A man like this needs to be put out of his misery. He misses you.

Look out for our exclusive interview with Guy Wright next week. The Rules of Engagement, *price £5.99, is available now.*

I'm aware that I've not said a word for at least five minutes.

'. . . *and publicly declares that he's in love with you.*'

I'm reading and rereading in a state of disbelief. There's a feeling beginning to bubble, deep down in the pit of my stomach. It's been a while, but I think it might be UTTER FUCKING DELIGHT. There's already 232 comments! I try to compose myself.

'Well? Cat, say something. I'm really nervous now.'

I place the iPad on the floor. 'I can't believe you did that.' I stand up and begin to walk towards the exit. He can't see me grinning like a fool.

'Where are you going?'

'Home. My bed is calling me.'

'Jesus, Cat, look, maybe the column was a stupid idea. I'm sorry. Don't go. Please.'

I'm almost at the exit when I turn to face him. 'You coming?' I raise an eyebrow and smile. We're the same two people we were when we met at the Filmhouse, only the tables have turned.

'What?'

'You heard.'

He laughs loudly and jumps up from his chair. 'Nicely played.'

'I think I've loved you since the moment you said that to me in the bar,' I continue. 'You made quite the impression that night. I remember everything.'

He walks towards me slowly. 'Then you know what's coming next.'

He's unbuttoning his shirt. I *do* know what happens next.

I kick off my shoes. If this dress wasn't so expensive I'd be already tearing it off me. I make my way back down the aisle towards him, letting the straps of my dress fall off my shoulders, reaching behind me for the zip.

He continues walking, undoing his belt. 'Stay exactly where you are.'

As he approaches me I think how weird it is that today I watched the first love of my life get married, and now everything has changed in a way I could have never predicted, thanks to one little, stupid book. I also know that there's no way in hell we're making it home tonight.

He reaches me – shirt open, throwing his belt on the floor, and before I can speak he pushes me back against Seat 5 Row C and firmly pins me there, his hands clasping mine. The look he's giving me is so intense I fear I might dissolve there and then.

'You know we're breaking at least four first-date rules here?' I say, my voice reduced to no more than a whisper.

He unclasps his right hand and moves it gently to the side of my face. 'Fuck the rules, Cat.'

And right there in Row C, accompanied by Johnny Cash,

Dylan leans in and kisses me, but unlike our kiss in the kitchen, this time I know what it means.

It's the kind of kiss that means something.

It's the kind that means *everything*.

ACKNOWLEDGEMENTS

Big love to the following people –

My wonderful agent Kerry Glencorse and my equally amazing editor Kathryn Taussig, along with all the staff at Quercus and Susanna Lea Associates.

I'd like to thank my brilliant parents for putting up with me and my sister for introducing me to a world where dating rules exist.

Finally, I'd like to thank my beautiful daughter for her endless supply of cuddles. Without them, I'd be far, far grumpier than I already am.

Keep reading for an extract...

It's been a year since Phoebe Henderson found her boyfriend Alex in bed with another woman, and multiple cases of wine and extensive relationship analysis with best friend Lucy have done nothing to help. Faced with a new year but no new love, Phoebe concocts a different kind of resolution.

The List: ten things she's always wanted to do in bed but has never had the chance (or the courage!) to try. A bucket list for between the sheets. One year of pleasure, no strings attached.

Simple, right?

Factor in meddlesome colleagues, friends with benefits, getting frisky *al fresco* and maybe, possibly, true love and Phoebe's got her work cut out.

JANUARY

Saturday January 1st

I emerged from my bed like Nosferatu about an hour ago
with a mouth like a stable floor. Since the minibar has
been cleaned out and I cannot find one cup in this entire
hotel room, I've been forced to drink water directly from
the bathroom tap. Fuck, I'm so hungover my face feels like
it belongs to someone else. Lucy is still asleep on the other
bed and I refuse to get dressed and venture out where
there are people with eyes who will judge me.

For once the hangover was worth it, as last night's
party was amazing! Every year we all stay at the Sapphire
Hotel (overpriced, trendy and slap bang in the middle
of the city centre) to bring in the bells and every year
I'm surprised they haven't banned us yet. The others
had already checked in by the time Lucy and I arrived
at half past three. We took the lift to our floor, dragging
our needlessly large suitcases behind us as we searched
for room 413. I've worked with Lucy for two years and

she's never on time for anything. 'I bet the others are pissed already,' said Lucy, 'and shagging. I bet they're all covered in Moët and wearing each other's underwear.'

Finally, we found our room and I fumbled with the key card in the door, 'Jesus, is that all you ever think about? Anyway, we're only half an hour late. Hazel's most likely pricing the minibar, Kevin will be ready for a pint and Oliver's probably . . .'

'Getting head off that Spanish girl,' Lucy interrupted. 'What's her name again?'

'Pedra. I've only met her once and called her Pedro by accident.'

She threw her coat on the bed near the window and turned on the television as I started to unpack, wondering why the hell I'd brought four pairs of shoes.

'Are you wearing your green dress?' I asked, looking at the plain black one I'd brought.

'Yup. Although with my red hair, I look like a Riverdance reject.'

I left her, mid-Irish jig, and went for a shower, excited about the evening ahead and thinking about last year's party: when Lucy got so drunk she fell asleep in the lift and Oliver hid behind my bedroom door and scared me so badly I wet myself.

My train of thought was interrupted by a knock on the door and a familiar Dublin accent.

'Phoebe, I'm coming in. Put your cock away.'

I grabbed the towel and wrapped it around me just as Oliver appeared from behind the door.

'Fuckssake, Oliver!' I shrieked, turning away from him. 'Give a girl some privacy! Go and peek at Pedro's tits.'

'It's Pedra, and I'm not here to see your tits, impressive as they are. I'm here to tell you that dinner is at 7 p.m., and there was something else but Lucy's Irish dancing has distracted me and made me homesick for mental redheads.'

'Fine, I'll see you when I'm dressed. Go and annoy someone else.'

An hour and two glasses of wine later, Lucy and I were still getting ready. The plan, every year, was to try to stay relatively sober until midnight, but generally we'd all be hammered by the time the bells chimed for New Year and do shots until we all fell over. I knew this year would be no different. 'At least you don't have Alex with you,' said Lucy, pulling on her tights. 'That man bored the shit out of everyone last year, going on about his bloody job. He's a physiotherapist, not a fucking wizard.'

'I know.'

'I mean, sleeping with his boss all that time, and he had the cheek to bring her into the conversation—'

'Enough!' I shouted. 'Don't kill my buzz talking about that dickhead. It's over now. I just need to concentrate on finding someone who isn't a total prick.'

'Don't set the bar too high,' Lucy laughed. 'And besides,

it's not a new boyfriend you need, Phoebe, it's a shag! Sex makes everything better.'

'My sex life is fine, thank you very much. What I need is another drink.'

We met Hazel and Kevin at the bar before dinner. They had already thrown half a bottle of champagne down their necks. Hazel saw me eyeing up the bottle.

'We have no child for the night. I intend to get shit-faced.'

'Hey, I'm not judging. I celebrate the fact I have no child every night,' I replied.

Hazel looked amazing in her pastel-pink evening dress. She'd swept her blonde hair up into a high ponytail decorated with tiny diamantés. Her husband Kevin was in his kilt and looked very handsome. They always looked so effortlessly groomed that I felt a tad thrown together in my black wrap-over dress, red heels and the same hairstyle I'd had since 1995.

'Oliver and Pedra not down yet?'

'From the way those two were slobbering over each other in the lobby, I'd be surprised if they've left the bedroom.' Kevin laughed and then paused, obviously trying to picture this in his head.

A flustered-looking waiter ushered us into the main hall, where we all sat around beautifully decorated tables covered in white linen with green and red centrepieces.

There must have been around a hundred tartan-clad guests and the atmosphere was electric. There were tables of hipsters wearing jaunty hats, ready to Instagram photos of their meal as soon as it arrived, the obligatory table of young lads who were pissed before the meal even arrived and the occasional middle-aged couple who weren't quite sure what to make of the whole thing. The meal itself was traditional Scottish: steak pie, haggis and some sort of tofu extravaganza for the vegetarians.

'That cutlery is immense,' said Lucy, lifting a silver spoon up to her face. 'I'd like these in my house.'

'Steal it then,' I joked, but then I saw the look on her face.

'Hey, klepto! Do *not* steal it. They made you pay for that dressing gown last year, remember?'

'Yeah, but they don't allocate cutlery to room numbers. That was a schoolboy error on my part.'

Ten minutes later Oliver swaggered in with a cheeky grin on his face, followed by Pedra, a woman so beautiful I wanted to punch her in the face and then myself. 'Finally! Did you two get lost?' I asked, knowing full well that wasn't the case.

'No,' Pedra answered quite seriously.

'I'm starving,' Oliver announced, stealing the bread roll Lucy was buttering. 'When's the food?'

'You better replace that with something carby in five seconds, Webb, or I won't be responsible for my actions,' she growled.

'You never are,' Oliver smirked, dropping another roll on to her plate. 'A toast, please!' He raised his glass and we all followed. 'To my good friends: Hazel and Kevin, who completely ruin my theory that all marriages are a sham; Lucy, the kind of woman my mother warned me about; Phoebe, my oldest and funniest friend; and finally to my lovely girlfriend, Pedra; I apologize in advance – this will get messy . . . oh, and not forgetting the new friends we will make and quickly lose this evening by being terrible human beings. Let's fucking do this.'

We ate, we laughed, we danced, by midnight my shoes were lying under a table, I'd been outside for 17,000 cigarettes and I was starting to get the 'I'm going to be alone forever' New Year's blues when the slower songs came on. Thankfully Hazel spotted this and was able to pull me back off the ledge.

'You thinking about Alex?'

'Yeah. I think I still miss him.'

'Nah, you miss the idea of him. The man you thought he was.'

'The man I hoped he'd be.'

'Exactly!'

'He was charming in the beginning.'

'So was Ted Bundy,' she quipped.

'I always thought Bundy would be a good name for a dog.'

'Focus, Phoebe.'

'Ugh, look, maybe I didn't try hard enough either. He did have moments when he was quite loving and tender. Maybe I—'

'Maybe you didn't, Phoebe, who knows, but *you* didn't screw around and he did! Alex was cheating on you for four months. That's four months' worth of lies for you *and* his mistress! That's not an endearing quality in any man.'

I knocked back my tequila. 'Why do I always gravitate towards arseholes? I'll never find anyone good.'

'You'll find someone new. Perhaps you need to go for someone who isn't your normal type.'

'Like a woman?'

'No. I mean someone you'd never usually consider, but, most importantly, someone who deserves you.'

'YES!' I shouted, startling a nearby man in an ill-fitting kilt. 'This year I'm going to find someone. Someone different. Someone brilliant!'

'You can do whatever you want. This is going to be your year, girl. Start living it. Now come and dance before we all turn into pumpkins.'

And so here I am, the first day of my brand-new year, and all I have to show for it so far is a hangover, a new spot on my chin and a handbag full of Lucy's stolen cutlery. I'm going back to bed.

Sunday January 2nd

Today I have decided to make my New Year's resolutions and become a better, more useful person instantly. But instead of the usual – lose weight, make money, unfollow everyone on Twitter who uses bastarding chat acronyms – I've decided to ask myself one question: if I could do last year again, what would I do differently? Every year I make the same lame resolutions, yet nothing really changes, and I end up wondering why I bothered. So, this year, the plan is to choose just one thing and actually get off my arse and do something about it. The question is, what? I've been brooding over where it went wrong with Alex, but the more I think about it the more I realize it was never right in the first place, even before he pissed off with Miss Tits. (I should really grow up and call her Susan, but that doesn't quite convey the level of my disdain). The first night we met, I was so grateful that this tall, handsome man had shown interest in me I bought every round of drinks and thrust my phone number into his hand at the end of the evening. I didn't hear from him again until two agonizing weeks later. I realize now that even that was significant. He kept me at arm's length for our entire relationship, occasionally pulling me in to give me a glimpse of what a funny, sensitive person he could be, but only when he chose to. So while I wanted to be swept off my feet, in reality I was just tripped up occasionally. That bastard has a PhD in manipulation, and I swear if you looked up 'fucker' in the dictionary, there would be a photo of him, holding my heart, and possibly my severed head, looking victorious and doing a little jig. I could never quite live up to his expectations . . . I wasn't educated enough or groomed enough or impressive enough. I just wasn't enough. I wasted four years with someone who was completely underwhelmed to be with me. That's the real kick in the vag. What a waste of time.

I spent over five hundred pounds on therapy in the last year with a forty-something-year-old American therapist called Pam Potter, whose name makes her sound like a garden gnome, but who happily listens to me bitch and whine in exchange for fifty pounds an hour (she was marginally cheaper than the psychologists with real names) and then says, 'I hear what you're saying, Phoebe.' The fact she had two working ears leads me to believe this was true, but not entirely helpful. However, it did help me come to the conclusions that a) I am still angry about the whole Alex thing, and b) although I wasn't completely blameless in our relationship, I did deserve better. No, I do deserve better. This year, I have to get Alex out of my system once and for all.

Monday January 3rd

It was Pam Potter's idea that I keep a diary. Apparently this whole 'writing down my feelings' lark should be therapeutic, but it just feels weird.

I haven't kept a diary since I was a fifteen-year-old loner with an ear cuff and a mono-brow. Back then my diary was hidden under my mattress and contained 13,000 different swear words to describe my parents along with some angst-ridden poetry about a boy in my class who never spoke and wore eyeliner. As it is, I still fancy boys who wear eyeliner, but I'm less inclined to insult my parents these days, except for when they send me those organic chocolates I hate at Christmas.

Despite it being a holiday, I had my first monthly session of the year with Pam this evening. She'd dyed her hair brown over Christmas and looked remarkably like Tina Fey.

'How was the New Year for you? In our last session you mentioned you were still struggling with your break-up. Has that changed?'

'God, no. I feel as if all I do is think about him . . . or moan about him . . . or just miss him. Recently I am seeing things more clearly, though.'

'In what way?'

'I threw myself into that relationship head first. I'll be the first to admit that I was lonely, and when he showed interest in me I clung on to him. I might have been needy, but he was worse – he was lazy. He was too lazy to end it so instead he just kept me there until someone better could replace me. He couldn't even be bothered to have his affair somewhere private. I remember when I caught them in our bed. OUR FUCKING BED!'

Pam just nodded, but I'm certain that if she wasn't being paid to sit through this story for the millionth time she'd have happily drop-kicked me out the office window.

I could feel myself shaking as I visualized the moment I caught Alex. I'd arrived home early from a concert that had been cancelled at the last minute. I came in and threw my jacket on the couch and watched it fall on top of a bra I didn't own. It was bright pink and about three cup sizes bigger than mine. The moaning from the bedroom gave me the answer to a question I hadn't even had time to ask myself. 'I walked into the room and stood there like an idiot. I couldn't even speak. He just shrugged and said, "This was bound to happen. You knew things weren't right between us." I stayed with Hazel until I found my own place. She's been very supportive. All my friends have.'

'Good. That's important. But it's been almost a year, Phoebe. How do you feel you can move on from here? You've expressed the desire to on several occasions.'

'I've been thinking about New Year resolutions. I need to change the way I think, otherwise I'm going to be stuck in this cycle forever. I'm *going* to change. I'm just not sure how yet.'

After my session with Pam, I called Oliver to tell him my plans. I could practically hear him rolling his eyes at me.

'You don't need to make a list of stupid resolutions you'll never keep, Phoebe. Remember last year you were going to start running?'

'I did start running. I totally ran. And anyway, I'm just making one resolution this year, one that matters.'

'You ran once round the park and then you vomited in a hedge, Phoebe. That doesn't count. You need to stop being so uptight and planning things. You never used to be like this. You used to be fun and carefree! We used to get pissed and you'd tell me all your secrets and we'd dance to really shit pop music at 5 a.m. Now you're like the anti-Phoebe.'

So much for the support of my friends. 'I got a little lost,' I said quietly. 'You know it's taken me a while to get back on track after I split with Alex.'

'I know that, but I suggest it's time you start getting found. And laid. You need to get your groove back.'

'Jesus, you sound just like Lucy. You two are obsessed.'

'You sound repressed.'

'I'm going now. Save your sex advice for Pedro. I have plans to make. Talk later.'

Trust him to piss all over my chips. He knows nothing.

Tuesday January 4th

Back at work today after my New Year break and I immediately wanted to set myself on fire. I've been working at this newspaper for three years, and approximately three weeks have been enjoyable. After running screaming from high school at seventeen, advertising sales was pretty much the only job for which my supposedly winning personality was more important than my qualifications. This was just as well, as I scraped a C pass in English and a Masters in forgery after faking my mother's handwriting on sick notes throughout my final year. I'm surprised they didn't have some sort of fun run to raise money for my recovery. The trouble with my job is that I'm meant to be good with people. Charming, even. Be interested in what they have to say and make them trust me, nay, LOVE ME to the point that they name their first child after me and then leave the kid out of their will because they love me more. But in fact I'm rubbish at small talk, I hate it, and if someone doesn't want to take advertising space that's fine with me; I honestly couldn't care less. That last statement perfectly sums up my attitude towards my job: *I couldn't care less.* But I do my best to talk a good enough game and sell my soul on a daily basis because I need to pay the rent. We share office space with ten other companies, most of which are in the financial sector, so I often have to share the lift with ball-bags who wear ridiculous ties and talk about numbers and golf. On the upside, the location is brilliant: a two-minute walk from the train station and upstairs from a pub and a sandwich shop where I'm found most mornings buying coffee and toast. The sales floor is mostly open-plan, and my desk is unfortunately directly in front of my boss Frank's office, giving him a perfect view of what I'm doing all day (which is usually nothing). Most of the other staff have pictures of their family on their desks, but my 'unkempt shambles that I call a workspace' (Frank's words) is decorated with a picture of a cat with a watermelon on its head, mostly obscured by empty coffee cups and aspirin packets. Today's regular morning meeting was painless enough – lots of encouragement from said boss, who is the most horrendous blowhard to have ever walked the earth, which no one paid any attention to. Then I caught up on four hundred emails that had arrived over Christmas and the skeleton staff had ignored. Lucy arrived late as usual, stuffing her face with a break-fast bagel and swigging coffee from her glittery flask. 'You all right, my lovely?' she shouted over. 'Recovered yet?'

'Yeah, I'm fine; you want to have dinner tonight? Sushi?'

'I can't. I already have plans.'

'New fella?'

'Old fella. That guy I was seeing last year, the one with that yappy dog I hated.'

'You said you'd never date anyone with dogs again. What changed?'

'His dog died.'

I am ~~43%~~ 97% sure that Lucy had nothing to do with that dog's demise. Lucy, like Oliver, is a serial dater. When I first started at *The Post* she was dating two men at the same time and this seemed perfectly acceptable to her. She's like the Pied Piper with men, they follow her wherever she goes and she has no intentions of becoming tied down any time soon.

'The dating part is the fun part. After you start all that living-together nonsense it becomes a drag, so I prefer to keep things simple. I love the "getting to know you" part.'

I, on the other hand, have never been very good at dating, and the 'getting to know you' part scares the shit out of me. I've had five dates in my entire life, and all of them ended up in some sort of relationship. There was Chris – my first boyfriend at school, which lasted precisely six months, until he went to university in Manchester; Adam with the exceptionally large penis, whom I dated for five months before he decided he'd rather piss off and join the air force than be stuck in Glasgow with me; Joseph, who only lasted three months as he had issues with intimacy and being shite in bed; James, whom I dated for a year, but who was profoundly annoying and had a crippling phobia of baked beans; and finally Alex, who turned out to be the biggest mistake of my life. Even though it's been nearly a year since we split, the thought of having to find someone new continues to be frightening and I don't see me rushing out to meet anyone anytime soon.